"I never should have done it. I should have left you out there to freeze!"

Kristin had been so full of emotion, so intent on getting out all the pent-up anger, she hadn't really been thinking about what kind of a reaction to expect from him—and for a moment Jake didn't do anything. He just stood there, staring down at her.

But then the most amazing thing happened. Suddenly he was coming toward her, reaching for her, pulling her close.

"I could have lost you," he growled, pulling her into him. "I could have lost you."

His words made their way into her heart and burst through her system like fireworks on the Fourth of July. She forgot about being angry, forgot about being careful and staying in control. Suddenly she understood there were some things worth suffering for—and in that moment she knew Jake Hayes was one of them.

Dear Reader,

Welcome to another fabulous month of the most exciting romance reading around. And what better way to begin than with a new TALL, DARK & DANGEROUS novel from *New York Times* bestselling author Suzanne Brockmann? *Night Watch* has it all: an irresistible U.S. Navy SEAL hero, intrigue and danger, and—of course—passionate romance. Grab this one fast, because it's going to fly off the shelves.

Don't stop at just one, however. Not when you've got choices like *Fathers and Other Strangers,* reader favorite Karen Templeton's newest of THE MEN OF MAYES COUNTY. Or how about *Dead Calm,* the long-awaited new novel from multiple-award-winner Lindsay Longford? Not enough good news for you? Then check out new star Brenda Harlen's *Some Kind of Hero,* or *Night Talk,* from the always-popular Rebecca Daniels. Finally, try *Trust No One,* the debut novel from our newest find, Barbara Phinney.

And, of course, we'll be back next month with more pulse-pounding romances, so be sure to join us then. Meanwhile…enjoy!

Leslie J. Wainger
Executive Editor

Please address questions and book requests to:
Silhouette Reader Service
U.S.: 3010 Walden Ave., P.O. Box 1325, Buffalo, NY 14269
Canadian: P.O. Box 609, Fort Erie, Ont. L2A 5X3

Night Talk
REBECCA DANIELS

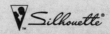

INTIMATE MOMENTS™

Published by Silhouette Books

America's Publisher of Contemporary Romance

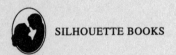 SILHOUETTE BOOKS

ISBN 0-373-27317-7

NIGHT TALK

Visit Silhouette at www.eHarlequin.com

Printed in U.S.A.

REBECCA DANIELS

will never forget the first time she read a Silhouette novel. "I was at my sister's house, sitting by the pool and trying without much success to get interested in the book I'd brought from home. Everything seemed to distract me—the dog, the kids, the seagulls. Finally, my sister plucked the book from my hands, told me she was going to give me something I wouldn't be able to put down and handed me my first Silhouette novel. Guess what? She was right! For that lazy afternoon by her pool, I will forever be grateful." From that day on, Rebecca has been writing romance novels and loving every minute of it.

Born in the Midwest but raised in Southern California, she now resides in the scenic coastal community of Santa Barbara with her two sons. She loves early-morning walks along the beach, bicycling, hiking, an occasional round of golf and hearing from her fans. You can e-mail Rebecca at rdaniels93111@hotmail.com.

TYVMFE! And for Jackson Jerome Phillips:
Aunt Nell has a place at the table for you.

Chapter 1

"*He* said he couldn't go that long, you know, without...er...without it."

"Without sex?"

"He's a man, he has needs."

"And this was while you were in traction."

"Right, for six weeks. He said it would just be for then, just while I...couldn't. H-he promised it would stop after that, he wouldn't see her anymore once I was...well, once we could...we could..."

"We get the idea. And that was okay with you?"

"He's a man, he has—"

"Needs, yeah, you mentioned that."

"But then, when I got home from the hospital I found it. The letter."

"The Dear Jane."

"Yes."

"And he was long gone, right?"

"He went with her to Alaska. They're going to look for gold."

"Gold? Oh brother!"

"Gold? You mean like prospect?"

"Yeah, that's why he said he needed my truck."

"Your truck?"

"It's four-wheel drive, he had to borrow it, you know, to get up into the mountain."

"He didn't borrow it, lady, he stole it."

"He took your truck without checking with you first?"

"He just borrowed it. He promised to bring it back once they struck it rich."

"I don't call that borrowing, Sally. I call it grand theft auto."

Jake smiled.

"But I miss him, Jane."

"Oh jeez, lady, give me a break."

"Sally, my dear girl, give me a break. You don't miss this guy, you escaped him. He didn't leave you, he did you a favor."

Jake's smile widened. It wasn't the first time they'd thought alike. "You tell her, Jane."

"Count yourself lucky all this relationship cost you was your truck."

"But…but I love him."

"Well, if you do, he doesn't deserve your love, Sally. But there will be someone who does. Anybody agree? Anybody out there have advice for Sally Sad in Savannah, or a story of the love you've lost that you'd like to share? Let's hear from you, 1–800–NIGHT TALK. This is 'Lost Loves' and I'm your host, Dear Jane—Jane Streeter—and here's a little smooth jazz to soothe those aching hearts."

Jake stretched back as best he could in the narrow lawn chair, listening to the sultry tones of the saxophone drift out from the speaker and up into the night sky. It was late, too late, and he needed to be up early in the morning, but he wasn't sleepy. He'd gotten caught up in the music and the stories from callers who had phoned into the late-night radio program, caught up in the soft, velvety voice of Dear Jane.

Of course, if anyone were ever to ask, he would deny it to the death that he was part of the legion of listeners across the country who tuned in to the popular call-in program. After all, *real* men didn't listen to programs called "Lost Loves." They went for things like sports and hard-core news. But when you live alone at the top of a mountain, the nights get to be long, and the low, sultry voice of Jane Streeter helped fill the hours.

A tiny flicker of light glimmered suddenly out of the blackness from the far side of the canyon below. Jake sat up, automatically reaching for his binoculars. No flame, no fire, nothing to get excited about, but he would check it out anyway.

He focused the high-powered lens on the tiny spot of light. Just the pale beam from the headlights of a lone vehicle on the narrow mountain road. Too late for campers to be out. Besides, it was off-season. The campground wasn't set to open for another six weeks yet. More likely one of the handful of locals who lived year-round in the tiny fishing village of Vega Flats, which was three thousand feet and fifteen very rugged miles below his mountaintop perch. It was probably Mac making his way back to his cabin on the ridge after closing up the tavern in town, or maybe Ruby from the bait shop, out looking for night crawlers or tracking down one of her stray colts from the small herd of free-roaming horses she raised.

Jake followed the headlights' slow progression along the winding mountain pass until they became lost in the dense overgrowth and disappeared. He had planned to swing by the Flats tomorrow to pick up his mail while he was out checking a report of a mudslide along the trailhead leading up the east ridge. He would give that stretch of road a look just to make sure whoever was down there had gotten to where they were going okay. The narrow gravel pass was treacherous in broad daylight; in the dead of night it could be a killer.

"We're back and we've got Miss Priss from Mississippi. What do you say to Sad Sally?"

"Jane, I've only got one thing to say to Sally and that's good riddance to bad rubbish. Let's hope she's seen the last of him."

The loud click on the line had a laugh coming from Dear Jane.

"Okay, Miss Priss, thank you for that. Rita in Rialto, what's your advice for Sally? What's a girl to do when her man takes off with her neighbor and her four-wheel drive?"

"Well I'm with you, Jane. Sally honey, if my man did that to me, he'd be doing some serious talking to the business end of my Colt .45."

"Colt .45, ouch!" Jake laughed, dropping the binoculars to his lap.

"Whoa, Rita, gunplay, that's a little harsh, isn't it? After all, isn't all fair in love and war?"

"Oh, I wouldn't shoot him, honey, just put the fear of God into him. And if that didn't work, I've got a friend over in San Bernardino who could turn that dude into a dudette."

Jake laughed again and shook his head. "They grow them mean in Rialto."

"Well okay, Rita in Rialto, thanks for the call. Let's go

to Harry, calling in from the East Coast. Harry, what's
the word?''

''I think you're right, Jane. There are a lot of good men
out there, Sally. Forget that creep. You're better than that
and don't let yourself be disrespected like that again.''

''Sage advice, Harry, thanks for tuning in. Now here's
a sad story from the Pacific Northwest. This is Tim from
Tacoma. You're on, Tim. Talk to me.''

Jake leaned back in the chair again and listened as the
story unfolded. He stretched out his long legs, hooking
his knees over the edge of the deck's railing. It had been
a mild winter and spring had come early. But despite the
clement days of early March, midnight on the mountaintop was always cold, and sitting on the deck, which en-
circled the lookout tower's dome, it was even colder.
Snow still dusted the ground in a few spots and the ther-
mometer hanging on the post beside the sliding door read
thirty-six degrees.

He pulled his Gortex jacket around him tightly and
reached for the glass of wine on the small metal table
beside the chair. He didn't mind the cold, but even if he
had he wouldn't have gone inside. The midnight sky was
brilliant with a million stars and worth risking cold ears
and a red nose.

He drained the glass, feeling the alcohol warm a path
down his throat, and listened while Dear Jane talked with
the caller on the line. There wasn't another sound on the
mountain and her voice drifted out into the darkness like
the wind through the redwoods. He'd been first drawn to
''Lost Loves'' by the jazz, an eclectic mix of new and
classic pieces, but it wasn't long before he found himself
listening to the rest of the show—in particular to Dear
Jane herself.

Jake wasn't one for talk radio and normally wouldn't

have much patience for the sad stories phoned in by listeners. But there was something in the way Dear Jane responded to her callers, something so practical, so down-to-earth and rooted in common sense that he could appreciate. She seemed genuine, real, and she refrained from the usual antics of the media to stir up controversy or feign concern in an attempt to promote ratings. It was her manner, her comments, her sense of humor that had him tuning in night after night—well, that and her sexy voice.

"So that winds down another one for tonight. Don't forget to tune in tomorrow and catch the irrepressible Sly Fox, who will be sitting in for me for the next few days while yours truly takes a little R&R away from heartache."

"Who broke your heart, Jane?" Jake asked, gathering up the glass and binoculars and slowly rising to his feet.

"But I'll be back on Monday night with the best in jazz and worst in love. In the meantime, you're in good hands with Sly Fox."

"But Sly Fox is no Dear Jane," Jake commented. The substitute host had filled in for Jane Streeter on several occasions in the six months he'd been listening and Jake would inevitably find himself losing interest in those broadcasts. But he didn't mind this time. With Ted's wedding, he wasn't going to be able to catch the program for the next few nights anyway.

The reminder that all too soon he would be heading down the mountain and returning to Los Angeles again had a mixture of emotions broiling up inside and he suddenly felt cold—the kind of cold that had nothing to do with the brisk night air. The sturdy Gortex could protect him from the elements but it didn't stand a chance against the dread that pushed itself up from the past.

"And don't forget, love may be a many-splendored

*thing, but when it's over, we'll be here waiting. This is
Dear Jane—Jane Streeter—and you've been listening to
'Lost Loves'. Until next time, dream, hope and love until
it hurts. Good night.''*

Jake took one last glance across the sky, but like his
disturbing sense of dread, the wind had kicked up, whistling through the trees and dropping the temperature another few degrees. He reached up, switching off the small
outside speaker mounted on the wall, and pushed the sliding glass door open. The blast of warm air that greeted
him from inside the tower felt delicious and inviting, causing him to shiver again.

Ranger Station and Fire Watch LP6, with its solid stone
walls and thirty-foot tower perched atop Mount Holloway,
was known as Eagle's Eye, and in the three years since
he'd been appointed its ranger, he'd grown accustomed to
the volatile weather conditions. The remote assignment in
the backcountry of California's Los Padres National Forest wasn't usually the first choice of rangers entering the
United States Forestry Service. Not many welcomed, or
could tolerate, the solitude and the rugged living conditions. But solitude was exactly what Jake had wanted
when he'd joined the Service three years ago. He'd
wanted to be by himself, wanted to be as far away as he
could get from people, from the LAPD and from the
memories.

Valerie had accused him of running away—from her,
from their marriage and from all the reasons that it wasn't
working. But things hadn't been working between them
for a long time, long before there had been a drug dealer
under indictment and a key witness to protect.

He'd been a cop for ten years and had considered himself a damn good one. He'd worked hard to make his way
up through the ranks, putting in long hours and many late

nights. But while his efforts had paid off, landing him in charge of an elite task force working to bring down a major drug-smuggling operation in the Los Angeles area, the strain it put on his relationship with Valerie had put their marriage in jeopardy. He'd promised her once the assignment was over, he would take some time off and work on making things right between them—and who knows, maybe if things had worked out as they should, they could have salvaged something. But as it was, he'd never know. Fate had stepped in and changed everything.

He hung the binoculars on a hook beside the door and switched off the lights and the stereo. The tower went black and he followed the pale glow of the lights along the spiral stairwell to make his way across the tower's dome. He didn't like thinking about those days or about that old life, but sometimes even time and distance couldn't block out the memories.

Ricky Sanchez. He'd been a man who had worked hard all his life, a kind, decent man with a wife and a family, a man Jake would never forget.

It had been a warm summer night in June when Ricky Sanchez had gone about his normal janitorial duties of waxing floors, emptying trash cans and cleaning the rest rooms after hours in one of L.A.'s towering glass and steel high-rise office buildings. But on that particular night it had been the wrong place to be at the wrong time. From an unseen spot in a maintenance closet, Ricky unwittingly became the eyewitness to a high-level drug deal that had turned deadly.

Ricky hadn't known at the time that it was notorious drug lord Donnie Hollywood whom he had seen put a bullet in the head of a rival, but instinct had told him the only way to stay alive had been to find a hiding place and stay there, which is exactly what he had done. He'd still been trembling in a crawl space when the police had found him the next morning.

Jake still remembered the rush of adrenaline he'd felt when he'd listened to Ricky tell what he had seen. They had been trying for months to get something on Hollywood, something that would put him out of commission for good, but he'd managed to elude them each time. But now they had him on a murder charge and Ricky's testimony was going to put him away for life.

It hadn't come as a surprise when word filtered in from the streets that Hollywood had promised a hefty reward to anyone who succeeded in taking out the prosecution's star witness. The authorities had already taken steps to protect Ricky, and Jake had been confident they had thought of everything to keep him safe. He'd been stashed in a safe house with around-the-clock security and no one outside of Jake, the D.A. and a small, select number of task force agents—all of whom he had trusted implicitly—knew how to find him.

Unfortunately, it was the one thing Jake hadn't accounted for that did Ricky in. It had been one of their own, one of *his* own task force agents who had betrayed him. Hollywood had managed to do the one thing Jake had thought could never happen, turn one of his men against him, and it was a mistake he would regret for the rest of his life. It had not only cost Ricky his life, but the lives of two more task force agents as well.

Jake paused at the top of the stairs, staring down the narrow passage. The sense of betrayal had been overwhelming but the sense of failure had been even worse. Ricky had known the risk, had understood the danger, but he'd agreed to testify anyway. He had trusted Jake and the other members of the task force with his life, and they had let him down. At the funeral, Ricky's wife had told

Jake she forgave him, and her words had haunted him every day since then. How could she forgive him when he hadn't been able to forgive himself?

He made his way down the stairs and along the corridor to his small apartment. It had been over three years since the funeral, three years since Valerie had left him and he'd decided to resign from the force. He'd failed—both in his personal life and at work. He'd dropped the ball. His wife had suffered and an innocent man had paid with his life. How could he ever forget that?

He'd hoped being alone would help him work through his guilt, would help him put the past behind him and allow him to get on with his life. But he was beginning to think that was never going to happen. Ted had told him he needed time to heal, but in three years the wounds still felt fresh.

He reached inside the door and flipped on the kitchen light. The station had originally been designed to house two rangers, with living quarters for each—one built into the stone base of the tower and another one above a detached garage about thirty yards across a small compound—but lean budget times allowed for only one ranger to be assigned. Jake had chosen to live in the apartment within the tower. While the actual living area was no larger than the quarters above the garage, the tower housed the main kitchen, laundry facility and a fireplace. Besides, it had just made sense that he be close to the station's elaborate communications systems, located in the tower, in the event of an emergency.

Setting the glass in the sink, he headed for the bedroom, feeling as though he could sleep for twelve hours straight. But despite his fatigue, sleep eluded him.

Maybe it was a good thing he would be leaving the mountain. Maybe he needed to test the waters a bit, see what it was like to be back in civilization again, to be among friends, eat a little junk food and maybe even drink a little too much—at least for a little while. While leaving wasn't exactly something he was looking forward to, he should try to make the best of it. Besides, he hadn't been able to say no to Ted.

Los Angeles police detective Lieutenant Ted Reed was like a brother to him and if it hadn't been for Ted, Jake wasn't sure he would have made it through those terrible months after Ricky's death and the divorce from Valerie. The two of them had grown up in a neighborhood in Los Angeles where it paid to know who your friends were and who you could trust to watch your back—and Ted had protected his on more than one occasion. Somehow the two of them had managed to survive the poverty and the violence, the dysfunction and the disadvantages, even though it hadn't been easy. They'd made the decision to enter the police academy together and had supported each other throughout the ten years they'd served on the force. The hard times had forged a permanent bond between them. It made them survivors.

It had been almost awkward when Ted asked him to serve as best man at his wedding. But he understood. As men and as cops they had learned to play their cards close to the vest and keep emotions to themselves. Ted hadn't told him much about the woman he was marrying but Jake could hear the emotion in his friend's voice. The feelings were there—powerful and deep—and it wasn't necessary for them to go through the uncomfortable ritual of talking about them.

The wedding was in a couple of days and Jake planned on heading down the mountain in the morning after he got back from checking the trailhead. While Eagle's Eye was remote, he was never really alone. The area wasn't

without inhabitants. There was Claybe Fowler, his nearest
neighbor in the Forest Service, who manned the Cedar
Canyon Ranger Station located eight thousand feet below
at the base of the mountain. And during Jake's regular
trips to Vega Flats, its motley crew of residents had all
become his friends. Of course, during the summer months
there were hikers and mountain bikers, campers and even
a handful of hunters and fishermen about, and with the
help of the tower's state-of-the-art communications and
computer system, he also managed to keep in touch with
the outside world. He talked to Ted, his co-workers, his
mom and his sister on a regular basis via his ham radio
and his cell phone, when he could catch a signal. The
satellite dish gave him more television channels than he
could count and, of course, there was the radio and Jane—
Dear Jane.

So, while isolated, he hadn't exactly been alone the last
three years. And while he didn't relish the thought of going back to L.A., he owed it to Ted.

"Go to sleep," he ordered himself, rolling onto his side
and pulling the comforter around him close.

He let his mind drift, thinking back over the stories he'd
listened to tonight on the radio. He wondered just how
many of them were real and how many were made up
just to get on the air.

He thought of Dear Jane's soft purring voice. Would
he make up something just to get on the air with her? Or
would he need to? If he were to tell her about Valerie,
about Ricky and how responsible he felt for his death,
what would her advice to him be?

"I know you're there Jane, I can hear you breathing.
Oh Jane, dear Jane, it's okay, you don't have to say any-

thing—you got plenty said on the radio tonight. It's my turn now. You can listen to me for a change.

"Did you get my letter? If you read it you will know it won't be long now. I'll find you. I'll find you and the—"

Her hand shook as she flipped the call button, cutting off the caller. The ringing in her ears was almost deafening and her heart beat so fast in her chest it was almost painful.

"Hey, you okay?"

"Hmm…wh-what?" She looked up into Dale's kind, round face. "Y-yes, I'm fine. Why?"

"I don't know, you look a little pale." Her producer regarded her for a moment, his gaze narrowing. "That was him, wasn't it? It was that psycho again. He used the call-in line, the son of a—"

"He just wanted to let me know he'd been listening."

Dale reached for the telephone receiver.

"No, please," she said, stopping him with a hand on his.

"We need to report this."

"It was just more of the same stuff as before, just him getting his jollies—nothing new."

"But the cops are going to want to know."

"And I'll tell them, I promise. Just not tonight. I'm exhausted and they'll keep me here answering questions until dawn."

He picked up the phone, offering it to her. "Call them."

"He's on tape, they can listen in the morning."

"They told you to report every time he called."

"I will, I promise," she insisted, taking the phone and lowering it onto the cradle. "First thing tomorrow."

Dale drew in a deep breath and gave her a skeptical look. "If you don't, I will."

"I will," she vowed with mock seriousness, raising a hand. "Scout's honor."

Dale made a face, and pushed away from the desk. "I got a bottle in my desk drawer. Feel like a drink?"

"No, that's okay. I've got a long drive home."

"Well, if you change your mind," Dale said, heading for the door, "give me a shout."

"I'll do that."

At the door Dale stopped and turned back to her. "And let me know when you're ready to leave. I don't want you walking out to your car by yourself."

She nodded. "Yes, Mother."

Dale snorted and shook his head. "You amaze me, sitting there so cool and calm. Doesn't it bother you knowing that nut's out there somewhere?"

"Sure it bothers me. But you said it yourself, he's a nut and more than likely he's probably harmless," she said, feeling her throat grow tight. "Although I admit, I'll feel a lot better when the police have him behind bars."

Dale smiled. "Believe me, we all will."

She laughed, but as Dale pulled the studio door closed behind him she let the smile fade from her lips. She glanced down at her hands, balling them into tight fists to stop them from shaking. She felt sick—shaky and sick—and it would take more than one drink for her to forget that horrible voice over the line.

"Don't think about it. Just don't think about it," she mumbled aloud.

She closed her eyes, pressure throbbing painfully at her temples, and squeezed her fists even tighter. Her nails bit into the flesh of her palms but she didn't care—anything to stop the shaking.

Who was she kidding? She wouldn't be able to get down enough alcohol to get that raspy, mocking voice out of her head. Besides, she had a client coming in early tomorrow. It was hard enough balancing a private counselling practice with a nightly radio program without throwing a hangover into the mix. Still, it might be worth a try. She could call her partner to cover for her and lose herself in a couple of bottles of wine.

She rubbed her fists against her temples, slowly massaging. If only Dale knew how terrified she really was—if only everyone did. But she was determined no one ever would. She was not going to allow herself to give in to the fear—she didn't dare. Keeping up a front was the only way she could cope. Besides, maybe if she pretended long enough the awful fear really would go away... only that hadn't happened yet.

When the letters first started showing up in the mailbag eight months ago, she hadn't been too concerned. After all, she received so much mail at the station it was only natural there would be a few crackpots in the bunch. But after several weeks, when the letters turned to phone calls, and the phone calls turned threatening, she'd gotten very concerned—and so had everyone else.

How foolish she had been in the beginning—and how naive. But he'd seemed so harmless at first, she'd honestly thought she might be able to talk some sense into the guy. She had taken those early calls, listening as he rambled on and on in that mechanical-sounding voice about why he believed they were meant to be together and why she should accept it. She never should have taken those calls, never should have listened. The calls had grown increasingly hostile and she was never going to forget those words or the images they left in her brain.

"I'm not going to think about it. I'm *not* going to think about it," she insisted, her hands starting to shake again.

"You say something?"

"Huh? What?" She jumped violently, startled by the sudden appearance of the station's young intern at the door. "N-no."

The young man shrugged, looking confused. "Uh, Dale said I should walk you out to your car. You ready to go?"

"Oh, right, y-yes." Her throat was tight and she cleared it with a small cough. "I'm…I'm ready."

She felt foolish following the young man down the corridor and into the elevator, but if the truth be known, she was grateful not to be alone. Of course, there was just the rest of the night to think about—the drive home, the empty house, the long hours until dawn. She would hear every noise, jump at every bump, wonder about every shadow—just as she had every night for the last eight months. It wasn't much better once she finally did drift off to sleep. Dreams filled with shadows and danger and dark, looming figures were even worse.

The elevator doors slid open, the sound echoing through the nearly deserted parking garage. And the hollow sound of their footsteps along the concrete made it feel even emptier.

"I like your car," the intern said as the automatic door locks opened with a chirp.

"Thanks," she said, eyeing the interior of the SUV carefully. When she was sufficiently sure no one was hiding inside, she slid onto the seat. "And thanks for walking me down. I really appreciate it."

"Not a problem. Take care," he said, raising his hand in a wave as he started back for the elevator. "Hasta."

"Yeah, hasta," she mumbled, slamming the door and quickly triggering the doors to lock again.

She hated living like this. It wasn't fair, her life was not her own anymore—and all because of that…that *creep*. He was out there somewhere, doing what he wanted, going where he wanted to go, no restrictions, no fears. *She* was the one living in a prison, constantly looking over her shoulder, afraid of what might be around the corner, and she resented it.

"And that's exactly what he wants," she concluded aloud into the silence of the car—which only added to the insult. He wanted to terrify her and he'd managed to do that very effectively.

Frustrated, she pulled out of the parking lot and onto the street, punching at the radio and turning up the volume to full blast. Maybe he was out there. Maybe he was watching right now—and she almost wished he was. If he wanted to see her cower and hide, he would be disappointed. She may be frightened, her nerves may be frayed and on edge, but he wasn't going to get the best of her— no way in hell.

"Finally! The mountain man has arrived" Ted made his way through the small cluster of people milling about in the church foyer, waiting for the rehearsal to begin. With arms outstretched, he grabbed Jake in a bear hug. "Am I glad you're here!"

"I'm late, I'm sorry," Jake apologized, returning Ted's hug. "The 405 was like a parking lot. I didn't think traffic would be so bad this time of day."

"Now I know you've been up on that mountain too long," Ted said, pulling back. "This is L.A., have you forgotten? Traffic is bad here—period! It doesn't matter what time it is." He rested a hand on Jake's shoulder and took a deep breath. "You've got to help me." He ran a hand over his stomach. "Honest to God, I think there are butterflies in there. I'm not cut out for this."

Jake couldn't resist the urge to smile. Ted's tall, lanky build and sun-bleached hair may have had him looking more like a California surfer than a seasoned cop, but that only proved just how deceiving looks could be. Typically restrained and self-controlled, not much ever ruffled his feathers, and even if it did, you would never know. But he definitely looked worse for wear now.

"Don't tell me you're nervous. A tough cop like you?"

"Felons I can handle. What I need is protection from the wedding planner."

Jake frowned. "What's a wedding planner?"

"Not what—who," Ted clarified, turning slowly and gesturing to a small, well-dressed woman chatting with a group of people in the church. "Although, if you ask me, she's more like the wedding *Nazi*."

Jake turned to look at the woman. "That tiny little lady? You're afraid of her?"

"Don't let her size fool you," Ted warned. "I've known prison guards who could take lessons from her."

"Want me to go over there and rough her up?"

Ted made a face. "Funny, very funny."

Jake laughed. "Well, calm down, the cavalry has arrived. I'll protect you if…" He glanced at the petite woman and laughed again. "If Minnie Mouse over there decides to get mean."

Ted laughed then too. He gave Jake's shoulder a good-natured pat and his smile faded just a little. "But I admit, I do feel a whole lot better now that you're here. I miss having you around."

Jake's face grew sober. Ted knew better than anyone this trip to L.A. wasn't going to be easy for him. "Maybe I've got a few butterflies too."

"No reason to," Ted assured him. "We're all friends here and everyone is really anxious to see you. They all miss you."

"You think so?"

"I know so."

"Yeah, well," Jake said with a shrug. "There's no way I was going to miss your wedding."

"I was banking on that. I don't think I could get through all this without you," Ted confessed. He looked at the activity happening around them and shook his head. "Just look—all this fancy, foofy wedding stuff—it isn't me. What am I doing here?"

Jake's gaze narrowed. "You're not having any... second thoughts, are you?"

"About marrying Cindy?" Ted shook his head. "No way. She's...well, she's...perfect! You're going to love her."

"As long as you do, that's all that's important."

"Oh, I do," Ted assured him, gesturing to the activity around them again. "Enough to put up with all this."

Jake looked around then too and nodded. "Must be true love."

Ted started to smile, but spotting the diminutive wedding planner headed their way, suddenly bolted to attention.

"We're starting in five minutes, boys," she declared as she breezed by. "Find a seat inside."

Ted's gaze followed as she passed, then slid to Jake. "You heard her, we better get moving."

Jake chuckled as they turned and started into the church. "But aren't we missing the bride? When do I get to meet this woman who has enticed you to endure all of this?"

"I don't know, she should have been here by now...."

Ted's words trailed off when he spotted the car pulling up to the curb outside. "There she is. Come on, I want you to meet her."

Jake followed Ted back outside and across the walk to where two women stepped out of the parked car—one brunette, one blond. In one smooth motion, Ted swept the brunette up in his arms and into his embrace.

"I take it this is the bride," Jake said when he'd reached the tall blonde standing by the car.

"Either that, or Ted has some explaining to do," she commented dryly.

A sudden chill had the hair on the back of his neck standing up straight. Something registered in his brain, something so...so peculiar it left him feeling a little unsettled. Turning to the woman beside him, he studied her as he extended a hand.

"I don't believe we've met. I'm Jake Hayes."

"Kristin Carey," she mumbled, ignoring his hand and slipping a pair of sunglasses over her eyes. "So when is this thing supposed to start?"

He'd admit to having been rebuffed by a woman a time or two in his life, but never quite as resoundingly as that. "According to Minnie Mouse over there," he said, nodding to the wedding planner, "in five minutes."

"Minnie Mouse?"

"Nothing," he said, shaking his head. "Just a joke." But from the look on her face, she obviously didn't think it a very funny one.

"Cin," she said, pushing past him and calling to the woman in Ted's arms. "I think the wedding planner is trying to get your attention."

But Ted was already pulling his bride-to-be in their direction.

"Here she is, Jake," he announced. "This is Cindy."

"Cindy," Jake said in a low, formal voice.

Reeling a bit from the rather rude encounter with the icy blonde, he wasn't sure what kind of reception to expect from Cindy. Should he try to shake her hand, bow or just stand there like a dope? But Cindy didn't seem to have any doubts. She completely surprised him with a hug and a kiss on the cheek.

"Jake, at last!" she gasped, her blue eyes bright and sparkling. "I can't believe I'm actually talking to *Jake!* Ted talks about you so much I feel like we're already friends."

"Just promise to give me a chance to defend myself," he said, liking her immediately. "There's no telling what this guy's been saying."

"Oh, it's all been very complimentary," Cindy assured him. She slipped an arm through his, shooting Ted a wink. "But I'm depending on you to fill me in on all the secrets."

"I keep telling her there are no secrets," Ted insisted. "I'm really a dull guy."

Jake turned to Cindy. "Well, he is right about that. He is dull—*really* dull. Which makes me wonder, what do you see in him anyway?"

Cindy laughed. "Anyone who knows me knows I love a challenge. Right, Kristin?"

"The bigger the better."

There it was again, that curious tickle in the back of his brain. Did he know this woman? Is that why she'd given him the cold shoulder? Only he couldn't imagine forgetting someone who looked like her. Ms. Kristin Carey may be a bit frosty around the edges, but the fact remained that the tall, slender blonde was probably one of the most striking women he'd ever seen. If they had ever met before, he was sure he would have remembered.

"Jake," Cindy said then. "This is Kristin, my sister."

Jake nodded. "Actually, we just introduced ourselves."

"That's great," Cindy said, reaching a hand out to her sister. "Because as best man and maid of honor, you two are going to be spending a lot of time together the next couple of days."

Jake felt something in the pit of his stomach go tight. "Wonderful."

"Okay, everyone inside. Time to get started." They all turned in unison as the wedding planner approached, clapping loudly. "There will be plenty of time for chitchat later. Everybody into the church."

"It seems the wedding Nazi has spoken," Ted grumbled, pulling Cindy to him. "And my advice to you is to do what she says."

Jake watched as Ted and Cindy started arm in arm up the walk. Turning slowly, he gave Kristin a hesitant look. "Shall we?"

"We probably better," she said as she passed. "Wouldn't want to keep Minnie Mouse waiting."

Chapter 2

Kristin stood in the church foyer waiting for her cue. She glanced down at the gaudy tissue-paper bouquet in her hand and steeled herself against a wave of nausea. Of course, tomorrow she would be holding the real thing—a spray of pale pink roses and baby's breath—and probably feeling even worse.

Her gaze shifted to the long center aisle leading to the altar and she felt her stomach turn again. How was she ever going to make it down that walkway without tripping, fainting or throwing up?

"Just breathe," she reminded herself aloud, drawing in a deep breath. This wasn't her. She wasn't a nervous, fidgety person. She'd always prided herself on the ability to keep a cool head and steady hand. But a stranger had come into her life and changed all that, a stranger who had her edgy and uneasy and seeing danger around every corner.

Wasn't it supposed to be the bride who got the jitters and the maid of honor who calmed her down?

Kristin turned around, watching her sister as she talked with Ted's father. With her sparkling eyes and radiant smile, Cindy looked anything but nervous. In fact, Kristin couldn't remember seeing her sister looking more beautiful, or more serene.

Which was only the way it should be. If there was one person on this planet who deserved to be happy, it was Cindy.

Cindy had barely been out of high school when their parents had died. Not many young women would have welcomed the responsibility of a thirteen-year-old sister, but Cindy had been determined that the two of them stay together. She had worked hard to make a home for them, and later, when Kristin had considered foregoing college because of the financial hardship it represented, Cindy wouldn't hear of it. She'd insisted Kristin apply for every scholarship available, and what they didn't cover, the money Cindy earned waiting tables in the evenings after a full day at her job with the Los Angeles Probation Department did.

Which was why Kristin didn't want to do anything to spoil Cindy's wedding. One way or another she was going to do this, she had to—for Cindy.

"For Cindy," she whispered, taking courage from the words.

Her gaze shifted to Jake Hayes as he stood in his position to the left of Ted. Thinking about how rude she'd been to him made her feel queasy all over again. He'd been friendly and pleasant and she'd practically cut him off at the knees.

He was watching the wedding planner, listening to her instructions and moving as she prompted him. He really did seem nice—not that she was surprised. Ted had described him as a good guy. Under normal circumstances she probably would have enjoyed getting to know him. The problem was, these weren't normal circumstances. Things hadn't been normal in her life for a very long time. Still, she hadn't intended to be impolite. It was just that despite all that Ted had said about him, to her he was a stranger, and the grim fact of her life was that strangers terrified her.

"That's your cue, dear."

The loud clapping sound had her looking up.

"Hello? Are you listening?"

"Oh, uh, y-yes," she stammered, feeling her cheeks flush red.

"That's your cue," the wedding planner said again. "Start walking now."

"Y-yes," she stuttered again. "I'm…I'm sorry."

Flustered and embarrassed, she clutched the paper bouquet tightly in her hands and took a few hesitant steps forward.

"No, no, no," the woman said, shaking her head, marching up the aisle toward her. "You're not trudging through mud. Try and smooth it out a little, dear. Nice and easy."

Kristin watched as the wedding planner demonstrated, then on stiff, wooden legs, Kristin tried again. She didn't think her awkward, wobbling gait was any better, but she did the best she could. She felt ridiculous and terribly self-conscious, and without having to look, she could feel Jake's gaze burning through her, turning the narrow aisle into an endless corridor of embarrassment. It wasn't until she'd finally reached the end and slipped into her spot alongside the altar that she actually dared to glance up. Almost instantly, Jake's gaze caught hers and he gave her a broad smile. She nodded stiffly in response, a move that only made her cringe even more.

"Pull yourself together," she muttered. She was acting as though she'd never been around a man before, clumsy and ungainly.

But when she looked up and caught sight of Cindy as she started down the aisle, she suddenly forgot about being embarrassed or uncomfortable. It was only the wedding rehearsal but her sister looked radiant and Kristin felt her eyes sting with tears. This was Cindy's time to shine and she was determined nothing was going to get in the way of that—not *her* problems, not *her* inhibitions….

Her gaze slid to Jake Hayes.

And certainly not her trouble with strangers.

Jake watched the wedding planner and waited for his cue. It would be all downhill from here on out. The mock ceremony was over and all he had to do now was follow Ted and Cindy back up the aisle and out of the church. Piece of cake. Although with Kristin on his arm he wasn't expecting it to be particularly pleasant. But she would only have to tolerate him just long enough to make it out of the church. After that, he would be more than happy to stay out of her way.

For the life of him he couldn't figure out why she seemed to dislike him so much. After all, they were virtually strangers—at least he thought so. She didn't know him well enough to dislike him. Granted, he wasn't the most charming guy in the world, but it usually took a woman a little longer to find him annoying.

Of course, his paranoia made him wonder if Kristin's attitude toward him had anything to do with what had happened three years ago, either with the shootings, the task force or his resignation from the police department. Had someone said something to her about any of it? But common sense told him that wasn't the case. For whatever reason, the woman had taken an instant dislike to him and he just had to accept it.

When the signal came, he was ready and moved slowly into the aisle. Looking at Kristin as he offered her his arm, he expected to see nothing but ice in those clear brown eyes of hers, so he was taken aback when he didn't. In fact, her face was full of emotion. Could it be the Ice Queen wasn't so icy after all?

Her hand on his arm felt warm as they moved together and he could feel the slight brush of her body along his as they walked. He wasn't sure what had brought about the change in her, but he wasn't about to look a gift horse in the mouth. Emotion had a way of softening her beautiful features and frankly he liked the effect.

Still, he had to admit, her transformation had left him feeling a bit unsettled. He wouldn't have pegged her as the sentimental type. Weddings had a way of getting to people, though. Even *he* had felt a tug of emotion and this had only been the rehearsal. And it was probably that same sentimentality that had him turning to Kristin and giving conversation another try.

"That wasn't as bad as I thought it would be," he whispered as they made their way up the aisle. "And the good news is that we only have to do it one more time."

"But the bad news is, the next time we'll be doing it in front of a church full of people," she pointed out darkly.

"You have a point there," he acknowledged. Since she hadn't snapped his head off, he boldly pushed on. "Feeling a little anxious?"

"Only about tripping, fainting or throwing up," she groaned. "Or any combination of those three."

"That could be a little embarrassing," he agreed with good humor. "But you did great this time. There's no reason to think tomorrow will be any different."

"No?" She released his arm as they reached the large double doors leading outside and tossed the paper bouquet aside. "Maybe you'd like to try it in four-inch heels and carrying a handful of flowers."

Just like that it was back—that hard edge, the sharp words—and he was surprised at how disappointed he felt. "Somehow I don't think they'd go too well with my tux."

She didn't so much as blink, let alone crack a smile. She simply turned and left.

He stood in the open doorway and watched as she ran down the steps and across the drive toward Ted and Cindy. He felt strangely winded, as if he'd just taken a punch in the stomach. What was her problem? Was there something actually *wrong* with her or was she simply incapable of being civil to him?

"You win some, you lose some," he muttered, doing his best to remain philosophical as he started down the steps.

He really shouldn't let her attitude bother him. After all, it wasn't necessary that they like each other. It just would have made the next couple of days a little more pleasant, that's all. It wasn't a big deal, certainly nothing he was going to lose any sleep over. It was just that there was something so...*what?* Familiar? How was that possible? He was certain he had never seen her before today. So why did he have this ridiculous feeling that he knew her, that there was a connection between them?

"You're frowning."

Jake glanced up at the sound of Cindy's voice. She'd

broken away from the rest of the wedding party, who had gathered outside the church, and her expression was full of concern. "Was I?"

"Yes, is everything okay? Was there something about the rehearsal you didn't like?"

"Absolutely not," he insisted, slipping a reassuring arm around her shoulders. The gesture was unusual for him but there was something vulnerable and soft about Cindy that made it okay.

He thought of Kristin's hand on his arm, how it had almost felt natural for a moment—but *only* for a moment. She hadn't welcomed his touch. In fact, she'd been able to stand it only long enough to get out of the church. How could two sisters be so different?

"Are you sure?"

"It went great and tomorrow it's going to go even better." He gestured to the others. "Ask anyone."

Cindy's face relaxed. "I hope you're right." She breathed out a long sigh, catching Kristin's eye in the crowd and motioning her over. "I'm just so nervous."

Jake followed Cindy's gaze, watching as Kristin made her way toward them. "I think it might run in the family."

Cindy turned to her sister as she joined them. "Kristin, what if I trip?"

Kristin shrugged. "What if I faint!"

"Oh brother," Ted said as he approached and immediately reached for Cindy's hand to pull her to him. "Talk about looking on the dark side. What if everything just happens to turn out fine?"

Cindy looked up at him and sighed again. "You think that's a possibility?"

"I don't know, let's show up tomorrow and find out," Ted said, placing a kiss on the end of her nose.

Cindy looked at Kristin. "I don't know. What do you think?"

"Oh what the hell," Kristin said with a careless wave. "We've come this far." She put a hand on her sister's arm. "How about we make a deal? I won't laugh if you trip and you promise to step over me if I faint. What do you say?"

Cindy laughed and patted Kristin's hand. "It's a deal."

"Well, I'm certainly happy we got that settled," Ted announced dryly. "And Kristin, I should have known that alter ego of yours would come up with a solution." He glanced down at his wristwatch. "But now we need to get moving. I told my folks we'd meet them at the restaurant." Turning to the group, he raised his hands. "Okay, everybody, time for free food—follow me!"

It was a long time before Jake had an opportunity to talk to Ted again—long after the rehearsal dinner had ended, long after all the old friends had been greeted and long after all the toasts had been made. The restaurant was nearly empty and most of the wedding party and friends and family had left. As the waiters stacked chairs around them, he and Ted sat alone at a table, watching while Cindy, Kristin and the small group that remained played a lively game of darts in the lounge.

Jake felt exhausted, but it was a good kind of fatigue. He'd been concerned about seeing everyone again— friends, family—about how they would react to him after all this time. But as it was, things had gone fine. Old friends seemed genuinely pleased to see him and it had been good to catch up again. Of course, he'd done his best to keep his distance from Kristin Carey throughout the course of the evening. Although he couldn't help noticing she didn't seem to have a problem being friendly to the others at the party.

"You mentioned something back there at the church I was curious about," he said to Ted as Kristin tossed a dart that missed the board and landed somewhere behind the bar.

"I did?" Ted asked drowsily, taking a sip of his beer.

"Something about Kristin."

Ted put down his glass and blinked sleepily. "I don't remember."

"You said something about an alter ego?" Jake leaned closer, lowering his voice. "Is there…well, you know. Is there something wrong with her? I mean, some kind of weird split-personality thing or something?"

Ted snorted out a laugh. "What? What makes you think that?"

"I don't know," Jake insisted, feeling silly now for having brought up the subject. "You're the one who mentioned an alter ego. What the hell else is that supposed to mean?"

Ted laughed again and took another drink of beer. "Well, you don't have to worry. There's nothing *wrong* with her. I was just referring to…well, she has this job. She doesn't like to talk about her work, but…well, she's on the radio—"

Jake felt the hair at the back of his neck stand on end and a strange-sounding tinkle rang in his ears.

"It's a talk show. Late-night sort of thing," Ted continued. "Called 'Lost Loves.' It's really very popular and…well, Cindy and I tease her about having an alter ego because she doesn't use her real name on the program. On the air she's known as Jane Streeter—Dear Jane."

Kristin took aim with the dart and let it fly across the room. But instead of sailing into the bristled board, it took a dramatic nosedive and landed snugly in the wooden leg of the bar stool. Covering her mouth with her hand, she grimaced. That one had surprised even her. Behind her, though, the group in the lounge erupted in laughter and cheers.

"I meant to do that," she deadpanned as she turned around, which only brought a barrage of hoots and whistles.

"Good form though," Cindy shouted over the noise. "And I don't think there's a person here who could have done that if they tried."

"I stink," she stated flatly, reaching for her wineglass.

Cindy paused for a moment, then nodded. "Yeah, you do." She leaned close, slipping an arm around her shoulders. "But I love you anyway, little sister."

Kristin smiled. "And I think you're a little tipsy."

"Me?" Cindy gasped dramatically, then shook her head. "Naw."

"Karaoke time!"

They both turned as Cindy's longtime friend, co-worker and bridesmaid, Dana Byrd, came rushing up.

"Come on, Cin, get up here," she said, grabbing Cindy by the hand and pulling her to her feet.

"What? No! No, no," Cindy protested, shaking her head. "I can't sing."

"Don't worry, it's not a requirement," Dana assured her as the rest of the group began clapping and chanting: "Cin-dy, Cin-dy, Cin-dy!"

"Kristin, help," Cindy pleaded as Dana dragged her off. "Don't let them do this."

"What can I do?" Kristin asked, tossing her hands up in a helpless gesture. "Your public won't take no for an answer." As Dana pulled Cindy farther away, she raised her voice to be heard over the din. "But don't worry about embarrassing the family. I've already taken care of that."

Kristin had to laugh as she watched Cindy stumble her way through a popular song. Her sister hadn't lied about the singing, she really was awful! But her sour notes only had everyone laughing that much harder and soon the whole room was singing along.

All in all, it had turned out to be quite an evening and Kristin had to admit she'd enjoyed herself. She hadn't exactly been dreading the event, but she had been concerned. Given all the chaos going on in her life the past several months, she'd had some serious doubts she would be able to enjoy anything anymore. But there was something about the raucous group, the camaraderie, the laughing and the loud music that managed to block out her concerns and she welcomed the respite.

It had been a long time since she'd felt this comfortable in a public place. Granted, her exposure was somewhat limited. She was hardly alone. The wedding party had all but taken over the small restaurant. And besides, with all of Cindy's friends from the probation department and Ted's friends from the police force, how much safer could she have been?

Her gaze shifted across the room to Jake Hayes. He was the only stranger and the only one there who made her uneasy. However, the reason he made her feel uncomfortable had nothing to do with the fact that he was a stranger.

She thought about her awkward performance at the wedding rehearsal and cringed. Why had she acted like that—so cold and unfriendly? And why was she so awkward? It wasn't as though she'd never caught a man's attention before. She'd dated often in college and would even go so far as to say she may have fallen in love a time or two, or at the very least, experienced several episodes of very ardent "like."

Of course that had been before she'd realized just how vulnerable love made a woman, before she'd learned how emotions could be used against you. That had been before Blake.

So instead of thinking about love, she had decided to focus on a career. It wasn't as though she'd started out looking for a career in broadcasting. After graduation, her focus had been on establishing a counseling practice and expanding her patient base. When she'd agreed to do a quick guest appearance on a local morning-radio program it had been to promote a new counseling hot line for teens. She wasn't sure why, but she'd been a natural behind the microphone and soon calls began coming in to the station for her. Dear Jane and "Lost Loves" had grown from there. It had all happened so fast she really hadn't thought about where the show was going or what the potential was—that is, until Blake Murray came into her life.

It was at a local broadcasters' awards dinner almost four years ago—her first—and "Lost Loves" had been up for L.A.'s Best Talk Radio. Winning had been a thrill, but meeting Blake had changed her life. Tall, handsome, charming and full of self-confidence, he came at her with both barrels and she hadn't been able to take her eyes off him. They became inseparable from that moment on.

As the manager of a small radio network, Blake had been a strong supporter of her radio show and she'd been thrilled when he'd shown an interest in promoting her career. But even beyond that, he had a way of looking at her that made her feel as though she were the only woman in the world. She had thought it was love she'd seen in his eyes. What a dope! It hadn't been love—it had been dollar signs.

To Blake, she must have looked like an innocent, ripe for plucking. He'd swept her off her feet with talk of building *their* life together. Thinking about it now, she honestly couldn't remember which had come first, the marriage proposal or the partnership proposal.

Blake had been concerned that the local radio network that broadcast "Lost Loves" wasn't doing enough for her, that they were taking advantage of her and holding her back. She needed someone to look out for her interests, to steer her career in the right direction, someone who cared about her, who had her best interests at heart. He had told her she deserved the best and he was going to see to it that she got it.

Kristin shook her head. How foolish she had been. She realized hindsight was always twenty-twenty, but how could she have ignored all the warning signs? How could she have let herself be taken in?

Only she knew why. That was what love did to her—it made her blind and stupid and made her forget all about common sense. That was a lesson she'd had to learn the hard way. Back then she'd been too starry-eyed, too much in love to see what was so painfully obvious now.

Even though she knew things were moving fast, she'd accepted when he'd asked her to marry him. It was only by coincidence that she'd stumbled across those papers on his desk, those papers dated weeks before they'd even met, papers outlining his plan to negotiate a merger with a national radio network. Of course, the merger was dependent upon him acquiring control over "Lost Loves" and control over Jane Streeter and her career.

She shuddered. It had been a lie from the very beginning—the romance, the relationship, the proposal. He'd set her up and she'd never seen it coming. Like a fool she'd trusted him, believed him when he said he loved her, when he said he wanted to help. But Blake's idea of helping her had been helping himself. He had set his sights high, and Jane Streeter and "Lost Loves" had been his ticket to the big time.

It hadn't exactly been her finest moment. The truth had been a shock, but she had needed a lightning bolt like that to shock her back to her senses. She had allowed her feelings to blind her to the truth and she should have known better. It had been a bitter pill to swallow to find out that the man she loved had cared more about what she could do for him than he did about her. But somehow she'd gotten through it. It had been a painful lesson, but one she would never forget. She wasn't the kind of woman who could fall in love; it was simply too dangerous. It made her lose too much of herself, made her defenseless and left her too vulnerable. Love was just too risky for her. She would never allow her heart to rule her head again.

She took another sip of wine and watched her sister, feeling a swell of emotion in her chest. Cindy had warned her it wasn't fair to swear off all involvements simply because of one failed relationship, and maybe she was right. Maybe the day would come when she would feel safe enough or confident enough to take a stab at love again. But that time hadn't come yet and as Dear Jane, she had listened to so many sad stories she wasn't sure it ever would.

"Care to make a request?"

Kristin stirred herself from the unpleasant memories and looked up, surprised to see that Ted and Jake had moved from the restaurant into the lounge.

"You're going to serenade us?" she asked, smiling up at Ted.

"Not yet, but I think after another couple of beers..."

Ted let his words drift, then nodded toward the bar. "What can I bring you?"

Kristin shook her head. "I've had my limit."

"Come on," he prompted with an impatient wave of his hand.

"I don't dare," she confessed. "Another drink and I just might want to try my luck at darts again."

Ted's hand shifted to a gesture of surrender. "Enough said." Turning to Jake, he raised an eyebrow in question. "Best buddy, name your poison."

"Designated driver, remember?" Jake said, lifting his glass. "I've been on mineral water for the last two hours."

Ted shuddered. "I don't see how you can drink that stuff."

"Hey, I'm not going to risk getting pulled over," Jake told him, giving him a sly look. "You know what those L.A. cops are like."

Ted considered this for a moment, then spun around and shouted to the bartender. "Another mineral water for my friend here."

"Do you mind if I sit down?" Jake asked.

When Kristin looked up, Jake was smiling at her and she felt herself becoming stupidly awkward. "Oh, s-sure."

"Turned out to be quite a party," he said, gesturing to the group and Ted weaving his way toward the karaoke stage.

"*Quite* a party," she agreed. Just then Cindy and Dana broke into another song. "And quite loud too."

He nodded and took another sip of water. It was really too loud for conversation, which was fine with her. She wasn't sure what to say to him anyway. She'd been so rude earlier she was a little surprised he was willing to speak to her at all.

It took a little concentration but she forced herself to focus on Cindy and Dana as they mugged it up onstage, but there wasn't a moment she wasn't aware of Jake beside her. She knew every time he took a drink, every time he laughed, every time he turned to look at her.

Why was she so supersensitive where he was concerned? He was a longtime friend of Ted's so it was obvious he wasn't the type of stranger she needed to be wary of. So why not relax and just enjoy herself? He was another member of the wedding party—no more, no less.

But when she glanced at him as Ted stepped up onstage and joined Cindy and Dana in their song, he was smiling at her and she felt her heart leap to her throat.

"If it even *looks* like they're coming anywhere close with that microphone," he said in a loud voice, talking over the noise, "I'm making a break for the door."

"I'll be right behind you," she called back.

He smiled at her and she felt her throat close off again. She quickly turned away in an effort to avoid the danger of any further conversation. She concentrated instead on Ted and Cindy as they entertained everyone with their best Sonny and Cher impersonation while murdering the song "I Got You Babe!"

Despite all the laughter and good feelings, Kristin felt herself becoming angry and frustrated. He was there. *Him.* That nameless, faceless stranger who had stolen her freedom, and it just wasn't right. As hard as she tried, she couldn't stop thinking about him. This should be one of the happiest times in her life. Her only sister was getting married. Cindy had found the man she loved and they were beginning a wonderful life together. Nothing should be more important and nothing should get in the way. Yet, there was something—some*one* who threatened to take center stage. The poison that touched her life touched theirs as well, and made her the angriest of all.

From her peripheral vision she was aware when Jake turned and looked at her, and felt a surge of frustration. How much longer was this going to go on? How much longer was she going to greet every new man she met as if he were *him,* as if he were the stranger who knew her only as Jane Streeter, who had muscled his way into her life and made it a living nightmare?

Chapter 3

Kristin leaned back against the chair. The last twelve hours had been a glorious blur of flowers, music, tears and wedding vows. It had been a beautiful ceremony, having gone off without a hitch, and with the reception in full gear now, she was ready to relax.

"I know who you are."

The whispered voice in her ear had Kristin's blood turning to ice. Frozen in fear, the champagne flute slipped from her hand, landing on her dinner plate and shattering into a hundred tiny pieces.

"Wha—wha," she croaked, but her mouth was too dry for words to form.

"Oh my God, I am *so* sorry," Jake said, quickly reaching for a napkin and stopping the stream of wine before it found its way to her dress. "I'm such an idiot. I didn't mean to startle you."

Somehow Jake's voice penetrated the dizzying ring in her ears, silencing the roar. "W-what did you say?"

Jake pushed the debris of broken glass to one side and sat down on the chair beside hers. With the dinner over and the dancing having just begun, the table was empty, except for the two of them.

"I feel terrible," he confessed. "Are you okay?"

"N-no."

Jake's forehead creased in concern. "You're not? What can I do? Can I bring you something?"

"No—I mean, *yes*," she stammered.

"What," he asked anxiously, reaching a hand out to hers. "Tell me what you want—I'll get it."

"No," she said, giving her head a shake, trying to regain her composure. "I don't want anything."

"How about a drink? Maybe some more champagne?"

"No, I don't want anything to drink," she insisted, pulling free of his hand. "Y-you said…you said you knew who I was. What did you mean?"

Jake pulled his hand back into his lap and felt heat crawling up his neck. Maybe talking to her hadn't been such a good idea after all. He was still having trouble believing all this, was still reeling from learning who she really was. Kristin Carey was Jane Streeter—*his* Jane Streeter. Dear Jane herself! What were the odds of the two of them showing up at the same wedding at the same time, let alone her sister marrying his best friend? They had to be astronomical—off the charts! The situation seemed almost too impossible to be true, and yet he knew that it was. There was no denying that voice.

That voice! It was unmistakable. The only thing that surprised him was that he hadn't figured out her identity for himself.

"Oh, that," he said with a dismissing gesture. "I just mean that I knew…you know…about…"

"About what?" she demanded, pushing her chair away from the table.

"A-about the radio show," he stammered, feeling a little as he had when he was ten years old and sent to the principal's office for having poured food coloring in the urinals at school. "You're...you're Dear Jane."

She leaped to her feet. "How did you know?" she demanded. "Have you been following me?"

"No, of course not." He rose slowly. He wasn't sure what he'd expected her reaction would be, but this certainly wasn't it.

"Then I demand you tell me how you found out," she insisted. "I want to know how you found me."

"Jane—" He stopped himself, confused and flustered. "I mean, Kristin. Please, sit down. I didn't mean to upset you."

He reached out, hoping to help ease her back onto the chair, but she yanked violently away.

"I am upset and I want you to tell me how you found out."

He drew in a deep breath, utterly and completely baffled by what was happening. Somehow, someway, he'd taken a sudden turn into the Twilight Zone. What other explanation could there be?

"Look," he said carefully, using a voice he hadn't used since he'd been a cop on the street. "Please, just sit down. We'll talk."

When she hesitated, glancing for just a second at the chair beside her, he took that as a sign to move.

"Here," he said, pulling the chair close and holding it for her. "Sit, please. I feel terrible. I didn't mean to upset you."

She slowly lowered herself to the seat, but glared at him suspiciously, as though she expected him to pull it out from under her at any moment. ''All right,'' she said as she watched him take the chair beside hers. ''Now tell me. How did you find out I am Jane Streeter?''

At that point Jake wasn't sure what to do. Did he tell her the truth? Should he tell her it was Ted who had told him? He'd said she didn't like talking about the show, did that mean she'd be angry with him?

He suddenly wished he could just rewind the tape on these last few minutes and start all over again. The wedding ceremony had gone off without a hitch. No one had fainted, no one had tripped and—gratefully—no one had thrown up. And given the fact that they'd been seated at opposite ends of the table during dinner, he'd been fairly successful in steering clear of her for most of the day. But dinner was over now, the band was playing, the dance floor was crowded and the reception in full swing. Only the high spirits and good feelings had lulled him into a false sense of security and he'd thought it would be safe to talk to her again.

Brother, had he ever been wrong.

''I really didn't want to start any trouble,'' he began, choosing his words carefully. ''It just happened to come up in a conversation last night. Ted mentioned—''

''Ted?'' she gasped. ''Ted told you about me?''

''Please don't be angry with him. Like I said, it was just something he'd mentioned. You remember, after the rehearsal last night. He talked about your alter ego. I was the one who asked him about what he'd meant and he told me about 'Lost Loves.'''

Watching her as she leaned back in her chair, he wasn't sure what to expect. Some of the fury had disappeared from her face and it almost looked as though some of what he'd said had sunk in, but he wasn't about to let his guard down. He'd made that mistake before.

"He said you didn't like talking about it," he continued. "I just thought I'd mention it because…well, because I've listened to the program. I'm…well, I'm a fan."

For a moment she did nothing. She just sat there staring at him, and he found that completely unnerving. Finally, after what seemed like an eternity, she slowly reached up and rubbed a hand across her forehead.

"Look, I'm…I'm the one who's sorry. I…" She breathed out a heavy sigh and shook her head, her voice trailing off. "This is an area of my life I try very hard to keep private." She rubbed her forehead again. "I have a counseling practice. My clients have no idea… I—I can't allow what I do on the radio to interfere or inhibit my work with them."

"You're protective of them, I can certainly understand that," he readily conceded. He rose to his feet. "And again, I'm very sorry to have upset you. Please don't worry, your secret is safe with me."

He turned around, weaving his way across the dance floor and headed for the door.

That definitely hadn't gone at all how he'd expected. He wasn't sure he'd even thought too much about what her reaction might be and maybe that had been his first mistake. He probably should have supposed she would be surprised, maybe even taken aback. He wouldn't have even been surprised if she'd been somewhat flattered to discover he was a listener. But that violent burst of anger had been completely unexpected.

He pushed open the terrace doors and stepped out into the crisp, evening air. If he'd been a smoker, he definitely would have needed a cigarette. If he'd been a drinker, he would have headed straight for the bar. But as it was, he wasn't either of those things. He was a mountain man and what he wanted was a little fresh air to help him regain his composure.

Drawing in a deep breath, he immediately coughed. He'd forgotten just what this city smelled like. The odor of smoke and automobile exhaust hung thick in the air. EPA regulations may have done a lot to improve the air quality in the Los Angeles basin, but it was still a far cry from fresh, especially compared to his mountaintop perch. Still, the urban landscape did have its advantages. There wasn't much good you could say about smog, but it made for some spectacular sunsets.

He walked across the terrace, watching the play of color and shadow across the sky. Not much had changed in the three years he'd been away. Ted was still Ted and the friends he'd had before were still friends now. There were still the good feelings, the easy camaraderie, the comfortable interactions and he was relieved at that. But judging from the reaction he'd gotten from Jane...Kristin...

He shook his head. Whoever she was, judging from her reaction to him in the last twenty-four hours one thing was glaringly obvious. He had completely lost his touch with women.

He thought about her violent reaction—or rather *over*-reaction just now. Granted, it had been awkward for him, even embarrassing, but that really didn't concern him. What he really found upsetting was his disappointment. She was Jane Streeter—*his* Dear Jane. She had been his sole companion every night for the last three years. But now, all that had changed. Dear Jane was no longer that smart, warm voice on the radio. She had a name and a face—a face that had looked at him as though he were the worst kind of monster.

He walked slowly to the terrace steps that led down to the parking lot. Dear Jane was gone and he was sure going to miss her.

Kristin stared at herself in the mirror, hardly recognizing the woman looking back at her. What was happening to her? Why was she letting this happen? How could she have let one innocent remark send her so completely out of control?

I know who you are.

She groaned, remembering how she had whirled around and all but accused him of threatening her safety. If she hadn't behaved badly enough with her curt remarks and rude behavior, she was certain she had done more than enough this time.

She reached down and turned on the faucet, cupping her hands and letting the cold water fill the small reservoir they formed. He was Ted's best friend. They had known each other since they were kids. He may have been a stranger when they met, but she could hardly qualify him as one now. So why couldn't she just let all the fears and uneasiness go? Why couldn't she just relax and forget about looking over her shoulder? Why couldn't she stop making such a fool of herself in front of Jake Hayes?

"There you are," Cindy said, pushing open the door of the ladies' lounge and stepping inside. "I wondered where you disappeared to."

"Just taking a little break from the party," Kristin said, bending low and splashing the water against her cheeks.

Cindy regarded her for a moment. "Is everything okay?"

"Of course," Kristin said, straightening up and pulling a paper towel free of the dispenser. "Everything about this day has been perfect." She patted her face dry and turned to her sister. "Especially you. You look so beautiful."

"Little sister," Cindy said, placing a hand on each of Kristin's shoulders. "Do you remember when you were a little girl and Mom could always tell when Bobbie Johnson had been teasing you at school? She was never wrong and she used to tell you she had physic powers, remember?" Cindy gave her shoulders a little shake. "She didn't have physic powers, sweetie."

"No?"

"No!"

"And the point of this story is…" Kristin let her words dangle expectantly.

"The point is that there are times, not always, but when you're upset, a tiny line forms right there." She reached up and gently traced a path along the bridge of Kristin's nose. "Right smack-dab between your eyes."

"There is not," Kristin scoffed, pulling free and turning to her reflection again. "You're making that up—" But her words were brought to an abrupt halt when she noticed the small crease along her forehead. "Wait a minute," she muttered, moving her head from side to side. "That wasn't there before."

"Like I said, it's not there all the time—just when you're upset."

Kristin's gaze slid to Cindy's reflection in the mirror. "Then how come I never noticed it before?"

"I don't know. Maybe because the only time it's there is when you're upset, and then you're too…*upset* to notice."

Kristin leaned closer to the mirror, squinting as she examined the small line that creased her skin. "So what you're telling me is I've pretty much been walking around all this time with a billboard on my forehead, is that it?"

"Not exactly a billboard." Cindy smiled and took Kristin by the shoulders, steering her around until they were facing one another again. "Just a little clue to those of us who love you, a little hint to let us know something isn't right."

Kristin's gaze narrowed. "Somehow that doesn't make me feel any better."

"But it does bring us back to my original question," Cindy pointed out, the smile fading from her lips. "Something's up, what is it?"

Kristin drew in a deep breath, turning away. "Other than me acting positively paranoid and making a complete ass out of myself?"

"Is that what you did?"

Kristin nodded. "Just now, with Jake." She sighed heavily, shaking her head. "Promise me once you and Ted settle down you'll make sure to keep me off the guest list whenever he's around. The guy has got to believe I'm a real nutcase."

"A nutcase, huh?" Cindy repeated slowly. "What happened?"

Kristin turned and looked in the mirror; the glum woman looking back at her was hardly anyone she recognized. "Oh, he came up behind me and whispered something in my ear."

"What do you mean, whispered something in your ear? You mean something…nasty? Offensive?"

"No, no," Kristin insisted, shaking her head. "Nothing like that." She turned back to Cindy. "He said…well, he said something about knowing who I was, knowing that I was—" She stopped, rolling her eyes. "And I thought—"

"Oh dear," Cindy sighed, cutting her off. "I'm beginning to get the picture."

"Oh, Cin, I am so embarrassed," Kristin groaned, continuing. "Of course I completely overreacted. I jumped all over him and—" She stopped a moment, thinking. "I—I actually think I accused him of following me." She groaned and turned away. "Oh, God, can you believe that? What must he think?"

"Don't worry about it," Cindy advised in a calming voice. "You're being too hard on yourself. After all, it's understandable, given the circumstances."

"But Cin, if you could have seen his face. The poor man...he was trying to do something nice. And it was such a sweet thing really, when you think about it, discreetly letting me know he'd listened to the show, telling me he was a fan."

Cindy straightened up, her eyebrows raising. "Jake's a fan?"

Kristin shook her head. "He was trying to be polite."

"Interesting," Cindy mused with a smile.

"Oh stop it, Cin," Kristin chided.

"Stop what? What am I doing?"

"You know what you're doing and I'm telling you to stop it."

"I'm just saying I find it interesting, that's all," Cindy said, her eyes widening innocently. "Frankly I'm surprised Jake Hayes would have even heard of 'Lost Loves.'"

"That's not the point, Cindy," Kristin pointed out in a deliberate voice. "The point is, he was being nice and I cut him right off at the knees."

"Oh stop, don't be so hard on yourself," Cindy said, gathering Kristin into her embrace. "You have every reason to overreact considering everything that's been happening."

"But he doesn't know that."

"Maybe not," Cindy conceded. "But Jake will survive. Okay, so maybe he thinks you're a little nutty. So be it. He was a cop for a long time. I'm sure he's seen his share of nutty things." She gave Kristin a little shake. "Things even crazier than a radio talk-show host gone postal."

"I suppose." Kristin smiled, coughing out a humorless laugh. But when she thought of the look of utter disbelief on Jake's face, she groaned again. "Oh God, I hate this. I hate that my life isn't my own any longer."

Cindy's face grew somber. "I know you do."

Kristin's gaze turned to her sister. Standing there in her glorious chiffon gown and silk veil, Cindy was the picture of a beautiful bride. Kristin hated that she had allowed all the turmoil and disorder in her life to spill over onto the special day. Her armor may have cracked a little, but it hadn't shattered completely. It would protect her long enough to make it through the rest of this amazing day. Once she was home, once she was alone in her own private space, she could fall apart, she could tremble and cry and do all those things she'd been doing for the last eight months, all those things no one needed to know about.

"But you're right," she said with resolve. "He'll get over it. In fact, I wouldn't be surprised if he's forgotten about it already." She slipped an arm through Cindy's and led her toward the door. "So let's get out there and dance like a couple of fools."

"You? Dance?" Cindy gasped. "This really is a special day."

"And was that a karaoke machine I saw out there?"

"What?" Cindy stopped. "I don't believe this."

Kristin opened the door, waving her sister through with a grand gesture. "I think I feel a song coming on."

"Ted says you live somewhere in the mountains?"

"That's right," Jake said with a nod.

"Really? That's interesting."

"I don't know," he said, shrugging. He'd only been talking with the young, voluptuous woman for a few minutes but already he was bored.

"Where?"

"I beg your pardon?"

"Where in the mountains?"

"Oh. Mount Holloway. I man the fire lookout tower up there."

"Is that in California?"

"Right," he said, pushing himself away from the terrace railing and turning to look out across the parking lot. The young woman had walked out of the reception a short time after he had. Her skimpy little dress and abundantly exposed bustline had gotten his attention, but even they weren't enough to hold his interest. Maybe Ted was right, maybe he had been out in the wilderness too long.

"Awesome wedding, huh?"

"Oh definitely," he agreed. "Definitely…uh…awesome."

"And aren't Ted and Cindy just the cutest couple? Ted looks so adorable in that tux and Cindy's dress—gorgeous. They're just adorable."

Jake thought this was probably one of those pivotal points in his life. At thirty-six, he hadn't considered himself old, but he hadn't realized until that moment just how little in common he had with someone obviously much younger.

"He's so quiet down at the station," she continued, stopping just long enough to take a healthy sip of her drink. "I work there, at the station, did I mention that?"

"Yes, I believe you did."

"Well, let me tell you, Ted is so serious at the station.

He barely even smiles.'' She took another drink, draining the glass. "Oh look at this," she said coyly, holding up her glass. "Time for another drink."

There was an awkward moment, one of those awkward moments that seem to stretch a few seconds out into an eternity. Jake knew this was his cue to do the gallant thing and offer to get her another drink. But doing that would mean he would have to continue this conversation.

"Well," she said cheerily when it became obvious he wasn't going to offer. "I'm off to the bar." She took a few steps, then turned back. "Can I bring you anything?"

"Nothing, thanks," he said with a little wave. "Nice talking to you."

Nice? It had been agonizing. There was a time he probably would have enjoyed her company, would probably have even extended their conversation all the way to his motel room, but for some reason he wasn't interested in just getting laid.

He turned and stared out across the darkening cityscape. Maybe that was another pivotal point he'd reached—the point where one-night stands just didn't seem as appealing as they once had. Was it possible to outgrow meaningless sex?

He drew in a lungful of city air, then pushed it back out again. Would he have felt the same way if that had been Kristin just now? Would he have been restless and bored and chomping at the bit to get away?

"Ha!" he snorted aloud, thinking about the encounter he'd just had with her. If it had been Kristin with him just now, he wouldn't have had to worry about getting bored. She wouldn't have let him get close enough to find out.

Just then, a car pulled into the lot and came to a stop just like the half dozen or so that had come before it while he'd been standing on the terrace. There was nothing much to distinguish it from any of the others, but Jake's keen eye had recognized it immediately as an unmarked police car. Of course, the appearance of a police car in itself wasn't all that unusual. After all, the place was full of cops. One of their own was tying the knot and the force would be well represented at the celebration. But when the two detectives stepped from the car, Jake could tell this wasn't a social call. Their body language was all business.

He had just decided to start down the terrace steps and wander across the parking lot to find out what was going on, when he suddenly saw Ted appear from out of the shadows to greet the men. Stopping on the stairs, Jake watched them for a moment.

Whatever it was they were discussing with him, it had to be serious. You didn't disturb a man on his wedding day unless it was big—and judging from Ted's reaction, it was. He had become agitated and for Ted that was serious.

Jake continued down the steps and soundlessly crossed the pavement. It really wasn't any of his business, but old habits died hard. Cops were nosy, even ex-cops like him. Something was up and he wanted to know what.

As he made his way across the blacktop, Ted looked up, spotting him.

"Jake, over here," he said, waving him close.

"Looks serious," he said as he approached the three men.

"It is," Ted said in a grim voice. "Jake, this is Tom Walker, Hank O'Brien. They're with CAP."

The Crimes Against Persons unit, a division of the LAPD's Robbery Homicide Division in which Ted acted as supervisor, meant it had to be a rape, battery or assault.

"Somebody get hurt?"

"I'm afraid so," Ted said. He turned to the two detectives. "I don't want to get anyone inside upset, so why don't you two wait here. Sit tight and I'll be back." He turned to Jake. "We need to find a place to talk."

The hair on the back of Jake's neck bristled. He recognized Ted's tone. This was something serious. "Sure. Want to go for a walk? Maybe around the block?"

Ted nodded.

"You know," Jake said after they'd been walking in silence for a few minutes, "I'm not afraid to admit you're scaring me a little."

"I'm sorry," Ted said with a heavy sigh, his pacing slowing. "I don't mean to. I've had something I've been working on turn really ugly."

"Someone I know?"

"Yes and no. A woman was assaulted about an hour ago."

"Somewhere close?"

Ted shook his head. "A parking garage out near Westwood."

"Rape?"

"No, but her attacker nearly killed her."

"Attempted murder."

"Actually, it's only by accident that it wasn't murder."

"You mean he got interrupted before he could finish the job?"

Ted slipped his hands into the pockets of his tux. "Not exactly. More like the guy realized he had the wrong woman before he killed her."

"Wrong woman?"

Ted nodded. "The guy was nice enough to leave the *intended* victim a little note scrawled across one of the walls in the garage, telling her he'd make sure he got it right next time." Ted's voice was ragged and his breathing strained and uneven. "Of course, he wrote it in the blood of the innocent woman, who just happened to be in the wrong place at the wrong time and bore a slight resemblance to the woman he was after."

"Sounds like you've got a sicko loose."

"Even worse than that. This sicko has been stalking the intended target for months—letters, telephone calls, stuff like that."

"Well, I'd say he upped the ante tonight." Jake was still troubled by Ted's reaction. They'd all worked cases that struck a nerve, that could get to you more than usual, but it wasn't like Ted to get personally involved—at least not to the point that he would allow himself to be pulled away from his own wedding. "Any leads?"

"Nothing of any significance."

"Any chance the victim tonight could ID him?"

"I doubt it. At least not for a while anyway. She's barely hanging on as it is."

"And you're worried about keeping the intended victim safe, is that it?"

"Something like that."

Jake couldn't seem to shake an odd sense of foreboding. As tragic as the situation was, Ted's reaction just didn't seem to match the circumstances. "So go back there and send Tom and Jerry—"

"Hank." Ted corrected.

"What?"

"It's Hank," he repeated, obviously missing the joke. "Tom and Hank."

"Okay, Tom and *Hank*," Jake said, regarding his friend carefully. "Send them out to pick up your intended victim and stash her until you pick the bastard up."

"It's not quite that easy."

"Sure it is. If the woman is interested in staying alive, it's damn easy."

"You don't understand. The attack tonight took place in the KLAM Building. The woman works there."

"Clam Building? Where is that? Out near San Pedro docks or something?"

"Not clam. K-L-A-M. They're call letters." He stopped in the middle of the walk and turned to Jake. "The building houses Wave Communications, the radio station where 'Lost Loves' is broadcast."

Jake's entire body went cold. "The woman tonight, this is someone Kristin knows?"

Ted nodded. "An assistant producer in the news division."

"And you have to tell Kristin about the attack," Jake concluded.

The growing darkness triggered the sensor on the streetlight and it suddenly flickered to life. A pale pink glow bathed the sidewalk around them and they both turned in unison and started slowly back toward the reception hall.

"There's more to it than that," Ted continued as they walked. "Like I said, the attacker was after someone else, another woman who works at the station."

It hit Jake right in the face. Suddenly it all made sense—the detectives showing up at the reception, Ted's reaction. He'd acted personally involved because he was.

"Kristin." Her name slipped from his lips without any conscious effort on his part.

"The calls started coming into the station about eight months ago, usually during the broadcast. Nobody thought too much about it at first. They get all kinds of crazy calls into the program, you can imagine—heavy breathers, crank calls. Of course, all calls are screened before they reach Kristin, and this guy never made it onto the air.

They were more of a nuisance than anything else. She even talked to him off air once, you know, confronted him, tried to reason with him to get him to stop. It seemed to work for a while, but then the letters started arriving.

"Like the telephone calls, they seemed pretty benign at first—your basic 'we're meant to be together' type of thing, but again, as the letters kept coming, they started getting darker, more violent."

Jake's mind was reeling. "There wasn't anything on those letters that could help you trace the guy—fingerprints, postmark?"

They had reached the parking lot. "Nothing. They were mailed from all over the country."

"All written by the same person?"

"As far as we can tell. Handwriting appears to be done by the same person, but beyond that we haven't been able to get anything else. Our lab here went over them and came up empty. I sent the letters over to the FBI lab for a look and they couldn't do much better."

Ted stopped before they reached the terrace steps. "The thing is, 'Lost Loves' is in markets in practically all fifty states. Stations all over the country broadcast it every night on a national network. All the calls came in on the national 800-number."

Jake closed his eyes. 1–800–NIGHT TALK. How many times had he heard Dear Jane call out that number?

"All the letters that came," Ted continued, "were addressed to the network's post-office box, which is announced numerous times throughout the program and can also easily be found on their Web site. When he called, he asked for Jane—you know, Jane Streeter, the name Kristin uses on the show. When he wrote, he addressed all the letters to Jane. We're fairly certain he didn't know who Jane Streeter really was or where to find her, but

now, after tonight..." He shrugged, letting his words
drift.

Jake could hardly believe what he was hearing. It explained so much. No wonder she had reacted so violently
to him earlier; she must have been terrified. She wasn't
unfriendly, she was frightened—and she had every reason
to be.

"And if he knows where to find her," Jake concluded,
"it's just a matter of time before he finds out who Dear
Jane really is, if he doesn't know already."

"I've got to find a way to keep her safe, Jake," Ted
said in a tightly controlled voice. "And I need your help."

Chapter 4

"I can't do this."

"Jake, you've got to. I need you on this one."

"No." Jake shook his head. "I'm not going to get into this armchair-philosophy-facing-your-fears sort of thing with you."

"Is that what you think this is?"

"That's exactly what it is." Jake paced back and forth between the coatracks, feeling like an animal caught in a trap. "I know what you're trying to do and it's not going to work."

"I'm *trying* to keep Kristin alive," Ted said, his eyes following Jake as he moved. "And I'm asking for your help to do that."

Jake stopped. "You're forgetting what happened the last time I was in charge of protecting someone. I blew it, remember? Or would you like me to call up his widow, have her remind you?"

The storage area behind the hatcheck counter was small

and cramped but it was private and out of sight of the wedding guests—and for what they wanted to discuss, they'd wanted no one listening. They'd sent the attendant on an extended break and hung up the Closed sign. They were completely alone. Only the light, lively music from the reception drifted through the array of coats, hats and wraps, a stark contrast to the intensity of emotion that filled the small space.

"I don't need to be reminded of anything," Ted pointed out. "What happened three years ago is over, done with, ancient history. Besides, despite how much you love to beat yourself up about it, the fact is it wasn't your fault. No one suspected Hollywood had someone on the inside. There was no way you could have known, and it's about time you stopped punishing yourself for the incident. You need to put it away once and for all."

"I'm living my life. Maybe it isn't the life you, or the department shrink, or anybody else thinks I should be living, but the fact is, I'm alive." He started pacing again. "That's more than I can say for Ricky or the two good cops who died trying to save him."

Ted was quiet for a moment, watching as Jake walked back and forth. "You know, I take it back. You're not still punishing yourself. You don't have time. You're too busy feeling sorry for yourself."

Jake came to an abrupt halt and stared at Ted, fists clenched. He wouldn't have tolerated that accusation from anyone else.

"So are you finished with the psychoanalysis?" he asked in a tightly constrained voice.

Ted turned away, shaking his head. "Did I tell you Cindy lost her parents when she was in high school? Three weeks before she was to graduate." He walked to one of the racks, resting a hand along the top. "Some guy blew through a red going about sixty and T-boned them in the middle of the intersection. Cindy pretty much raised Kristin after that. Except for a few distant cousins, there was no other family.'' He glanced back at Jake. ''I promised her I wouldn't let anything happen to Kristin. I'm asking you as a favor to help me, Jake. Help me keep my promise to my wife.''

Jake felt the anger seep out of his body and his hands go limp. Why was he even bothering to argue. He owed Ted—a lot. Ted had always been there for him and there was no way he could turn him down. But fear had his stomach knotting into a tight ball. He understood how much this meant, not just to Ted and Cindy but to Kristin as well.

Kristin. He thought of the nights he had listened to her on the radio, of that low, sultry voice drifting out along the mountaintop. It seemed impossible to think that at the same time there had been someone else listening, a madman bent on harming her. Ted had told him how remarkable she had been, coping with all this for the last eight months. She had complied with all the restrictions they'd asked of her, curtailing her activities, halting public appearances and changing her daily routines. But Jake had seen the terror in her eyes, he had see the suspicion and the anxiety. Everything in him responded to the threat to her safety. He wanted to protect her, wanted to keep her safe—he just prayed he wouldn't fail again.

''I'm...I'm afraid,'' he confessed in a whisper.

Ted took the few steps to bring them together, resting a hand on Jake's shoulder. ''I know.''

''What if I...if I can't—''

''You can,'' Ted said, not even giving him a chance to finish that thought. ''If I had any doubts, I wouldn't ask.

This is family—*my* family. Do you think I'd ask if I had even a shred of doubt?''

Ted's faith in him was almost enough to make him believe too. ''Tell me what you want me to do. Tell me about this plan of yours.''

''Where are you taking us?'' Cindy giggled as Ted took an abrupt turn in the foyer and steered her toward the door of the hatcheck counter. ''What is going on?''

''Come on, we're going in here for a minute,'' Ted said, opening the door and stepping to one side to allow Cindy and Kristin to pass.

''What?'' Cindy laughed as Ted gave her a little push through the door. ''What for?''

Kristin started to follow but couldn't quite shake a sense of uneasiness. Ted had found them and hustled them out of the reception, offering very little explanation. She was suspicious but cautioned herself not to overreact, especially given how she'd embarrassed herself earlier with Jake, but something just didn't feel right.

''Jake? What are you doing here?'' Cindy asked, spotting him as she walked inside. She turned back to her husband, eyebrow arched. ''What are you guys up to?''

Spotting Jake, Kristin came to a dead stop at the door. ''Something's happened, hasn't it?''

''What?'' Cindy said, confused, her smile faltering. ''What are you talking about?''

Kristin's gaze slid from Jake to Ted. ''I'm right, aren't I?''

Ted shifted his weight, motioning her inside. ''We'll talk in here.''

Kristin moved through the door on legs that felt like water. Ted had his ''cop face'' on now and the sense of dread she felt was almost palpable. But she'd become adept at masking her emotions, had mastered the art of maintaining control when all she wanted to do was fall apart, especially in the last eight months. She had no doubt as she walked into the small open area behind the counter that no sign of the terror that clawed at her stomach showed.

She glanced up at Jake as she entered. There was something about him though, something that made it more difficult to maintain control. It was as if he saw too much, could tap into those thoughts and fears she preferred no one see.

"What *is* it?" Cindy demanded. She was visibly agitated now and Ted reached for her in an effort to calm her down. "Something terrible has happened, hasn't it? Tell me!"

"First I want you to sit down," Ted insisted, leading her to the attendant's chair. "Kristin, let me find you a chair—"

"Ted, for pity's sake, just *say* it," Kristin snapped. The anger felt good and helped tamp down the fear that wanted to bubble over and consume her. "What the hell is going on?"

Ted glanced up at Jake, then turned back to Kristin. "There's been an assault. Someone at the radio station."

"Oh God," Cindy groaned.

Kristin's body went numb. "Was it him?"

Ted nodded. "We're fairly certain."

The world seemed to shift suddenly then, causing her to lose her balance, and it wasn't until she felt Jake's strong arms around her that she realized she'd been about to faint. There was a blur of noise and action around her, Cindy was saying something but she couldn't seem to concentrate or respond. She wasn't sure if she wanted to cry, or scream or just drift away. The only thing she could be certain of were those arms around her, solid and secure.

"Ted, that chair over there," Jake shouted, nodding to the folding chair leaning against the back wall.

"Just lean on me," Jake told her.

"I'm…I'm fine," she insisted as he helped her to the chair, but she wasn't sure about that at all. She hated being weak, hated that she couldn't stand up to all this on her own. But even as the ringing in her ears subsided, a wave of nausea replaced it.

"Here," Cindy said, shoving a glass into her hand. "Drink this."

She wasn't sure where the ice water had come from, had no recollection of Cindy leaving to get it, but it didn't matter. It felt cool and refreshing going down her throat and seemed to revive her clouded perception.

"W-who?" she stuttered after she'd taken a few sips. "Who was hurt?"

Ted reached into the breast pocket of his tux, bringing out a small tablet.

"Her name is Victoria—"

"Tori Peters," Kristin mumbled, leaning back in the chair. She closed her eyes, picturing the bouncy young woman in her mind—smart, funny, full of life. "Is she…"

"She's in surgery right now," Ted said. "They'll know more once she's out."

"Surgery? Was she shot?" Cindy asked.

Ted shook his head. "Multiple stab wounds to the upper torso."

Kristin groaned. "But why? Why would he want to hurt Tori?"

Ted hesitated for a moment. "She's tall, she's blond. He thought—"

Kristin groaned. "He thought she was me." This couldn't be happening. It just kept getting worse. When was it going to end?

"But I don't understand," Cindy said, pushing Kristin's hair back from her face. "How can you tell it was him? I mean, how do you know it wasn't a random attack?"

Kristin felt the apprehension building and felt sick to her stomach. "Because there's something more, isn't there?"

Ted knelt down in front of her. "He'd mistaken the victim for you. He left…he left evidence at the scene that said as much."

"Evidence?"

Ted's gaze shifted to Jake for a moment. "It's clear this guy isn't fooling around any longer. He means business and we have reason to believe he's going to make another attempt."

Kristin looked from Ted to Jake, and back again. "How can you know that? What's this evidence you found?"

"He left a…communication at the scene," Ted hedged.

"A communication? What kind of communication? A phone call, a note?"

"It's not important," Ted said finally with a dismissive gesture. "Just believe me when I say he's planning another attempt."

"Then we have to do something," Cindy demanded. "You have to find him and stop him."

Ted stood up, taking Cindy by the arm. "That's what we want to do, what we intend to do." He turned to Kristin. "Jake and I have come up with a plan but we're going to need your cooperation to make it work."

"What kind of plan?" Kristin asked. And what does Jake have to do with it was the question she didn't ask.

"Until tonight, we had no way of knowing just how serious a risk this guy presented. It was important to take precautions, to not take any chances, but for all we knew, these could have just been idle threats and all the guy was interested in was getting his jollies thinking he might have frightened you." Ted reached down and gave Kristin's arm a pat. "Now we know that wasn't the case. Now we know how dangerous he is and we're going to have to take some serious steps to ensure your safety."

Kristin thought of the precautions she'd been taking for the last several months—check-ins with her boss and Cindy; circling the block before going home; altering her routes to and from work; not answering her phone—precautions that had all but made her a prisoner in her own life.

"I've done everything you've asked me to," she pointed out. "What more is there?"

Ted straightened up, slipping an arm around Cindy's shoulders. "I want you to go away for a while."

"What?" Kristin leaped to her feet. "What do you mean go away?"

"Wait a minute, wait a minute," Cindy said, reaching for her. "Let's hear what he has to say."

"I won't wait," Kristin snapped, pulling her arm back. "I won't discuss it. It's out of the question."

"We're talking about your safety here, maybe even your life," Cindy snapped back. "*Nothing* is out of the question." She took a deep breath, gathering her control. "Let's just listen."

Kristin glared at her sister, but she knew she was right. After a moment, she turned to Ted. "All right, I'll listen."

"Kristin, this guy isn't playing around, and he seems to know what he's doing. The show is syndicated in markets across the country. Finding the station where it's broadcast couldn't have been easy, but he did it. He also knows what you look like, has probably seen pictures of you on the Internet taken at various awards shows. Also, he's probably watching the studio, or has someone watching it for him, and it's just too risky for you to try and continue doing the show from there.''

"Then I'll do the show from somewhere else. I'll talk to Dale, he'll make the arrangements.''

"We need to get you away from here, someplace where he can't find you.''

"But what about my practice, my clients? Ted, I have people who depend on me, who need my help.''

Ted hesitated for a moment, looking to Cindy and giving her shoulder a squeeze. "Well, hopefully it won't be for very long. Maybe you could think of it as a…a vacation.''

"A vacation?'' Kristin shook her head, tossing her hand in the air and pacing a few steps back and forth. "This is crazy. You're going way overboard here.'' She stopped, her hands on her hips. "This guy is looking for Jane Streeter, not me. He doesn't know my real name.''

"You can't know that for sure.''

She turned at the sound of Jake's voice behind her. In the back of her brain she thought of those strong, solid arms and how secure they'd made her feel. "It's not common knowledge.''

"Maybe not,'' he admitted. "But it's not exactly something you can control either. You know how it goes, one person knows—a friend, a co-worker, and they tell someone, who tells someone.'' He shrugged. "I found out and I wasn't trying.''

She couldn't argue with him. She may have told him she didn't like people knowing she was Jane Streeter, that she'd been concerned about protecting her clients who came to see her for help, but the truth was that up until eight months ago she hadn't cared who knew.

"So okay," she conceded, turning back to Ted. "It's a lot more dangerous now. I'll take a lot more precautions—I'll call in every hour, I'll put bars on the windows—whatever."

"You just don't get it," Cindy cried, her voice wavering with emotion. "There's someone out there who wants to hurt you, who maybe wants to kill you. This isn't the time to be thinking about your practice or your radio program. It's the time to start doing what you need to survive."

Kristin sighed, the fatigue of many long, sleepless nights taking its toll. "Cin, I'm sorry. You're right, you're right," she said quickly, reaching for her sister and giving her a hug. Knowing she had upset Cindy only made the situation worse and she just wanted to make it better. "What should I do? Go to a convent somewhere? A desert island?"

Cindy turned to Ted. "Why doesn't she come to Mexico with us?"

"I am *not* going on your honeymoon with you," she stated flatly.

"Then we won't go," Cindy continued without missing a beat. "I've got the time off work, you can come stay at our place."

"No," Kristin said, stepping back and shaking her head. "You two are going on your honeymoon as planned."

"You expect me to get on a plane and leave now?" Cindy shook her head. "No way."

Kristin looked at her sister. There she stood in her wedding dress, the shoulder-length veil pushed back, surrounding her face like a halo. This was her wedding day, she should be beaming with happiness and hope. Instead, she looked miserable, her face pale and eyes red from tears. Kristin wanted to scream, wanted to pound on the wall, pound on her chest, pound on *something* in protest. This whole awful nightmare was like a poison in her life, spreading and touching everyone and everything she cared about. Wasn't it enough that a nameless, faceless stranger had made her life into a living hell? Did he have to tarnish the lives of the people she loved as well?

She thought of the young woman in surgery fighting for her life. That should have been her in that hospital bed, not Tori, not lovely, wonderful, innocent Tori. The woman had done nothing wrong, her only crime being that she bore a slight resemblance to her—to Dear Jane.

She reached out and took Cindy's hand again. Now the poison had reached her sister, had turned a bride's smile to tears, marring this wonderful day. It wasn't right. She had to put an end to it, had to stop the poison from spreading before it ruined all their lives.

"You have to go, Cin," Kristin concluded. "It's your honeymoon."

"We can go some other time," Cindy insisted.

"But everything's all planned."

"It doesn't matter," Cindy insisted. "It was only a week, there will be other trips."

"But not like this—"

"Stop!" Ted's voice boomed loudly in the small room, causing them both to be quiet. He picked up the stool from behind the counter and slid it beside the folding chair. "Both of you, sit down."

Kristin would have normally chafed at such blunt orders, but there was something in Ted's tone that made her think better of it. Following Cindy, she returned to the folding chair and sat down.

"As I said," Ted went on, "Jake and I have come up with a plan. It isn't perfect but it could work." His gaze slid purposefully to Kristin. "As long as we *all* cooperate. We've worked out a plan for you to stay at Eagle's Eye."

"Eagle's Eye?" Kristin felt the tingling of apprehension again.

"The ranger station at Mount Holloway. It's remote, hard to find and Jake would be there to protect you."

"You want me to stay up there?" Kristin literally choked, her hand going to her throat. "With…with him?"

Jake reminded himself it was a good thing he wasn't taking Kristin's reaction to Ted's proposal personally, because if he was, he would have had to be pretty darned insulted. Watching the woman choke at the thought of spending time alone with him was hardly flattering and no doubt would be a blow to any man's ego. But she was upset, her nerves were on edge, so he'd give her the benefit of the doubt.

He hadn't really expected her to jump at the idea. After all, dropping everything and walking away from your life wasn't the easiest thing to do—he knew that from personal experience. But serious times called for serious measures and this was about as serious as it got. There was plenty of motivation for her to agree to the plan. Whoever it was who'd been stalking her wasn't about to give up easily. He had too much invested to just give up and go home. Ted had sought help from the FBI and the case had been moved to the front burner in both agencies. All efforts would be directed to finding the stalker. The trick would be making sure he didn't find her first.

He had to admit he'd been a little taken aback when Ted had first suggested the idea to him, but actually, the more he thought about it, the more sense the plan seemed to make. After all, Eagle's Eye was certainly off the beaten track. The miles of wilderness alone would offer considerable protection, and with the tower's sweeping views, it would be virtually impossible for someone to approach without being observed.

But exactly what he was going to do with the woman was a different story. Of course, he understood no one would expect him to entertain her. After all, he had a job to do and his daily work routine couldn't change. She would have to find something to occupy her time.

Except for an occasional visit from another ranger, a hunter or a camper or two, he was alone at the tower. He would have difficulty imagining what it would be like to have anyone else around, let alone her. Of course, given the separation between the tower's living quarters, they would hardly be tripping over one another. In fact, he could almost assure her complete privacy. But having someone around, whoever that might be, would take some getting used to.

"I couldn't," Kristin was saying. "I really couldn't. It would be too much of an imposition." She turned to him. "Thank you, honestly, it's very sweet of you to offer, but it's too much to ask."

"I think it's a terrific idea," Cindy said, jumping up. Some of the strain had disappeared from her face, and her eyes were wide with excitement. "Oh, Jake, you're a godsend. Would that plan really be possible?"

"No, it's not possible," Kristin insisted before he could answer. "You can't ask that of him. This isn't his problem, it's *mine*. Too many innocent people have been affected by this situation already. I will not ask anyone else to take the risk."

She spoke with intense resolve and determination, but not everyone was on such an intimate basis with her voice as he was. He heard the slight quiver, the momentary hesitation, the uncertainty he was sure she thought she'd disguised.

"You're not asking," he pointed out after a moment. He would have to proceed slowly. He knew her better now, understood a little more why she behaved the way she did. She could also be stubborn and unwavering, and pushing her would only make her dig her heels in deeper. "I'm offering."

"I appreciate it," she said in a quiet voice. "I really do."

That voice was so familiar to him and hearing it was like finding an old friend again. He couldn't help but respond. "Then I wish you'd reconsider. Did you ever think that staying here is putting everyone else at risk?" It was obvious by her expression that she hadn't, but he didn't give her time to counter. "I realize the whole thing sounds extreme—it *is* extreme—but it just might be the best solution for everyone." He knelt down in front of her. "The risk if you go is minimal. Staying is what would be dangerous. With you safely in one place, law enforcement could concentrate all their efforts on getting this guy." He shrugged a shoulder. "And maybe Ted and Cindy would even feel good enough to still go on their honeymoon."

He'd dealt her a low blow and the crack in her resolve was apparent, but she still wasn't ready to give up.

"But I can't just pack up and be gone indefinitely. A few days, a week maybe, that would be one thing, but who knows how long this could go on."

"Kristin," Ted said solemnly. "We're going to nail this guy, I promise you that. It may take a week, it may take a month, two months, I don't know, but we will get him. I hate asking you to do this, but believe me, it's necessary.''

"And, sweetie," Cindy added, reaching down and taking her hand, "wouldn't you do whatever it took to get your life back?"

"You know I would." Kristin's shoulders slumped. She pushed the chair back and rose slowly to her feet. "But I've got clients who are at critical stages in their therapy. What about them? What about all those who listen to the show every night, who phone in? Do I just walk away from them?"

The latter struck a chord with Jake. He knew she wasn't suggesting anyone would shrivel up and die without their daily dose of Dear Jane, she was grasping at straws, grabbing at any excuse to hold her ground.

"Didn't you say you had a partner in your practice?" he asked, straightening up.

"Not a partner exactly," Kristin said. "We share office space."

"You two ever on call for one another?"

"Of course they are," Cindy jumped in. "You and Nancy are on call for each other all the time." She turned and looked up at Jake. "Nancy has even filled in for her at the radio station."

Nancy, Jake thought, remembering another voice over the radio waves. The Sly Fox.

"You don't think she could fill in for you with your more critical clients?"

"I'm sure she could," Kristin snapped, defenses up again.

"Well, if she could do that, I think I might be able to help with 'Lost Loves.'"

As though on cue, all three of them stopped and turned to him.

"What do you mean?" Kristin asked.

"Eagle's Eye may be surrounded by hundreds of miles of wilderness, but it also has state-of-the-art radio communications."

"Brilliant!" Ted shouted, tossing his hands in the air. "Why didn't I think of that?" He turned to Kristin. "You could do the show from there. Dear Jane would be broadcasting from the top of the world."

And with that the plan was solidified.

Chapter 5

Kristin opened her closet door and stared at the row of clothes hanging inside. She didn't even know where to begin. What did you pack when you were heading for the wilderness—down jackets, wool socks, thermal underwear?

She pulled down a couple pairs of jeans from the shelf where she'd stacked them and reached for a hooded sweatshirt from a hanger. Jake had advised her to bring warm clothes. These would have to do.

She still couldn't believe she was doing this, that she was actually packing a bag and leaving. She felt as though she was giving in, as though she was letting him win. That creep, that *bastard* who had been terrorizing her was driving her from her home and from her work. But Jake had been right, staying only put everyone else at risk and she couldn't bear to do that.

She thought about Jake, about how rude she had been to him, how unpleasant. Tossing the jeans and sweatshirt onto the bed, she sank down beside them and buried her head in her hands. She felt so foolish now, so embarrassed. It was a wonder the man was willing to speak to her let alone offer to help.

She didn't doubt for a moment that Ted had done some heavy-duty arm-twisting, that he'd taken full advantage of his longtime friendship with Jake to coerce him into agreeing to this plan. The poor man probably felt he had no choice.

She opened her eyes, fell back and stared up at the ceiling. She'd tried to give him an opportunity to back out, tried to make it easy for him to change his mind, but he hadn't budged. Instead, he'd done his best to convince her this plan was a good idea, making it all but impossible for her to refuse. Why would he do that? What sense of duty would have him reaching out to a stranger, especially one who hadn't been particularly nice to him?

"I don't know," she muttered in answer to her own question. She sat up, picking up the clothing beside her and tossing the items into her nylon athletic bag. "Maybe it's some kind of ex-cop thing."

"What's some kind of ex-cop thing?"

She turned, hopping up from the bed. "Nancy, thank goodness."

"I came as soon as I got your message. What is going on around here?" Nancy Fox asked, motioning with a nod out the bedroom door. "It looks like you've got the entire LAPD out there."

She was joking, of course, but the two black-and-white units and two unmarked sedans parked outside her house were hard to miss.

"Don't forget the FBI."

Nancy's dark eyes narrowed. "It's got to be him, your stalker."

Kristin had met the petite brunette in college, having shared a number of classes together. While they'd never been close friends, they had often studied together and when, after graduation, they each decided to open private counseling practices, it had only made sense that they both save overhead by sharing a suite of offices. It became even more convenient when the late night radio show went on the air and Kristin's hours changed. Nancy could book her clients in the morning, leaving the afternoon free for Kristin.

"Did you hear about Tori?"

"Oh my God," Nancy gasped. "That was him?"

Kristin closed her eyes to a surge of emotion—a cocktail of anger, outrage, guilt mixed with terror. "He thought she was...he mistook her for me."

"How awful," Nancy commented, shaking her head. "Well, that explains the police then."

She reached out and gave Kristin's arm a pat. Nancy wasn't openly affectionate, a skill Kristin had often thought served her well as a therapist.

"They seem to feel he'll make another attempt."

"Do they have any suspects?"

She shook her head. "I don't know, and frankly, I haven't asked," she admitted with a tired sigh. "They're going to be studying the tape from the security cameras in the parking garage and they're talking to people who were in the area at the time of the attack."

"Well, at least they're working on it. That sounds encouraging," Nancy said, walking over to the bed and gazing down at the athletic bag. "What's this? Are you going somewhere?"

"Believe me, not by choice," she said dryly. "Ted and Jake—"

"Jake?"

Kristin gave her head a small shake. "I'm sorry. Jake Hayes, he's a friend of Ted's. He used to be with the LAPD."

"The ex-cop thing," Nancy concluded with a nod.

Kristin breathed out a small laugh, feeling foolish to think Nancy had caught her talking to herself. "You're right, the ex-cop thing. Anyway, they seem to feel it would be better if I got away for a while, you know, safer."

"I think they're right," Nancy agreed. "There's no telling where this guy is. So where are you going?"

The words were almost out before she remembered Ted's warning. "I'm sorry, I'm not supposed to tell anyone."

"Not even me?"

Kristin cringed, embarrassed. "I know, it all sounds so cloak-and-dagger but the police feel it would put those who knew in too much danger. If he thought you knew my whereabouts, he might try and…well…" She shrugged. "You know."

"I guess that makes sense."

"Which is why I asked you to come by. I need to ask a huge favor."

Nancy smiled. "If it's about doing the radio program, don't worry about it. I'll take care of it. The show went off without a hitch last night and—"

"Well, actually, it's not about that," Kristin said, cutting her off.

Nancy's eyes widened. "No?"

"Don't ask me how, but Jake and Dale have worked out a way for me to do the broadcast from…well, from where I'll be. It may take several days to get things set up, maybe a week so, if you wouldn't mind filling in until then?"

"Of course not, you know I'd be happy to." She regarded Kristin for a moment. "But are you sure you're up to doing the show?"

"To be honest, if I wasn't able to continue the broadcasts, I'm not sure I'd be able to leave." She grabbed a sweater from the closet shelf and tossed it into the bag. "I have to have something of my life to hold on to, something to do while I'm away."

"But what about the practice?"

"I've been on the phone all morning. I've arranged for the majority to attend group sessions at the counseling center until I get back, but there is one critical case I was hoping you'd be able to help with." She walked over to the bureau and picked up a thick manila file folder. "The chart is in the office but these are my notes. If you have a few minutes, we could go over them now."

"Of course, I'll help in any way I can," Nancy assured her, taking the file from her and flipping through it. "Have you spoken to the client yet? Is she going to be okay with this?"

Kristin thought of the young teen she had been working with. After many months of counseling, she had felt the young woman was about to open up. It was a critical point in her therapy and definitely not the best time to be switching counselors.

"I have, and I'll be honest with you, I'm worried. I'm not sure how she's going to deal with the change."

"I see what you mean." Nancy nodded, perusing the file. "This kid has some problems."

"I know, and she's come a long way already. I feel so guilty leaving right now but…" She let her words drift, tamping down another rush of emotion. "But I had a thought. I'll have my cell phone, I'll be able to check in with you, we can discuss the sessions, we could even think about doing a conference call during a couple of them.''

Nancy nodded again. ''That certainly sounds doable. Why don't you finish packing while I go find someplace quiet to read this over, then we can talk.''

Kristin breathed a sigh of relief. ''Thanks, Nancy.''

''Get packing,'' Nancy scoffed with a dismissive gesture as she headed through the bedroom door. ''I'll let you know when I've finished reading.''

Kristin turned back to the closet. It had been a frantic morning, but for a plan that seemed impossible twelve hours ago, things had come together remarkably well. She felt enormously better to have most of her clients taken care of, and with Nancy's help, and the help of her cell phone, she could still stay in touch with her most critical case.

She looked at the down jacket hanging in the closet, the price tag dangling. She had bought it for a ski trip a couple of years ago, but for some reason the trip had been canceled and she'd never had reason to wear it.

She walked to the window and glanced outside. The March sun was bright and the temperature warm. It was hard to believe she would need such a warm jacket this time of year, but Jake had said to pack warm.

She walked back to the bed, looking down at the bag stuffed with sweaters, socks and jeans. She couldn't even imagine what it was going to be like up there on that mountain. She'd always enjoyed the outdoors, enjoyed riding her bicycle, taking nature walks—she'd even camped a time or two in her life. But this would be the wilderness, some of the harshest and most unforgiving country in California. Nothing she had ever done prepared her for this.

Things had been rushed last night. After she'd—reluctantly—agreed to Ted's plan, they had all returned to the reception. She'd been too distracted to do little more than sit and stare, but she hadn't wanted to disappoint Cindy. It was no doubt due to Jake's sense of obligation as best man that he felt he had to sit with her. She would have protested but it seemed to ease Cindy and Ted's concerns knowing she wasn't alone, at least long enough for them to enjoy the rest of their wedding reception.

Of course, Jake had been a perfect gentleman throughout the rest of the evening. But his kindness had only made her feel all the more uncomfortable. She suspected he had no idea when he'd agreed to be best man that he would end up having to baby-sit her as well.

So she was relieved when the evening finally wound down. At Cindy's insistence, she agreed to stay in a hotel near the reception hall as a precaution last night, where two uniformed officers kept watch outside her room. Another pair replaced them this morning to drive her home, where they'd remained ever since, sipping coffee in her kitchen. She'd gotten on the phone the moment she'd walked in the door, and by the time Cindy and Ted had arrived, she'd made arrangements for most of her clients. The plan called for her to be packed and ready to leave by noon. Once she and Jake were headed for the mountains, Cindy and Ted would leave for their honeymoon.

"Knock, knock."

The deep voice startled her and she jumped. "Jake!"

"I'm sorry," he said with regret. "I can't seem to stop scaring you."

"Don't feel bad," she said with a sigh. "I can't seem to stop being so jumpy."

"You'll feel better when you're up on the mountain."

Kristin doubted that. "You're early."

"I am, but I'm not rushing you," he added quickly.

"It didn't take as long with your producer as I'd thought."

"Dale? What did he say? Is the remote feed possible?"

"Doesn't seem to be a problem. In fact, I've got the equipment loaded in the Jeep."

She was thrilled. There was so much uncertainty ahead of her. She had no idea what awaited her up on that mountain, no idea what to anticipate, but at least she had something—she had "Lost Loves" to hold on to. It was something familiar, something she recognized, a part of her that creep hadn't been able to touch.

"You finish up," Jake was saying. "I'll be talking to Ted, so just give me a shout when you're ready."

"I will."

He stopped as he started for the door and turned back around. "I thought, if we get away early enough, you might like to stop by the hospital on the way out. You know, to see your friend."

"I'd like that," Kristin whispered. "Thanks."

It was a struggle, but she'd managed to blink back the tears until he'd left the room. She hated to cry, hated to get all weepy and emotional. It made her feel weak and powerless, but for some reason she couldn't seem to help herself. His offer to visit Tori had been so thoughtful, so unexpected, and had taken her completely by surprise. Kristin Carey might be cautious when it came to strangers, but Jane Streeter had a feeling about this guy. She was beginning to think he just might be one seriously nice man.

Jake pushed the door open, lowered the bag to the floor and reached for the light. The bare bulb cast a dim, yellow glow across the small apartment.

As he set Kristin's laptop computer down at the table,

he glanced up and stopped. Had he ever really noticed just how rustic the place looked with its open-beamed ceiling and green-painted wooden table and chairs? Add to that the fact that he hadn't been expecting to bring a guest back with him when he'd left and therefore hadn't had a chance to get rid of the cobwebs or air the place out at all, and it hardly presented a welcoming picture. He wouldn't be surprised if she took one look and headed right back down the mountain.

He deposited the rest of her things on the bare mattress, stretching his stiff and aching muscles. The drive had been long and not exactly the most pleasant one he'd ever made. He hadn't expected her to be chatty during the trip, but she'd barely spoken. He'd been relieved when she'd finally fallen asleep. It had helped ease the strain of those awkward silences.

But it hadn't made the trip any easier, or any shorter. He'd hoped to make it up the mountain before dark, but with traffic and the stop at the hospital, that hadn't been possible. Though it had probably worked out for the best. She'd been through a lot already today and someone not used to the narrow, twisting mountain road leading to the station might find the drive a little harrowing at first. As it was, it had been too dark for Kristin to see just how high up they'd climbed or how steep the drop-offs really were.

Her visit to the hospital had been a difficult one and he still wasn't sure exactly what had prompted him to suggest it. She hadn't said it in so many words, but he knew she felt responsible, and he couldn't help feeling sorry for her. Because some nutcase had become fixated on her, her entire life had to change. She'd put up a valiant effort to avoid accepting Ted's plan, but she'd been fighting a losing battle from the beginning. He understood her guilt and sense of responsibility at what her ordeal had brought to the people in her life. He remembered all too well attending Ricky's funeral and the funerals of the two officers who had died along with him, remembered the crippling sense of regret and responsibility he had felt for their deaths and wouldn't have wished that feeling on anyone. How many times he wished he would have been given the opportunity to talk to those men, to have been given the chance to apologize. He'd thought he would at least give Kristin the chance he'd never gotten.

Of course, it was hard to tell if the hospital visit had helped or not. She seemed so stoic, so unemotional, it was hard for him to know what she was feeling. He had waited in the corridor outside Victoria Peters's room while Kristin had gone in for a visit. She'd looked a little pale when she'd stepped out of the room a few moments later, but other than that, she'd revealed little else. In his years on the force, he'd seen people—including cops—go to pieces after a lot less than what she'd been through. He couldn't decide if the woman had enormous strength, or had ice water flowing through her veins.

Even with his jacket on, the room felt cold. He reached down and flipped the switch on the small, electric space heater in the corner but it was going to take more than that to bring the temperature up. He turned to the potbellied stove along the far wall. It was stone cold and the wood box was empty. But he wasn't worried. There was a stack of ages-old newspapers beside the wood box and a couple of cords of wood stacked outside. He would have a fire going in no time.

Turning around, he stared at the open doorway. He could have sworn she was right behind him when he'd started up the stairs. What the hell happened to her?

He found her at the foot of the stairs, staring up at the

night sky. He cleared his throat and made his steps noisy as he climbed down, not wanting to startle her again.

"Need some help?"

"Oh, I-I'm sorry," she said, giving her head a shake. "It's just…I've never seen anything like it." She gestured upward. "I don't think I've ever seen so many stars in the sky."

"It's beautiful, isn't it?" But there was something in her expression, something in the sound of her voice that caused a tightness in his chest. He wouldn't have expected the cool, curt Kristin to have noticed the stars. She was too practical, too down-to-earth. But Jane was a dreamer, *she* would notice.

"And it is so black out there." She pointed out into the darkness. "Are you sure there are mountains out there?"

"Why don't you ask me that question in the morning," he suggested dryly. "In the meantime, you better head inside. I'll grab some wood and be right up. We'll want to get a fire going before the temperature drops."

Kristin shivered and snuggled her jacket around her. "Does it get much colder than this? Because I'm freezing already."

He had to laugh. "Just a little," he lied. "But don't worry, we've got plenty of wood."

Just then a gust of wind swept up the side of the mountain, sending a blast of cold air swirling around them.

"Listen," she said, her eyes widening. "Do you hear that?"

"Hear what? The wind?"

"No." She shook her head as another gust buffeted them. "There! Do you hear that?"

He was so accustomed to the sounds of the area it took

him a few minutes to figure out what she was hearing. "You mean that whistling sound?"

"Yes!"

He pointed to the top of the lookout. "It's too dark to see much right now, but it's the antennae tower. It makes that sound when the wind blows through them."

She looked up into the direction he pointed, then back to him. "Kinda spooky."

"You'll get used to it," he assured her. "And you'll feel better once you've warmed up." He watched as she started up the steps. "And like I said earlier, the rooms are a little rough, but we'll get them cleaned up in the morning. I'll bring you some clean bedding and some towels. There's hot water if you want a shower."

"Thanks," she called back with a small wave as she disappeared inside.

He turned and headed across the driveway to the mountain of firewood he had chopped and stacked under the overhang of the tower. He walked quickly and with assurance despite the darkness. In three years, he'd come to know every square foot of the small compound and didn't doubt he could walk it in his sleep if he had to.

The tower was dark and the only light burning below was the small one above the main door that Claybe would have left on for him. He and Claybe would fill in for one another when either had to be away. But Claybe would have left hours ago, wanting to be down the mountain before nightfall. He suspected things had been quiet while he was away, but he would touch base with Claybe by radio tomorrow just to be certain.

He quickly gathered up an armful of wood and made his way back across the gravel driveway. At the top of the stairs he stopped. The door was closed. Without a hand free to knock, he hesitated, trying to decide the best way to get her attention.

"Kristin? Hello?" he called out. He waited several seconds, shifting the weight of the wood, then tapped gently against the door with the toe of his boot. "Hello—"

The door opened so quickly he jumped, nearly unbalancing his load.

"I'm sorry," Kristin said, pushing the door open wide. "Let me help."

"No, it's fine," he said, rushing inside quickly. A momentum had started, throwing off his balance and he made a beeline for the wood box. It was only luck that had him aiming the tilting load just right and filling the box up in one smooth motion. "That ought to be enough to get started." He knelt down and opened the cast-iron door of the stove. Reaching for the newspapers, he crumpled up several large sheets and tossed them inside. "Once we get the fire going, I'll bring up some more wood."

"I can help," Kristin offered, closing the door to a cold gust of wind. She rushed over to the small space heater and warmed her hands. "If you show me where the woodpile is."

"You concentrate on getting warm," he advised, stacking several small pieces of wood on top of the crinkled papers. "It's too dark out there to see much anyway."

"I don't want you to feel like you have to wait on me."

"I don't."

"Because I know you have work to do around here. Please don't feel you have to entertain me. I don't want to be a bother."

"Thanks, I appreciate that."

"And if you need some help, just let me know."

"Okay," he said, reaching for several larger logs.

"Would you mind seeing if you can find a box of matches in one of those drawers over there?"

"What? Oh, sure," she said, jumping to attention. She eagerly rushed into the small kitchen and began pulling out drawers and searching through the cabinets. "Found them!"

"Why don't you keep an eye on this," he said once the papers and the kindling had started to burn. "I'll bring some more wood up but I'll go get you some linens first and—" He stopped, vaguely remembering the burgers they'd had many hours ago on the road. "Are you hungry? I've got food over at my place. I could fix you something."

"Oh no, don't bother," she insisted. "I'm fine."

Somehow he didn't quite believe her. "I'll bring a couple cans of soup just in case, and some coffee for you in the morning," he said, heading for the door. "You should find some pots and pans in the cupboard." At the door he turned around and watched her as she knelt down in front of the fire. It suddenly hit him then. Jane Streeter had come to his house. "I'll be right back. Don't let the fire go out."

The light was blinding, like sunshine and then some. Squinting, she scooted up, wincing as every muscle in her body protested. She looked around the small apartment. Awareness was immediate. Something was different but it had nothing to do with the unfamiliar surroundings. There was something drastically different about this morning, something missing.

She sat up as realization hit like a rock. Fear. It wasn't there. She didn't feel that nagging, gnawing monster in the pit of her stomach. She had lived with it for so long, had greeted each morning with a growing sense of dread, she'd almost forgotten what it was to wake up and feel…safe.

Was it possible Ted had been right? Could it be that getting away from L.A., away from the telephone calls and the letters and the precautions and the check-ins and the million other things she'd had to deal with for the last eight months might actually be better?

"Amazing," she sighed, sinking back against the pillows. She had been so concerned about being displaced, about having to leave her life and her work and her family behind in L.A. it hadn't even occurred to her she'd also be leaving behind the fear. It had been the overriding emotion in her life for so long, she'd almost forgotten what life could be like without it. This morning she was hundreds of miles away from all of that, from the threats and the dread and the fear.

She took a moment, savoring the feeling. This was what her life had been like before, and a glimmer of hope brightened at the thought that maybe someday soon the whole nightmare would end, that her life would be her own again.

As her eyes grew more accustomed to the light, she looked around the small room. The place looked better in the daylight—not great by any means, but better. Coming in last night it had felt gloomy and a little spooky. Now it just looked a lot like the cabins she remembered from summer camp as a kid—functional and rustic.

She glanced at her down jacket tossed at the foot of the bed. When Jake had suggested she pack warm, he'd obviously known what he was talking about. It seemed impossible now to think she'd actually considered not bringing the jacket. She didn't even want to think what it would have been like without it. In fact, before the fire started creating some heat, she'd even considered wearing the garment to bed.

She glanced at the stove beside the bed. Embers still glowed red inside. She had gotten up several times in the night to add more wood, and she had to admit she'd been surprised at just how much heat that little black thing could put out. The cold was definitely something that would take a little getting used to.

"Although let's hope that won't be necessary," she said out loud, her voice sounding hollow as it echoed off the bare walls. The only way she was going to get through this was to concentrate on the time when it would all be over, when she could have her life back and try to put this whole nightmare behind her.

She glanced down at her watch.

"Eight a.m." She groaned. She had slept amazingly well last night, just not long enough. It had been only a little after eleven when she'd crawled under the covers. She'd been grateful for the two cans of chicken noodle soup Jake had brought with him when he'd delivered the linens for her bed. Immediately after he'd left, she'd opened one can, tossed it into a small saucepan she'd found and heated it up on one of the two burners atop the tiny gas stove. The soup had tasted so hot and delicious, when she'd finished, she'd promptly opened the other can and did the very same thing.

She leaned back against the pillows, thinking about Jake. Along with the soup, he'd also brought crackers, a bar of soap, coffee, sugar and dried nondairy creamer. He'd been a perfectly gracious host, thinking of everything. It was almost as if he did this sort of thing all the time.

She sat up again. Did he? The thought hadn't occurred to her before, but the man was attractive and unattached.

It was probably not unreasonable to think he entertained a woman up here from time to time.

"None of my business," she mumbled to herself, sinking back against the pillows and pulling the covers up tight, but she couldn't quite shake the thought.

He'd offered to stay and help her make up the bed last night, but that would have simply been too awkward. It was bad enough that she'd landed in his lap, the least she could do was be as self-sufficient as possible and try to stay out of his way as much as she could.

Besides that, she still felt uneasy around him—only not like before, not like the uneasiness she'd felt when he'd been a stranger. This was different and in some ways much worse. There was something that happened when he was around, something that affected the oxygen supply to her lungs, something that made it difficult to breathe.

Her body ached, and everything was telling her to bury herself under the covers and sleep for another couple of hours. After all, she wasn't used to early mornings. Doing a live broadcast each night, she usually didn't get home and into bed much before two. Add to that, she was in a strange place, she was frankly surprised she had gotten any sleep at all last night. In the darkness, the small apartment had come alive with sounds, which conspired to keep her awake and on edge. Of course, some sounds she could recognize—the wind blowing outside and the wood snapping in the fire. Those hadn't bothered her. It was all the other ones that kept her teeth rattling, the ones she didn't even want to guess at.

"No, better get up," she ordered herself when she felt her lids start to grow heavy again.

She pushed the covers aside and sat up. She had no idea what the routine was around the station but she suspected sleeping late probably wasn't part of it. Besides,

Jake didn't strike her as a late sleeper. He had that rugged outdoorsy thing going on and she would bet his day started early. The least she could do was make an appearance.

It took her a moment to realize the tiny tapping on the door wasn't just one of those hundreds of miscellaneous sounds she'd been listening to all night. Someone was knocking very lightly on her door.

Not someone. Jake.

Chapter 6

There was one freaky millisecond of indecision. Kristin leaped to her feet, then quickly sat back down. She forgot about feeling tired, forgot about the cold, about her aching muscles and too little sleep. What did she do—answer the door or hide under the covers and pretend to be asleep?

She frantically glanced around the room. She was in her underwear and a T-shirt. Had she even packed a robe—or a hairbrush?

There was another small tap, fainter than the first.

"C-come in?" she stuttered, hurriedly slipping back under the covers.

"I hope I didn't wake you," Jake said, cracking the door open an inch.

She cringed and pulled the covers up, wishing she could pull them over her head. She didn't even want to think about what she might look like, and told herself not to be surprised if the man took one look and hightailed it in the opposite direction.

"No, no...I wasn't asleep."

"You're up early," he said, stepping inside. In one hand he held the straps of a large, burlap carrier filled with a load of wood. "Did you get any sleep?"

"Some," she said, pulling the blanket to her chin.

"I thought you might be cold," he said, lifting the carrier full of wood. He walked to the stove and emptied the wood into the box. Reaching for the poker hanging from a hook on the stove, he knelt down and opened the iron door. "Would you like a fire this morning?"

"Sure, thanks," she said, running a hand through her hair. Her fingers encountered a major snarl and she worked quickly to try to smooth it away. "That...that would be nice."

He tossed several small logs into the stove, working the embers until they flamed and engulfed the new pieces.

"That ought to warm you up," he said as he straightened and returned the poker to the hook. "Feel like some breakfast?"

"I think I'm fine." She sat up. "I was just about to start coffee. Could I get you a cup?"

"Why don't you relax for a while, get warm," he said, gathering up the burlap carrier. "When you feel ready, get dressed and come on over to the tower. I've got a fresh pot of coffee made and I'll give you a tour of the place."

"Okay." She nodded. "That sounds great."

He walked to the door and opened it. "Give me a shout if you need anything."

"I'll do that," she said as she watched him leave.

She stared at the closed door for a moment. He'd been perfectly polite and perfectly thoughtful. So why was she feeling disappointed? What more did she expect?

"Just knock it off, Jane," she warned her alter ego with

a shake of her head. She pushed the covers aside and swung out of bed. "Stop analyzing everything."

The bare floor felt frigid and she moved quickly as she pulled out a pair of jeans and a sweater from her athletic bag. By the time she had her clothes on and had brushed her teeth, the fire was putting out a steady stream of heat.

Fumbling quickly through her bag, she found a pair of thick cotton socks. Taking them, she grabbed a wooden chair from the table and pulled it across the room to the stove. She sat down, and dangled one icy bare foot inches from the hot cast iron until her skin felt warm and toasty.

"Mmm," she moaned, quickly slipping a sock over her warm skin and savoring the heat. Pleased with herself, she repeated the process with the other foot. She was lacing up her running shoes, when she suddenly stopped and straightened.

"He didn't look at me," she said out loud. That was it! He'd been friendly, he'd smiled, he'd been a perfect gentlemen, but... "He didn't look at me. Why didn't he? What does that mean?"

With an exasperated sigh, she stood up and dragged the chair back to the table. It was only natural she'd be aware of the man. They were the only two people at the ranger station, the only two people for miles around. But that didn't mean she needed to analyze his every move.

"Dear, *dear* Jane, you're working overtime," she warned herself, taking a deep breath as she headed for the door. "Give me a break this time, please? Don't!"

It was probably a good idea she'd decided not to pursue a life of crime, because he suspected she would have made a very successful criminal. She had the unique ability to show nothing of what she was feeling—not just mask her emotions, but simply not show them at all! It was a device he'd seen used by one or two particularly clever criminals to evade capture. They'd succeeded because they had always looked so innocent, no one had ever suspected them of doing anything wrong. And no doubt hiding her emotions came in handy in her line of work as well. Counselors, therapists, psychiatrists probably all became adept at controlling their feelings so as to reveal nothing to their patients.

But there was no way she'd been able to hide her reaction when she'd stepped out of her room. The look on her face said it all.

"Oh my God!" she gasped as she climbed down the stairs and started across the compound towards the tower. She turned around once, twice, a third time, taking in the breathtaking panorama.

"Welcome to the top of the world," he said, walking across the gravel to meet her. His frail, mortal hand had played no part in the creation of such grandeur, but he couldn't help feeling a sense of pride, as though it had.

"I had…I had no idea," she said. She spread her arms out wide and did another three-sixty. "This…this is *incredible.*"

"It's pretty amazing," he agreed, trying not to notice just how alive and how beautiful she looked. "What was it you asked me about mountains last night?"

She laughed, covering her mouth with her hands. "I did, didn't I?"

At nearly eight thousand feet, Mount Holloway towered above the landscape as far as the eye could see. The March morning air was cold and crisp, but the sky was clear, making the view from the peak spectacular.

"Unbelievable," she sighed, the wind blowing her hair across her face. She grabbed at her hair, turning to look up at him. "Just unbeliev—" But she stopped abruptly, forgetting about her hair and pointing behind him. "That isn't…I mean, is that…?"

He turned around, following her line of vision to the towering stone structure that was his home. "That's Eagle's Eye."

She walked slowly across the gravel driveway. "It's so beautiful. Last night it was so dark. I just saw the small light above the door." She looked up at the tower, shading her eyes against the sun. "It's so…tall."

"A lot of stairs to climb," he commented dryly. "The stone stands around fifteen feet. Steel reinforces the enclosed wood tower above. The whole thing stands just under thirty feet."

She shook her head, turning to him. "I hate to keep saying this but I had no idea."

"Most people don't," he said with a shrug. "We're a little off the beaten track."

"I guess," she said, her gaze scanning the panorama again. "What's that over there?"

"The road?"

She blinked. "That's a road?"

He smiled. "It's the road we drove up on."

She spun around and looked at him. "You're kidding."

She looked so utterly aghast at the thought, it was all he could do to keep from laughing. "I'm not."

She turned back, grabbing her hair again as she stared at the narrow, twisting route carved out of the mountain. "It was darker last night than I thought."

"Come on," he said with a laugh. "I'll show you around."

He led her up the stone steps and into the tower. The door led to a small porch where an ancient-looking washing machine and basin stood.

"This is the pantry," he said, pointing to the white

wood-slate door just inside the porch. "I try to keep the pantry pretty well stocked, canned goods mostly. Help yourself to anything you can find. I usually do a run down the mountain for supplies once a month or so, six weeks, depending on the weather or the time of the year. Fresh foods—fruits, vegetables, things like that—are a little hard to store, but there is a small basement or root cellar. I try to keep some apples, bananas, potatoes, onions, things like that, down there when I can get them." He pulled open a narrow door on the opposite wall, a gush of cool air rushing out. Reaching up, he pulled the string hanging from a bare bulb just inside, its dim light exposing thick, rough-hewn steps leading down into darkness. "It also doubles as a wine cellar—mostly reds, but there are a few bottles of white if you're interested." He turned off the light and shut the door. "If you need something in the meantime, I make a weekly patrol to Vega Flats down the other side of the canyon."

"Vega Flats? You mean there's a town around here?"

"I wouldn't exactly call it a town. More like a fishing village—bait shop, tavern. Only about a half dozen or so residents year-round but it can get a little lively during hunting and camping season. Mac owns and runs the tavern. He makes a supply run about every week. He can always pick up something." He started out, tapping on the basin as he passed. "The washer only looks like it's on its last legs but it does work. Not very fancy, but it gets the clothes clean. No dryer but there's a line outside—and when it's windy, a few minutes outside is about all it takes."

He stepped through another open doorway into the kitchen. "Are you sure you're not hungry?"

She shook her head. "I'm not much of a breakfast eater."

"Cup of coffee then?"

"I would love that," she said, following him in. "Smells great."

"This is the main kitchen—a lot bigger than the little convenience one in the other apartment," he pointed out, opening a cupboard and bringing out a mug. He filled the cup and offered it to her. "If you are ever in the mood to cook, feel free. I'm no Emeril Lagasse and hopefully I wouldn't poison you, but I'm not making any promises."

"Well, I don't expect you to cook for me," she insisted, taking the mug from him. "Or wait on me. I meant it when I said I don't want to bother you. I've been taking care of myself for a long time and can pull my own weight, honestly."

"Whatever you say," he said, returning the coffeepot to the stove. She had been very polite, very friendly, but the message had been clear. She wasn't interested in spending time with him. "You do your thing and I'll do mine. Deal?"

"Deal."

"You eat when you want to eat and I'll eat when I want to, how does that sound?"

"Perfect!"

"Want some creamer for your coffee?"

"That would be nice, yes."

"In the cupboard above the sink," he said, nodding in the direction. "Get it yourself."

She laughed. "Good, you're getting the idea."

Despite the smile and pleasant disposition, he recognized the change in her. Like a shade coming down and blocking out the sun, she revealed nothing. That small window of insight he'd had earlier had closed; she was in control again, showing him only what she wanted him to see.

"When you're finished," he said, heading through the kitchen toward the spiral staircase, "come on up if you want. I can show you the tower."

He didn't wait for an answer, but left her there stirring her coffee. If she wanted, she could follow, but he wasn't about to force her to do anything she didn't want.

Taking the steps two at a time, he climbed quickly. He was overreacting, he understood that, but he couldn't seem to help himself. He had thought finding out about the stalker and the ordeal she'd been dealing with had answered all his questions as to why she had been so cool to him at the wedding. He'd used it as a way of explaining why she'd been so distracted, so jumpy and uneasy whenever he'd been around. But now he wasn't so sure.

At the top of the stairs his heart was beating fast but it had nothing to do with the exertion of having climbed the long, twisting flight of stairs. He was upset. He was acting like an idiot. He was being unreasonable, expecting too much. He understood what kind of toll the stress of the last eight months would have taken on her, understood the kind of pressure she'd been under. So why did he insist on taking it personally? He was acting as though they were friends, and they weren't. She seemed familiar to him only because he'd listened to her for so long on the radio. She hadn't come to Eagle's Eye because she wanted to be his friend; she'd come because she needed his help. Why couldn't he seem to get that straight?

He reached for the binoculars, taking them to the window and scanning the sprawling landscape. He knew why. If she were just some ice princess with a prickly personality, he could deal with it, but she wasn't—at least he didn't think she was. That was what he found so unnerving. She could be icy and prickly and all the rest, but every once in a while that shade would lift and she would look the way she did this morning.

He put down the binoculars but continued to stare out into the distance. But it wasn't the blue sky or the white, fluffy clouds he was seeing, it was her face and the way she had looked when she'd stepped outside this morning. Why did she do that? Why did she give him just a glimpse, just enough real emotion to make him think Jane Streeter was really in there somewhere?

"That's quite a climb."

He turned just as she reached up the last step, coffee mug in her hand. "It's cut down my time on the StairMaster."

"Wow," she said, walking to the window and surveying the view. "Just when I thought the view couldn't get any better."

"Here," he said, offering her the binoculars. "Give these a try."

Setting her coffee mug down, she took them from him. "Talk about a million-dollar view," she said, looking through the glass. "And you do this every day?" She peeked over the top at him. "They pay you for this?"

"It's a dirty job," he said with a shrug.

"So what is all this?" she asked, gesturing around the tower.

He walked through the room, pointing as he went along. "Maps, charts, log, computer—"

"Computer?"

"Hey, we may be mountain folk, but we're not rubes," he joked as he continued. "This is the two-way radio, the GPS, global positioning system, television—"

"Television! You've got to be joking." She picked up her coffee and took another sip. "You have a television?"

"Two actually. One here and one downstairs." He

walked across the tower and pointed down. "And the satellite dish out back not only brings us about two hundred channels, it will also shoot Dear Jane to the towers over there on that mountaintop and then out to the rest of the world."

She walked to where he stood and peered outside. "You mean we'll do the broadcast from up here? In the tower?"

"Is that going to be okay?"

She breathed out a small laugh, looking around again. "Are you kidding? I think that's going to be more than just okay." She set her coffee cup back down and reached for the binoculars again. "Will the feed take long to set up?"

He shook his head. "A day or two maybe. It's really just a matter of coordinating with the radio station, doing a few test runs."

"That is so great," she said. After a moment, her expression turned serious and she took a hesitant step forward. "Jake, in case I haven't said it already, I really want you to know how much I appreciate this—everything. I don't know how I can ever repay you or—"

"Stop, stop," he said, raising his hand in surrender. "There is no need for you to repay anything. I'm just glad I was able to help. Besides, I'm doing this for purely selfish reasons."

Her expression turned curious. "Oh?"

"The Sly Fox may be fine as a replacement once in a while, but your listeners need Jane Streeter. We're Dear Jane junkies."

She laughed, but gave him a skeptical look. "You've really listened to the show?"

"I listen all the time. I told you, I'm a fan."

She regarded him for a moment. "I'm flattered."

He shrugged a shoulder. "Are you really?"

Suddenly it was as though the air had become charged, the way it did just before lightning was about to strike. His heart thundered against his rib cage and pressure pushed against his chest.

"So tell me, what do you do when you spot a fire?" she said blithely, turning away suddenly and bringing in the binoculars.

The moment shattered like a mirror into a thousand pieces and he felt strangely unsettled and out of breath.

"Uh…a lot depends on what kind it is," he stammered, struggling to regain his composure. "Whether any populated areas are being threatened or even if the tower itself is threatened." He walked to the small desk and arranged several of the maps sprawled across it. "Basically I'd radio down to Cedar Canyon for an aerial run, let them check it out. If they determine crews need to be called in, I help coordinate ground crews, evacuations, things like that."

She put down the binoculars. "Evacuations? Does that happen very often?"

"Gratefully no, but when it comes to fire, it's best not to mess around. It's a judgment call. You have to be cautious, but at the same time you can't call in the troops every time someone strikes a match. Where there's smoke, there's fire, but not every fire is a forest fire." He turned and pointed. "See those pines over there, on that ridge?"

She peered through the glass again. "You mean by those big rocks?"

"Just above them, yeah. That's Big Chumash Campgrounds. During camping season, you often see smoke from campfires. There are also trails that run up and down these canyons—you've got hikers, mountain bikers, hunters all through here."

She focused the lenses. "And you watch over them all."

He laughed. "Just like a guardian angel."

"No, I'm serious," she said, setting down the binoculars and reaching for her coffee cup again. "That's quite a responsibility."

He wasn't sure if her flattery was sincere or out of some misguided sense of gratitude, but either way it made him uncomfortable.

"We've got company," he said, pointing out the window, anxious to change the subject.

"What? Is someone here?"

"Right there," he said, pointing to a family of raccoons as they made their way down a tree and across the driveway below.

"Oh my gosh," she gasped, spotting them. "They're so adorable."

"They're so nosy," he corrected, picking up one of the large maps and rolling it into a tight cylinder. Opening the slider, he stepped out onto the deck and whacked the rolled-up map noisily against the rail.

The furry little dark-eyed creatures jumped and scrambled, making a mad dash back to the tree.

"Oh, no," she lamented, stepping out onto the deck behind him. "You frightened them away. How come?"

He nodded to the Wrangler parked in the driveway below. "I left the window open when I moved the Jeep this morning. Believe me, there's nothing adorable about what they would do to the inside of my car."

She laughed, grimacing. "I hadn't thought of that. I suppose you're right."

"Which reminds me," he added. "It's probably a good

idea to keep your door closed and windows shut if you're going to be out of the apartment for any length of time. Otherwise you just might end up with a close encounter of the critter kind, if you know what I mean.''

''Critters, huh?''

''Yeah, and some may not be so adorable.'' He followed her back inside, sliding the door closed behind them. ''I don't want to frighten you or anything, but this is the wilderness. There's a lot of wildlife around, it just pays to be careful.''

''Gotcha,'' she said with a nod. She walked around the tower again, slowly perusing the maps and equipment as she continued to sip her coffee. ''Well, this is something,'' she said after a moment. ''This had to have been quite an adjustment for you, being so far away from everything.''

''It took a little getting used to.''

''And to think you actually survive without pizza delivery, I'm impressed.''

That was a Dear Jane remark and he had to smile. ''Not without a struggle.''

She laughed, but then her face grew serious. ''A big change from L.A.''

''It was,'' he said, his gaze turning to the horizon. ''But I was ready for a change. Now I can't imagine being anywhere else.''

''You don't miss being a cop?''

It was a therapist's question and he couldn't help wondering just how much Ted had told her about him. He hadn't liked it when the department's shrinks had tried to psychoanalyze him and he wasn't crazy about the idea of her trying to either.

''Sure, sometimes,'' he said matter-of-factly.

He could see her in his peripheral vision, quiet and

patient, giving him plenty of time in case he cared to elaborate. He didn't.

"I think I'll go help myself to some more coffee, if that's okay."

The fact that she'd dropped the subject so quickly surprised him. She had either picked up that it was a topic he wasn't interested in discussing, or she simply wasn't interested enough to pursue it. Either way, he was grateful.

"Of course. Help yourself."

"Can I bring you a cup?" she asked as she started for the stairs.

"No thanks, but while you're down there you might want to check out the strawberry preserves in the jar on the counter. Ruby, down in Vega Flats, keeps me supplied. It's pretty good on an English muffin."

She nodded, giving the idea some thought. "I just might do that."

"Am I sure I want to quit?" She thought about that for a moment. "I do unless you're ready to deal me some decent cards." She moved the mouse, sending the little arrow on the computer screen to the No tab, and clicked. "All right, I'm giving you one more chance." At the prompt, playing cards scattered across the screen. "But could you at least give me a fighting chance this time?"

She had unloaded her client files and plugged in her laptop with every intention of going through each file and updating them in the computer, but she found it hard to concentrate on anything more than the computerized solitaire game. It had been such a beautiful day outside—clear and sunny. It had made her feel restless to stay inside all day.

After Jake had found her in the kitchen, drinking coffee

and stuffing her face with English muffins and strawberry jam, he had shown her around the rest of the station. She hadn't been kidding when she'd told him she was impressed. Eagle's Eye was beautiful, both the structure and the location, with far more modern conveniences than she had expected. She had been hoping for indoor plumbing, but not only did it have that, it also had hot water, television and a microwave oven, to boot. Had she known that two days ago, she didn't think she would have resisted the idea of coming nearly as much.

She had turned down his offer of lunch. She'd taken up enough of his time. She didn't want him to feel obligated to entertain her or treat her as a guest all the time. Besides, she was a little embarrassed at what a pig she'd made of herself with the muffins and jam. She'd told him the truth when she'd said she wasn't much of a breakfast eater, but that hadn't been the case this morning.

"All right. Black queen over the red king. It's about time."

She moved the cards across the screen. She'd never been great at solitaire, and her luck this afternoon had been particularly bad, but not all of it had been a result of the draw. She'd had trouble keeping focused on the game. Her mind kept drifting back to that moment this morning in the tower.

She still wasn't exactly sure what had happened. They'd just been standing there talking about the broadcast, talking about Dear Jane when…when it happened. Suddenly he was looking at her and it was as if the air had turned electric. Everything in her reacted—her heart, her lungs, every nerve ending in her body.

She'd realized she had developed a certain…*awareness* of the man in the last couple of days, but there had also been a lot to distract her and help her to put what she was feeling aside. Now, however, away from the city, from the fear and the nightmare, there was a lot less distracting her from what might be happening.

"Just what *is* happening?" she demanded of herself aloud. But she already knew the answer to that. What was happening was all too clear. The awareness she had of him was all too quickly becoming full-fledged attraction, and that was something she simply couldn't allow to happen. The man was dangerous, posed too great a threat. Unlike the danger of a stalker bent on harming her, Jake threatened to make her care.

She couldn't allow herself to fall into that trap again, couldn't allow her feelings to leave her wide open and vulnerable the way they had with Blake. No one was ever going to have that kind of control over her again. She'd made that mistake once.

The situation wasn't hopeless. Being forewarned was being forearmed and she understood the pitfalls and risks in a way she hadn't before. She could protect herself against this attraction, could control it and not allow it to get the better of her. She just had to be careful, that's all, careful to keep things in perspective, careful not to let her feelings get the better of her. But just to be on the safe side, it probably wouldn't be a bad idea to keep to herself and avoid the man as best she could. No sense tempting fate.

The knock on the door made her jump, her heart leaping into her throat. "C-come in."

"I startled you again, didn't I?" Jake said as he walked into the apartment. "I'm sorry. Would it help if I made some noise climbing the steps?"

"It would help if I could just stop being so darned jumpy, get over this a little."

"It'll happen," he assured her. "It just takes time."

"I suppose."

He nodded to the computer. "Working?"

From where he stood he couldn't see the screen and she quickly folded it down. "Just a little."

"Look, I know we agreed to just coexist, to do our own thing, but I just made a huge pot of chili and you didn't have any lunch..." He shrugged. "Want to have a bowl with me?"

She almost smiled. It was a good thing she'd had that little talk with herself, because now she was prepared for situations just like this. She had already decided what her course of action would be, what was allowed and what wasn't. She was going to keep to herself. She was going to avoid the man whenever possible. She was in control.

So it took her completely by surprise when she opened her mouth and heard the words that came out.

"Sure, I'd love to."

Chapter 7

"*I just can't bring myself to sign them.*"

"*The divorce papers.*"

"*Yes.*"

"*Why do you suppose that is?*"

"*I—I don't know. It's over. I know it's over. But a divorce, it's just so final.*"

"*You want to get back together, is that it?*"

"*No, I really don't. I know that will never happen, I just can't...*"

"*Can't what, Pamela?*"

"*I just can't let him go, Jane. Help me to let go.*"

"*You heard it, we're talking with Pamela from Peoria and she needs help letting go of her lost love. Let us hear from you 1–800–NIGHT TALK. I'm Jane Streeter, give me a call.*"

On cue, Jake switched off the mike and gave her the all-clear sign. Over the speakers, soft jazz began drifting out into the night, broadcast from the L.A. radio station miles away. The precisely timed, coordinated effort between the tower and the radio station had this first broadcast of "Lost Loves" going off without a hitch.

"That seemed to go okay, don't you think?" Jake asked in a low voice.

"You know," she said in an equally low voice, leaning across the makeshift desk he'd set up for her, "it's really not necessary that we whisper." She smiled as she straightened up, tapping the dead mike in front of her. "This thing isn't on," she told him in a normal voice.

"You're right." He chuckled. It was only then that he realized just how tightly he'd been holding himself during the broadcast. "I guess it's going to take me a little while to get the hang of this."

"You're doing great," she assured him. She glanced at the timer, which counted down the seconds until they went on the air again. "How does the call queue look?"

"Lit up like a Christmas tree." He stretched his arms, easing the taut, tense muscles in his neck and shoulders. "I think America missed Dear Jane."

"Well, it's been six long days, let me assure America that Jane is very happy to be back," she said, making a few notes.

"Crazy calls tonight, though, don't you think?" he asked, rolling his shoulders back.

She laughed. "They do seem to be out in force tonight. What was that one from…who was it…?" She put her head down, thinking for a moment. "Was it Sammy? Something about his girlfriend being jealous of his dog?"

"Scotty," he corrected. "Scotty from Scottsdale. Don't you remember, he's the guy that called a couple of months ago talking about how his girlfriend was threatening to leave him because he would let the dog watch whenever they…well, you know, when they made love. He couldn't understand why she got so mad, because the dog would just end up going to sleep anyway."

Her eyes widened. "Okay…Scotty from Scottsdale…I think you're right. I remember now. That was him?"

"Yeah, I remember because his dog was a Scottie too." He laughed. "And you told him if he put the dog to sleep, he should check on his girlfriend too."

She laughed with him. "Wow, I *am* impressed. You've got a great memory. You really have been listening to the broadcasts, haven't you?"

If she only knew, he thought, feeling foolish now. He watched as she adjusted her headset, pushing an errant strand of hair out of her eyes. The whole night had a fantasy-like feel to it. Despite the work it had taken to set up the makeshift studio, despite the numerous tests they'd done and the careful planning it had taken, he was still having trouble believing he was actually seeing Dear Jane in action.

It had been almost a week since Kristin had first arrived at the tower, and to say she'd been as quiet as a mouse would have been an understatement. Except for that first morning, when he'd given her a tour of the place and they'd shared a dinner together, he'd barely seen her. She would occasionally come into the tower in the mornings to fix a small breakfast, or collect a few pieces of fruit. The rest of the day she would spend in the apartment above the garage working on her computer. He would maybe catch a glimpse of her again in the evening, when she would emerge to fix herself an equally small dinner, maybe watch a sunset, then disappear into her room for the night.

Thinking she might be bored, he'd taken one of the television sets and hooked it up in her apartment. She'd been very grateful and had thanked him profusely. But when he'd asked if she'd like to join him in the tower for some spaghetti and meatballs he had simmering, she'd promptly declined the invitation.

At the wedding she'd acted as if she didn't like him. That wasn't the case any longer. There was nothing rude or impolite in her behavior now. On the contrary. She'd been a perfect guest—cordial, affable, pleasant. Also, too perfect. He almost wished she would give him one of those barbs of hers, one of those icy stares or chilly comebacks. At least he would have known she felt something for him, even if it was only contempt. Anything would be better than indifference.

"Ninety seconds," she signaled, glancing at the timer.

It was hard to believe he was watching the same woman now though. The transformation was almost unsettling. The person sitting on the opposite side of the desk was like an old friend. She didn't act anything like Kristin. There was nothing cool or indifferent about her. She was warm and passionate and capable of displaying myriad emotions. This was Jane Streeter—his Jane—and watching her as she worked was amazing.

He glanced at the timer, watching with her as the seconds counted down. He could feel his muscles tensing as he inched his thumb closer to the switch. He'd been in some tight situations in his life, but this kind of stress was a killer.

Ten...nine...eight...his heart sped up...six...five... four...beads of sweat popped out along his forehead... two...switch and...

"And we're back. You're listening to 'Lost Loves' and I'm Jane Streeter, your shoulder to cry on. We've got someone on the line. Hello, caller, this is Dear Jane, thanks for phoning in to 'Lost Loves,' talk to me."

"Hi, Jane, this is Anthony, glad to have you back."

"Thanks, Anthony, what should we talk about to-night?"

"I wanted to say I think I know how Pamela feels. I had a hard time signing my divorce papers too. They sat on my desk for almost a month and I couldn't bring myself to put my name on them until I realized I wasn't afraid of letting go, I was afraid of admitting failure."

"And as long as you were still legally married, you didn't have to do that?"

"Exactly. But then I got out the dictionary and looked up failure. It means catastrophe, fiasco, collapse. My marriage hadn't been a catastrophe or a fiasco. It had been great while it lasted. It just ended, that's all. It hadn't failed. It just ended."

"Sage words, Anthony, and no doubt ones that were hard to come by. Did you hear that, Pamela? Maybe what you really need to do is reexamine what you're really hanging on to. We've got someone else on the line. Caller, you've got Dear Jane, talk to me."

Jake watched and listened. She made notes as she talked, jotted down names of the callers, reminded herself of things she'd wanted to say, even doodled. He could imagine she had been doing much the same things all those nights he'd been listening.

She had looked so surprised when he'd reminded her of the caller earlier—Scotty with the Scottie in Scottsdale. He'd actually felt a little embarrassed. Had she thought he'd only been flattering her when he'd told her he was a regular listener?

He closed his eyes, listening to her voice, hearing the expression, the wit and the emotion in it. It was hard to believe someone listening to that voice would want to harm her. What was it the stalker had heard that would make him want to kill?

He opened his eyes, watching her expression as she talked. He could see becoming fascinated by her, even just from hearing her voice. Was it possible that a desperate, disturbed personality had taken that fascination one step further and really wanted to harm her?

In many respects, her stalker had followed a predictable pattern, becoming possessive, expressing feelings of love, his belief that they were soul mates. But where he seemed to break the pattern was that his fascination had turned so rapidly to violence.

He had studied Ted's notes and the official file on the case before they'd left Los Angeles and he found a number of things that disturbed him. The stalker's initial contact with her had been through the call-in line at the radio station, but even then he had used a mechanical device to disguise his voice. It struck him as odd that he hadn't used his own voice. If he had feelings for the woman, had become obsessed and believed them to be soul mates, wouldn't he want her to know him? It was almost as though his intent from the beginning had been to harm her, that those early professions of love and devotion to her had been merely a cursory attempt to hide his true intentions.

But why? Who would want to hurt her?

"Oh, friends, another heart has been broken. This first-time caller hails from the wilds of Washington State. Sad Sheila, you're among friends. Tell us your story."

"Hi, Jane. Well, we met a few weeks ago, our sons play on the same Little League team, and we just started talking during the games. We had a lot in common, both divorced, both in our early forties, both worked in the health-care industry. After one of the games, he suggested we all go out for pizza and the four of us had a great time. I'm no raving beauty and it had been a long time

since a man had paid any attention to me. It made me feel..."

"Like a woman again."

"Yes, yes, like a woman again. I started looking forward to going to the games, you know, to see him. I even started paying more attention to how I looked, fixing up a little more. Anyway, I had to work late and was late getting to the game. He was there, waiting for me. I was thrilled. Then he asked me if I'd do him a favor and—oh, I just feel like such a fool...I—I thought—"

The caller became very emotional and Jake watched the play of emotion on Kristin's face as she listened. The show took its fair share of crank calls and she listened to a lot of crazy stories, joked with a lot of the callers and everyone was entertained. But not this time. This was the kind of call that made her show a success, the reason her listeners tuned in night after night. This was a real person in real pain and there was nothing amusing or manufactured in Kristin's response. She wanted to help and you could hear it in her voice.

"Finding out something isn't what you thought it was doesn't make you a fool, Sheila."

"But I just feel so stupid. H-he asked me if I'd do him a favor and of course I said I would. I thought maybe he was going to ask me for a date or something."

"But he didn't."

"No, but you know what he wanted? He wanted me to baby-sit his son for the night so he and his girlfriend, Bambi, could go to Vegas—you see, it was a special weekend. Bambi was turning twenty-one."

"Sheila, Sheila, you met someone who represented himself as being one kind of person but turned out to be somebody else. You shouldn't be the one who feels foolish."

"But I thought he liked me."

"I'm sure he did. But, Sheila, let me ask you something. If I told you I had this man I wanted you to meet, he was your age, divorced, in the throes of a crippling midlife crisis, was trying to convince himself he has something in common with women half his age, would you want to meet him? Of course not.

"Sheila, that's the man you met. He may have told you he was somebody else, but that was a lie. No reason to feel foolish for having been misled."

"You think so, Jane?"

"I do. Any of you out there have something to say to Sheila? If you do, the number is 1–800–NIGHT TALK. Let's hear from you. In the meantime, here's a little something to smooth out the night."

Jake flipped the switch, giving Kristin the all-clear sign as the timer began its countdown.

"You're getting pretty good at that," she said, slipping off her headset. "You'll be a pro in no time."

"I don't know," he said, rubbing the muscles in his neck again. "I'm not sure I have the nerves for it. Live radio, how do you do it every night?"

"You get used to it," she said, making a few notes on the table in front of her. "And it helps knowing we're on a thirty-second delay. That way, if I do something truly stupid, we've got some time to rethink it."

"That's right, I forgot about that. They're able to screen the calls then, at the station, right?"

"Yes, thank goodness."

He noticed the change in her immediately. "That's why he never ended up on the air with you."

She had stopped writing, but didn't look up. "Once we realized he was using some sort of device that distorted his voice, Dale pulled the plug." Leaning back, she tossed her pencil down and glanced up. "So he got frustrated and started writing. Sometimes I wish I'd just let him talk. Maybe that's all he wanted, to hear himself talk."

"Maybe," he acknowledged. "Or maybe it would have just made it too easy for him."

"What do you mean?"

He shrugged. "He wanted your attention. The harder it is for him to get it, the greater the chance he'll trip up and Ted can be there to snag him."

She thought about that for a moment. "I never thought of it that way. I hope you're right. Even though I know Dale is down there screening each caller, it will be a long time before that creep isn't in the back of my mind every time those call buttons light up."

"Having him behind bars might help, too."

"That's good advice," she said, glancing down at the timer and adjusting her headset back into place. "You know, you better be careful or you just might end up on the radio."

"Don't even *think* about it," he warned, the thought alone causing every muscle in his body to tense up.

But she merely smiled and held up one hand, counting down. "Five, four, three…"

Switch flipped.

"And we're back."

"Hold on a minute, I want to put some more wood on the fire. I'm freezing."

"What? You're breaking up."

Cell phone service at the top of the mountain was sketchy and weak at best. "I'll be right back," Kristin said again, louder this time. "I'm freezing. I'm going to put more wood on the fire."

"Careful now," Nancy warned between the bursts of

static. "Don't give me any hints now. Your whereabouts are a matter of national security these days."

"Very funny," Kristin scoffed, pulled the blanket over her shoulders and set the cell phone down next to her laptop. She ran quickly across the frigid floor, loaded up the stove with wood, then ran back to the table. "Okay, I'm back."

"Let's see, it's mid-March, sixty-eight degrees around here and you're freezing. Do I take that to mean you are no longer in the Greater Los Angeles Area?"

"You were the one who didn't want any hints," Kristin reminded her. "Top secret, remember?"

"I think you've watched—"

A loud blast of static drowned out Nancy's voice. "Hello?" Kristin shouted. "Are you still there? Nancy? You there?"

"What was that?"

"This cell phone is doing weird things."

"You want to hang up and call me back on a land-line?"

Kristin hesitated. Letting Nancy know she was without traditional telephone service might be too much information for her to have. "That might be a little difficult."

"No phone in your room?"

Kristin laughed as a distraction. "You're getting no clues from me. Top—"

"Secret, I know, I know," Nancy conceded, cutting her off. "And like I started to say before, I think you've watched one too many James Bond movies."

"I just like being mysterious," Kristin joked.

"Well, wherever you are, though, I take it you're doing all right? You sound good, your spirits certainly appear high."

"I'm doing okay. Going just a little stir-crazy maybe but doing fine otherwise."

"Well, try and take advantage of the downtime," Nancy advised. "Rest, relax, destress a little. God knows you could use it."

"I'm trying. And Cindy and Ted are due back tomorrow. I'll feel better when I can talk to my sister again," Kristin confessed, pulling the blanket up close around her shoulders. "And things will be much better now that I can do the show again. Did you listen last night?"

"Of course, and I have to say, my dear, you amaze me."

"It sounded okay then?"

"Are you kidding? It sounded great. I'm jealous. I didn't even get a full week on the air."

Kristin smiled, pleased. "I was a little worried how it would go, working remotely and all. So many things to go wrong. The timing between here and the station had to be just right."

"Well, from where I listened, which was cuddled up in my bed, it certainly sounded as though everything was. Actually, it sounded remarkably normal. You sure you didn't sneak back into the studio? That this whole remote thing isn't just an elaborate ruse?"

"Don't I wish." Kristin laughed, but she had to admit the cramped broadcast booth at the radio station held little appeal compared to the unbelievable view of that remarkable night sky from the tower. "But it sounded *that* good?"

"I don't think anyone could even tell there'd been a change."

Kristin let out a sigh. "That's a relief. I know Jake spent a lot of time on the radio—" She stopped suddenly. Knowing the only communications from the tower were weak cell phone reception and two-way radio might be more information than was safe for Nancy to have. "He spent a lot of time talking with Dale, coordinating things."

"Ah yes, Jake, the ex-cop. How is our mystery man?"

Kristin felt her cheeks flush with color. "He's hardly a mystery man."

"He is to me. Who is this guy anyway? He seemed to come out of nowhere and sweep you up and disappear with you into the sunset."

"I told you, he's an old friend of Ted's. They used to work together."

"But the question is, is he a friend of yours now, or is that top secret too?"

Kristin was grateful she could control the sound of her voice, because she seemed to have none over the heat that continued to burn her cheeks. "I hardly think he is interested in my friendship."

"Why, is there a Mrs. Ex-cop?"

"No, although I do believe there is an ex–Mrs. Ex-cop. I just feel like I'm a bit of an imposition for him, having me around all the time."

"Oh really," Nancy mused. "You two not getting along?"

"It's not that. He's been a perfect gentleman."

"Maybe that's the problem."

"Oh, stop," Kristin chided her. "I guess I'm a little uncomfortable, that's all. He became involved as a favor to Ted. I feel a little like he got roped into something he really didn't want to do."

"I wouldn't be so sure," Nancy said. "There's nothing a man likes more than to come to the aid of a damsel in distress. He's probably loving it."

"I just hope it won't be for much longer."

"Any word from the police?"

"Not really. I called one of the detectives yesterday, but he didn't have much to report. Hopefully I'll get some information once Ted gets back." Kristin leaned back in the wooden chair, peering out the small window. The sun was bright, sending a beam of light darting across the wooden floor. "Have you had a chance to go by and see Tori?"

"No, not yet, poor thing. From what I hear they're still not allowing many visitors. But she is supposed to be doing better."

"Thank God." Kristin closed her eyes and heaved a big sigh. "Oh, Nancy, I hope they find him. I hope they find him and make him pay for what he did to her." She stopped, opening her eyes and giving her head a shake. "When I think about it..."

"Well, don't," Nancy advised when Kristin's words drifted. "It only upsets you."

"I'm upset. And I'm angry. Look what this guy has done, look how many lives he's affected with his sickness."

"Well, with any luck it will all be over soon and then we can all get on with our lives."

Kristin took another deep breath. "I hope you're right."

"And in the meantime, you just concentrate on doing the show and staying safe. I've got an appointment later this week with the client you've been concerned about. Let me work with her for a while, get a feel for what we're up against and then we can discuss the situation."

"Sounds good, and, Nance, I hope you know how much I appreciate all your help—with the clients and filling in on the show. It means a lot."

"Hey, we've been friends for a long time and what are

friends for?'' Nancy said after a moment. ''I gotta run now. Talk to you later in the week?''

''Absolutely.''

Kristin clicked off her cell phone and thought for a moment. What are friends for? It was a perfectly normal phrase, one she had heard hundreds of times before. Just...

She set the phone down next to the computer and pushed herself away from the table. Just not from Nancy. Their professional relationship had been good for them both. It had just never been particularly personal.

Hiking the blanket up, she shuffled to the window and peered out. It was silly but she felt oddly emotional. Maybe it took extraordinary circumstances for people to realize what was really important in their lives. It wasn't like Nancy to be sentimental. Knowing she thought enough of their friendship to mention it was rather touching.

She watched as a gust of wind blew a cloud of dust up and across the driveway. It was a beautiful morning— clear and cold—but there hadn't been a bad one in the week that she'd been there. Eagle's Eye was a very special place. Its vast, pristine beauty held a peace, making the world and all its problems seem far enough away not to matter. It seemed impossible after less than a week, but it almost felt as though the whole nightmare of the last eight months had happened somewhere else—to someone else. She was beginning to understand what had attracted Jake to a place like this.

Jake. She wasn't sure she would have been able to get through last night if he hadn't been there. Despite all her experience, she had been nervous about the broadcast, nervous about whether she could get back into the swing again after all that had happened. But he'd been there with her every step of the way, helping, supporting. So why, after he'd been so nice, was she dreading seeing him again?

She closed her eyes for a moment. They had stayed up in the tower long after the broadcast had ended, talking. It must have been because she'd been riding so high after they'd gone off the air, because she'd been so pleased at how well things had gone, that had started her talking. The truth was, she hadn't been able to shut up. She was embarrassed now thinking about how she'd gone on and on about one thing or another. What had she been thinking?

Of course, it hadn't helped that he'd been just a little too easy to talk to. Besides, he had been so helpful during the broadcast, so willing to help, and after long days and six very long nights of trying to stay out of his way, it had just felt so great to talk to him again.

She groaned, remembering how she had chattered on. Conversations like that were simply too dangerous and she needed to be more careful. She couldn't afford to feel that comfortable with the man, to reveal too much of herself to him. It made her vulnerable and the last thing she wanted was to be vulnerable to a man again.

She thought of Jake and how he had watched her as she worked. His knowledge of the program and how it operated had been obvious and she didn't doubt he'd been telling her the truth when he'd said he listened on a regular basis.

The thought seemed to form somewhere in a dark corner of her subconscious, disturbing and unpleasant. It had probably been there before but somehow she'd managed to push it aside and not think about it, but remembering the conversation, recalling how much she had enjoyed herself, it suddenly burst like a rocket into the forefront of her brain. Exactly what had he been doing last night? What had been his intention in drawing her out? Did he want something from her? Or did he want something from Jane Streeter?

She caught sight of a little squirrel as it scurried across the driveway, darting over a massive boulder and up the side of the tower. Was it the past coming back to haunt her or was she just being overly suspicious? She couldn't afford to be naïve, but at the same time it would be egotistical for her to overstate just how impressed he was by her. Cindy had always said that since Blake she had become jaded and cynical when it came to men and their motives, but she had disagreed. She had told herself she was just being smart, just protecting herself from falling into the same trap, from making the same mistake all over again. So, was she being jaded to wonder why? Was it unreasonable to question his motives? Was she just being paranoid to wonder if it was really her he'd wanted to talk to last night, or was he really caught up with some fantasy he had about a radio personality?

But the disturbing thoughts scattered when Jake suddenly appeared from around the corner of the tower. He must have just gotten out of the shower, because his hair was wet and clung close to his head, and a picture flashed momentarily in her mind of soap suds on wet skin.

"For crying out loud, Kristin," she scolded herself, disgusted. "What are you doing?" Only, as she spoke, her breath had made little patches of fog along the glass. "Oh *no!*" She winced, quickly rubbing at the moisture with the sleeve of her sweatshirt. Except, Jake caught sight of the movement in the window, causing him to look up. Thinking she had waved to him, he gave her a wave back. "Oh my *God!*" she gasped, realizing now he was starting across the driveway toward her room. "He's coming over here. He's coming over here."

Panic was swift, immediate and caught her completely off guard. She stepped back away from the window, her heel catching the end of the blanket and throwing off her balance. Her arms flailed about in a desperate attempt to regain her balance, but the backward momentum was simply too great. After a few wild steps to the rear, she landed on the floor with a thud.

She groaned as a dull pain radiated up her spine. For a millisecond, she almost wondered if she'd cracked her tailbone, but she had far more pressing issues to worry about at the moment. She could hear him on the stairs and realized to her horror that she not only hadn't brushed her hair or had a lick of makeup on, she hadn't even brushed her teeth yet.

Kristin scrambled to her feet, ignoring the dull throb emanating from the region of her bottom, and tossed off the blanket. All she could think about was getting into the bathroom and to her makeup bag before he made his way to the door. It was probably because she was so distracted that she didn't bother to look where she was going, and when her foot hit the other end of the blanket at top speed, it sent her one leg shooting forward and she ended up in a quasi-splits maneuver that even the most adept gymnast would have envied.

"Good morning," Jake called from the other side of the door.

"I'll…I'll be right there," Kristin shouted, struggling to her feet and taking a few hesitant steps forward. The muscles in her leg and groin protested with every step and her bottom didn't feel much better. "Will you get a hold of yourself?" she muttered, under her breath. By the time she hobbled to the door and opened it, she felt completely undone and utterly stupid. "Hi, sorry to keep you waiting. Come on in."

"Thanks," he said, stepping across the threshold and closing the door behind him. "I saw you waving from the window. Did you need something?"

"What? Oh, no," she insisted, all too aware of the wrinkled T-shirt and sloppy sweats she had on. "No, I was just…"

Just what, she thought. Just watching him?

Giving her head a small shake, she hobbled back across the room. "Just saying good morning."

"Oh," he said with a nod, his gaze narrowing. "You okay?"

"Of course," she said in a voice just a little too high to be believable. "Why do you ask?"

"No reason, I just thought you seemed a little out of breath."

"No, no," she insisted, pushing her hair back with the shake of her head. "I'm fine."

"Well, that's good," he said, smiling. "Actually, I was a little surprised to see you up so early. You had a big night last night, doing the show and everything. Thought you might want to sleep in."

The blanket was still in a heap on the floor and she snatched it as she walked by. "No," she said, holding the blanket in front of her with one hand and doing what she could to push her hair into shape with the other. "A little too much adrenaline, I guess."

"That's good."

"It is?"

"It's just that I'm planning on making a trip down to Vega Flats this morning. Maybe you'd like to ride along?"

"You mean now?"

"Well, not this minute," he said with a smile. "Whenever you're ready."

"Oh, uh, okay, sure," she said quickly.

Just then the blanket started to drop but as she reached out to grab it, her bottom bumped painfully against the edge of the table, upsetting the cup resting there and sending coffee spilling in all directions.

"Ouch!" she groaned, reaching behind her to her sore bottom only to discover a stream of coffee was now making a beeline for the laptop. "Oh my gosh!" she shrieked, desperately looking around for something to sop up the flow. She could hardly believe what was happening. Things had gone from bad to worse and her mind had shut down completely. She was absolutely stumped as to what to do. She just stood there, watching the coffee inch closer and closer to the computer, when Jake calmly reached down with a paper towel and dammed the stream.

"You sure there's nothing the matter?" he asked again.

She stared down at the table and watched as the paper towel absorbed the brown liquid. What sort of nightmare had she gotten herself into? She'd been fumbling around and acting like some sort of slapstick clown ever since she saw him walk around the corner.

"Everything's fine," she lied. "I'm fine." But she wasn't fine—wasn't fine at all! Her bum was sore, her leg ached and she felt really, really stupid.

"So in a half hour maybe?"

"Hmm—what?"

"Vega Flats," he reminded her, picking up the loaded paper towel and tossing it into the trash. He pulled another off the roll on the counter. "That give you enough time?"

"Oh sure, yes, that would be fine," she said, trying to snap herself back to sense. "I-I'll be ready."

He had finished wiping up the last of the coffee and

headed for the door. "It's usually a little warmer down the mountain, but I'd still bring a jacket."

"Okay, I will," she said, watching him as he walked outside and pulled the door closed behind him. "What kind of an idiot have I turned into?" she said under her breath as she wadded up the blanket and tossed it onto the bed. He may not have witnessed the acrobatic stunts she'd just performed, but that didn't matter. She wasn't sure she could have felt any more embarrassed if he had. "Of course you could always try, Kristin," she muttered dryly, disgusted. "I have faith in you. Maybe next time you could try knocking yourself out. I'm sure that would *really* impress him."

How was it that in the space of a few short minutes her lazy morning had turned into such a circus act? She hadn't fumbled and fallen all over herself in…in *forever*. What was it about Jake Hayes that reduced her to idiot status? She was supposed to be a mature, professional business-woman. But something happened to her when she came into proximity of that man, something that had her acting stupid, talking stupid and feeling stupid.

Rolling her eyes to the heavens, she tossed her hands in the air in a gesture of frustration and headed for the bathroom. Reaching into the small shower, she turned on the water and let it run, waiting for it to heat. She thought about the image that had flashed in her mind, the image of water flowing over his hard, wet body.

Sometimes when he looked at her, sometimes when they were talking, she thought…it was almost as if…

"Oh, don't be ridiculous," she told herself.

Tossing off her T-shirt and sweats, she stepped into the hot spray. She had no idea what Vega Flats would be like, but she was grateful to be going. She needed to get away. A week cooped up in this tiny apartment was getting to her. She was beginning to see things that simply weren't there. Thoughts were creeping into her head that had no business being there.

What was she doing thinking about Jake in the shower? What was she doing thinking about him at all? Hadn't she inconvenienced the man enough? He hardly needed her to make his life any more complicated by letting her imagination run away with her.

"It will be better now," she reminded herself aloud. "Dear Jane is back. That will keep you busy."

Only, just at that moment another one of those thoughts crept into her brain. Jake had been so helpful working with Dale to get the equipment for the broadcast set up and helping her out last night while she was on the air. But while it may have appeared that he had been enjoying himself—listening to the callers, keeping a line of communication going with Dale on the two-way radio, talking with her during the breaks—she had to remind herself not to make any assumptions.

She knew all too well how appearances could be deceiving. It may have looked as though Jake had been enjoying himself, but he simply had been making the most out of the situation, been following through on the promise he had made to a friend.

The water stung her skin, but she welcomed the sensation. It helped clear her mind, helped her to remember the only reason she was here was that Jake had made a commitment to Ted. Maybe she was being suspicious and unreasonable and just plain cynical, but she didn't care. She couldn't afford to think there had been something in the way he watched her last night, because just like Blake, he hadn't been watching her, he'd been watching Jane Streeter. He'd made no bones about the fact that he was a fan of Dear Jane's—he liked her. She wasn't so sure the same could be said of Kristin.

She let the water flow over her head, plastering her long blond hair against her back. She had thought Blake had been interested in her only to discover it was Jane he'd really been interested in. And she wasn't about to make that same mistake again.

Chapter 8

"Oh," she said, coming up short as she started across the driveway. She had expected to find him waiting in the SUV he'd driven before. Instead, he sat behind the wheel of an olive-green pickup truck that sat high off the ground and had the emblem of the United States Forestry Service emblazoned on the door. "Were did this come from?"

"You've been living on top of it for the past week," he said, leaning across the seat to push open the door for her.

"The garage?"

"That's right," he said. "Hop in."

She tossed her jacket up into the cab, but when she raised her leg to climb in, she stopped suddenly, wincing.

"You all right?" he asked, reaching a hand out across the seat to help her.

"Fine," she mumbled, but her acrobatics earlier had left a few reminders in her tender muscles. Taking his hand, she let him pull her up.

"How come we're using this?" she asked, looking over the utilitarian interior of the cab. The seat wasn't nearly as soft as the one in the Jeep he had driven before, and her bottom could use all the cushioning it could get.

"On business trips I always take the company car," he joked, handing her the end of the seat belt. "Pleasure trips I use my own."

"The Jeep belongs to you?"

"Yup."

"And this?

"Compliments of the United States Forestry Service."

"So this is a business trip," she concluded. Looking at him, she suddenly realized he had changed clothes too. "Oh my gosh, you're wearing a uniform? I haven't seen you wear one before."

"I don't usually," he said, glancing down at the olive jacket he wore over a khaki shirt and pants. "At least not this time of the year when I'm around the tower most of the time. It's rare anyone ever gets up this far. But on patrol things can come up. I may be checking fishing licenses, hunting licenses, Adventure Passes, may have to cite campers or hunters for violations, that sort of thing. It's a good idea to look official for that."

"Forest cop?" she joked, hoping the humor would help her not notice how handsome he happened to look.

"Smokey the Bear with a badge," he smiled. "That's me." He glanced down at the leather running shoes she was wearing and his gaze narrowed. "Those look new. It may be a little muddy where we're going. You didn't happen to bring a pair of boots, did you?"

"I didn't," she said, glancing down at her feet. "I'm afraid it's either these or a pair of sandals."

"Then definitely those," he said, shifting the truck into

gear. "But we'll check with Mac. See if he has any boots in stock."

"We're going shopping?" she said, her eyes lighting up. "I love it."

He laughed. "I'm not sure picking something up at Mac's would exactly qualify as shopping."

"Hey, any port in a storm."

He laughed again and she couldn't help thinking what a nice sound that was. It was real and genuine, but there wasn't much about him that she'd found that wasn't. How different he was from Blake, who could charm the scales off a fish. But his practiced lines and polished routines had grown old fast. Jake didn't stand on ceremony, didn't try to say or do what he thought you wanted. He was upfront and spoke his mind and you could pretty much tell where you stood with him.

She thought again of how he looked at her, how his gaze would hold hers. There was something very comforting in his eyes, they had a kind of confidence that made her feel safe. When he looked at her, she couldn't help feeling that she mattered to him, couldn't help feeling he cared—

Suddenly the truck lurched sharply as he turned across the driveway, scattering her thoughts and jerking her back to reality with a harsh jolt. What was the matter with her? She was doing it again, letting her imagination run away with her. She had slipped into those forbidden thoughts without realizing, and it had to stop before she made a complete fool of herself. Besides, until she figured out just who it was this guy saw when he looked at her—Kristin or Jane—it would be wise to try not to think about him at all.

Grabbing hold of the door handle, she hung on for dear life. The "company car" left a lot to be desired in the luxury department and she suspected the ride down to Vega Flats was going to be a rough one. But that was okay. At this point she needed something else to concentrate on besides Jake.

"So do you ever have to do much of that? Cite campers or hunters?"

He shrugged. "Sometimes. Most of the time it's pretty quiet up in this area. It's so far into the wilderness that usually the people who make it back here are pretty serious about the sport. But occasionally…"

She turned to him when his words drifted off. "Occasionally what?"

"You can get some crazies up here once in a while. They get drunk or doped up and then like to start shooting it up."

He turned onto the road and started down the back side of the canyon. To say it was a bumpy ride would be a gross understatement, and she braced herself against the dash and the door, forgetting about what the hard seat was doing to her sore bottom. She peered out her window and shuddered at the nearly straight drop-off.

"Kind of steep, huh?" he said.

"Are you sure we came up this way?"

He laughed. "Just keep talking, keep your mind off it. Don't look outside, just look at me."

That hardly seemed like a safe alternative, but he had a point about the conversation. She did feel better when she kept talking. "So what happens then?"

"When?"

She found a benign spot on the dashboard to concentrate on, making it possible for her to avoid looking at either the rugged terrain or him. "When you get a rowdy bunch up here. I would think it could get dangerous."

"It can, I suppose, but you can usually get them quieted

down. It just takes a little convincing sometimes.'' He turned the steering wheel in a crazy zigzag motion, avoiding a huge pothole. ''The ones you have to worry about are the urban farmers.''

She looked up at him. ''Urban farmers?''

''Marijuana growers. It doesn't happen very often but every once in a while we get a few enterprising individuals who find a nice little isolated spot to plant their crop.''

''That sounds scary. You don't cite those guys, do you? I mean, it's not like catching someone with an expired fishing license.''

''You're right, I don't cite them. I arrest them.''

''Really? But you don't have a gun.''

He steered around another pothole. ''I don't carry a sidearm. But, just in case it comes up.'' With a free hand, he reached behind the seat and lifted a leather-covered rifle.

''Wow,'' Kristin gasped, turning in the seat. ''Have you ever had to use it?''

''Sure, lots of times.''

Her eyes widened. ''You're kidding.''

''No,'' he assured her, shaking his head. ''Bottles and cans—I've even scared off a mountain lion or two.''

She made a face. ''Oh, you are so funny.''

He laughed and this time she forced herself not to notice. Instead, she concentrated on the road ahead. And while the steep terrain was still daunting, she found herself growing more accustomed to the narrow, twisting route, at least enough to allow herself to enjoy it a little.

''You said you were going to patrol?'' she asked after a few moments.

''Well, it's not a set patrol. I'm making my weekly trip to Vega Flats, to pick up the mail at least once a week, check on the group down there. Then I do a spin by the campgrounds. It's pretty empty this time of year but in the summer it can fill up.''

"So, do I go on patrol with you?''

"Sure, if you want. But don't think that means you'll be getting a badge or anything.''

The joke surprised her and she couldn't help laughing. "So I guess a sidearm is out of the question.''

"Definitely.'' He smiled as he joked, but then his smile faded. "But seriously, you're welcome to ride along with me or you can hang out at Mac's, maybe have a little lunch or something, explore the village, even though there really isn't much there to explore. I'll introduce you to Ruby. She runs the bait shop but also raises a small herd of free-roaming horses.''

"Not to mention putting up some dynamite preserves,'' she pointed out.

He smiled. "And that too. So whatever you decide to do is fine with me.''

"Okay, thanks.'' She nodded. Although as far as she was concerned, it was no contest. The less time she spent with him, the better. No matter how tempting it was accompanying him on his patrol, limiting her exposure to the man really was the best idea. The less she found about him to like, the better off she would be.

She turned and looked out the window, letting him concentrate on maneuvering down the narrow pass. The road wound its way along the side of the mountain, becoming less steep and the drop-offs less dramatic as they descended into a canyon green with pines and manzanita. She saw a dozen things she would have liked to ask him about, but managed to resist the temptation. It was stupid, she knew, but it seemed the more she talked to him, the better she got to know him, and the better she got to know him, the more she thought about him, and the more the thought about him... Well, that was when fantasy started to mix with reality and she kept getting herself in trouble.

It was fortunate he had invited her to come with him when he did. While she may have talked to Nancy on the phone this morning and a number of callers during the broadcast last night, he had been the only person she had actually seen or spoken to face-to-face in the last seven days. Her fantasies and silly little daydreams about him probably shouldn't worry her too much. Given the circumstances, the seclusion and the remoteness of their location, it was only natural that he would take up a large portion of her thoughts. Once she got back to civilization, once there were other people in her life, other distractions and interests, she was confident she would gain a little perspective again and be better able to control herself. At least that was what she was depending on.

"See the smoke over there, above the trees?"

She turned and looked in the direction he pointed, her eyes growing wide and round. "A forest fire?"

He shook his head and laughed. "No. Lunch."

"What?"

"Mac's got the barbecue going. That means burgers and ribs."

She turned back. "So we're almost there?"

"Less than a mile." He pointed up ahead of them. "See? We're hitting blacktop again."

Kristin felt her heart quicken with anticipation as they made their way over a river crossing and into the small settlement of Vega Flats. The village was hardly more than a collection of cabins and shacks with a few pickups parked here and there, but with lights in the windows, smoke in the chimneys and a dog barking somewhere in the distance it showed signs of life—and life was what she needed to help her gain some perspective again.

She needed to touch base with the real world again. It would help her see the situation as it really was, see him as he really was. *If* there was something in the way he looked at her, *if* she picked up on a certain vibe or a certain feeling, was it based on fact or fantasy? Whoever or whatever he thought Jane Streeter was, she was beginning to think he liked her a whole lot better than he liked Kristin Carey.

Jake pulled out of the campgrounds and headed back toward Vega Flats. He hadn't expected there would be much going on at Big Chumash Campgrounds and he'd been right. He'd driven through the site, moved a few boulders that had dislodged in the last storm and fallen onto the roadway, did a check of the pit toilets and chatted with a handful of hunters who had set up camp. All in all it had been a pretty uneventful trip, but still he'd found himself reluctant to head back.

He'd been relieved when Kristin had elected to stay at Mac's instead of going with him to the campgrounds, even though it wasn't exactly the way he'd thought the day would go. It hadn't felt right leaving her, but Mac had promised to keep an eye on her; he wouldn't let anyone harm her.

Jake suspected the break would be good for Kristin too. They both had been a little "high" after the broadcast last night and were happy everything had ran as smoothly as it had. Being part of the action been quite an experience for him and the adrenaline pumping through his system had kept him up long after the program had ended.

Just the fact that he'd sat in that very tower and listened to that program so many times before was pretty remarkable, but watching as she came alive in front of the microphone was something he wasn't likely to forget. Whatever it was in her voice or in her on-air persona that had attracted him to the program in the first place paled when compared to actually seeing her work. She had been in her element—relaxed, capable and content.

Only, as exciting as the broadcast had been, it was the time after the program ended that he'd enjoyed the most. Maybe it was just that everything had gone off without a hitch, or maybe it was just that she was back doing what she loved, he wasn't sure. After they had gone off the air and he had begun breaking down the equipment, they had started talking.

At first their conversation had been about some of the calls that had come in, then it moved to the topics that had been discussed on the air, but then somehow it had taken a more personal turn and they'd both started talking about things that had happened in their lives. He'd learned about the death of her parents and he found himself telling her about a few of the rough times he and Ted had seen each other through. After nearly a week of having her barely look at him, having her talk and laugh and smile at him had been like the sun after a long, cold night.

He'd begun to suspect that while Jane Streeter was a smart, classy, together woman, Kristin Carey was all that and more. She had a sensitivity and a vulnerability he wasn't sure he'd ever encountered before. Was that what she hid behind that icy wall of indifference from time to time? She joked and made light of her work on the radio, but the truth was, she really cared about the people she talked to, the people who looked to her for advice.

It was because of last night that he even had the nerve to suggest she come with him today. The trip had actually started out pleasant enough. They had chatted and made jokes and he'd actually thought when they got to town he could introduce her to a few locals, spend a little time at Mac's, maybe even end up having a little lunch together. Only, just when he'd actually started to enjoy himself, just when he'd started thinking they had turned a corner and he'd finally broken through that icy wall she kept around herself, she just stopped talking, just clammed up and acted as though he'd suddenly become invisible.

He made his way slowly along the rough blacktop, in no particular hurry. But as he drove, he felt himself growing more annoyed—only not with her. He was angry at himself. He really had no business feeling insulted, or even frustrated. After all, this wasn't exactly a pleasure trip for her. He was acting as if she *wanted* to be at Eagle's Eye with him, which was a mistake. She needed his protection, not his friendship, and he'd do well to remember that. He wasn't about to have a reenactment of the last time he'd been in charge of protecting someone.

Bringing the truck up to a normal speed, he concentrated on the drive, feeling better after the small lecture he'd given himself. He didn't know why he was making such a big deal about it anyway. She wasn't going to be there forever, so it really didn't matter if she liked him or not. Once Ted and his boys did their thing and brought in the creep who'd been stalking her, she'd be on her way back home and he'd never see her again.

He slowed down as he caught a glimpse of Vega Flats in the distance. The thought didn't settle well with him, never seeing her again. It probably wasn't entirely true. After all, her sister was married to his best friend. The chances were pretty good that he would meet up with her from time to time. And there was always "Lost Loves." He would always have Jane to listen to at night in the tower, just like before.

Only it wasn't going to be just like before. Now he knew her, had watched her work and had seen the warmth and compassion in her eyes. He would never forget that— and he suspected that when he was sitting alone in the tower listening to her over the airwaves, he would probably wish that he could.

Catching sight of Ruby on the porch of the bait shop, he gave her a wave. There was no sign of life as he pulled the truck to a stop in front of the tavern, but that didn't worry him much. Mac didn't get many customers this time of year anyway.

But when he walked into the small tavern/restaurant/ general store, there wasn't a soul around.

"Mac?" he shouted, walking toward the back room and peeking inside. "Anybody home?"

When he got no response, he turned and walked back out into the store. He spotted a couple of empty glasses on the bar—one beer, one soda—and there was a buzzing sound coming from a fly trapped inside the front window. Other than that, the place was empty.

He walked outside, a sick feeling of dread washing up from the back of his memory. He remembered with horrifying clarity how he'd felt the instant he realized the safe house where they'd stashed Ricky had been compromised.

In something very close to panic, he ran down the tavern steps and out to the road. He never should have left her alone, not even with Mac.

At six foot four inches, Mac Mackenzie was a force to be reckoned with. He more or less kept the peace around Vega Flats by his size alone, and when that didn't work, the double-barreled shotgun he kept behind the bar usually did. By the man's manner and demeanor, Jake suspected Mac might have had some training in law enforcement, even though he never would have asked. Vega Flats wasn't the kind of place you got nosy. People respected each other's space and their privacy. While he hadn't said anything to Mac about the stalker or the reason Kristin was with him, Jake had asked him to keep an eye on her while he was gone and he'd felt confident she would be safe. Only now he wasn't so sure.

Glancing up and down the deserted road, he felt his stomach tighten into a hard knot.

"Kristin?" he shouted. He ran down the road, not really sure where he was going. "Kristin, where are you? *Kristin!*"

"What's all the shouting about?" Mac stepped around from the side of the tavern, the sleeves of his red flannel shirt rolled up to the elbows. "What's all the commotion?"

"Kristin," Jake called out, turning and heading toward Mac Mackenzie on a full run. "Have you seen her?"

"Hell, man, of course I seen her. You dropped her off here yourself not even an hour ago."

"What happened to her?" Jake demanded, skidding to a stop. "Where is she?"

"Nothing's happened to her as far as I know." Mac's weatherworn features made him look older than his thirty-seven years, but his brown eyes were clear, sharp and didn't miss a thing. "What's going on? You need some help with something?"

"Mac," Jake said, hearing the panic and desperation in his own voice, "I need to find Kristin."

Apparently Mac did too. "Sure, sure, okay," he said quickly, pointing to the rear of the tavern. "She's down in the garden. Right there, see her?"

Jake's gaze searched in the direction Mac pointed. Kristin's blond head in a sea of lush green was not hard to spot, and the relief that flooded his system was almost overwhelming.

"Thank God," he whispered, his shoulders sagging.

"You know, buddy, I think you just might need to come inside and sit down for a little while," Mac said, his brown gaze squinting as he regarded Jake closely. "I swear you look as white as a ghost."

Jake pulled in a ragged breath and shook his head. "No, I'm...I'm fine."

"I don't think so," Mac disagreed. "You look like you could use a good stiff drink."

"I'm okay," Jake insisted, even though he felt anything but okay. He stood there for a moment, watching her as she talked to another woman in the small plot behind Mac's tavern.

He felt foolish at having overreacted so violently. As a cop he had learned to control his emotions, to hold them in check and keep his head in a crisis. But when he couldn't find her just now...

He closed his eyes and swiped an arm across his sweaty forehead. The thought that he might have put her in danger, that he hadn't been there when she'd needed him had done something to him. He should have been thinking about notifying the authorities, about plotting out search grids and rounding up volunteers, but he hadn't done any of that. Frankly, he'd barely been able to think at all. He'd simply lost it completely.

A raw, gnawing feeling clawed at the pit of his stomach. Maybe he'd been out of the game too long—lost his edge, his instincts. Maybe he couldn't be of help to anyone any longer.

Suddenly he caught sight of something moving behind a scrub of ratty-looking bushes and all his senses sprang to full alert. "Wait, is that someone with her?"

"Carolyn," Mac said in a quiet voice as a petite woman stepped into view. "Carolyn Hammer."

Jake turned to him. "Who is that? Do I know her?"

"Probably not. She's Ruby's niece. Been staying with her for about a month or so, helping out with the stables and the shop." Mac turned and took a few steps in the direction of the two women. "Asked me if I'd mind her doing a little work in the garden." He rubbed a hand along his beard. "I don't mind saying, that woman has some kind of green thumb. That old weed patch has never looked so good."

Just then Kristin looked up and caught sight of him and smiled. Jake had to struggle to tamp down the deer-in-the-headlights reaction he had, forcing himself to lift a hand for a casual wave instead.

"She seems to have hit it off pretty good with Kristin," Mac said as he watched the two women start towards them. He turned then and looked at Jake. "She mentioned she's a counselor of some kind?"

"Yeah. In L.A."

"Old friend?"

Jake shook his head. "We met at a wedding a week or so ago."

"That's right, your buddy. The cop, right?"

"Yeah, Ted."

Mac nodded. "Visiting up at Eagle's Eye for a while?"

"A little while."

Mac nodded. "Interesting."

Even if he had been curious and wanted to know more, which Jake wasn't entirely sure that he was, he knew Mac wouldn't prod any further and he was relieved. He wasn't sure how he should explain Kristin's presence at the tower. Instinct told him the fewer people who knew who she was and why she was with him, the better. The likelihood of someone poking around Vega Flats asking questions was slim, but he didn't like taking chances of any kind with her safety.

"Back so soon?" Kristin asked she as headed around the tavern toward him. She stopped when she reached him. "You're done with your patrol?"

Jake hadn't fully recovered from the panic, and being so close to her made him feel off balance and awkward. It didn't help either that he had to resist the urge to catch her up in his arms and hold her tight.

"There's never much going on up there this time of year."

The wind had kicked up, blowing a long strand of hair across her face. She reached up and pulled the hair back, the golden strands pressing against her lips as she did.

"Well, I think I've met everyone in town. We just got back from Ruby's. Carolyn was just showing me the garden out back," she said, gesturing with a thumb over her shoulder. She turned to Mac. "Looks like you'll have some nice artichokes ready in a few weeks."

Mac's gaze slid from Kristin to the woman standing beside her. "I'll look forward to that." He took a few steps forward. "Carolyn, you haven't met Jake Hayes, he's the ranger up at Eagle's Eye. Jake, this is Carolyn Hammer."

"Jake, hello," Carolyn said, extending a hand to him. "Nice to meet you."

"Nice to meet you too, Carolyn," Jake said, taking her hand with a small bow. She was an attractive woman, with a nice smile and warm, brown eyes beneath a mass of curly, golden hair, and he was particularly grateful for the distraction she presented. He could safely concentrate on her and avoid Kristin for the moment. He needed to buy himself a little time to pull himself together and avoid that penetrating gaze of hers. He suspected she saw far too much when she looked at him, and there was too much to see at the moment. "Visiting Ruby, I hear."

"You hear right."

"Plan on staying long?"

She shrugged a shoulder. "I'm not sure yet. Just going to take a little time and get reacquainted with the place. My folks used to bring my sister and I up here when we were kids, and Aunt Ruby would put us to work brushing down the horses, cleaning out stalls and digging for night crawlers." She laughed and shook her head. "I think I forgot how beautiful it was up here."

Jake nodded, looking around at the tree-lined canyon. "It is that."

"Kristin mentioned she was staying with you on the mountain. Sounds like a beautiful spot you've got up there."

Jake couldn't help wondering what else Kristin had mentioned to her about him. "It is. You should come up for a tour sometime during your visit."

"That sounds nice, but I don't know if I'm that adventurous," Carolyn confessed, giving Kristin a wink. "Kristin just happened to mention something about the road. I grew up on a farm in the San Joaquin Valley. I guess you'd call me a flatlander. Not a lot of twists in the roads around my part of the country."

"You get used to it after a few miles," Jake dismissed.

"Of course, a good seat belt and a few prayers don't hurt either," Kristin added.

"Well, you'd need them with Aunt Ruby's old truck, that's for sure," Carolyn pointed out with a smile.

"You know, I'd bet we could talk Mac into bringing you up," Jake suggested. "Then you could keep your eyes closed the whole way."

Carolyn laughed. "Well, that's an idea. It's something to think about, thanks."

Kristin had taken a step closer and, strangely enough, he felt a sense of panic again. In desperation, he turned to Carolyn. "Mac tells me you're quite a gardener."

"Just a hobby," she said with a wave of her hand. "But I enjoy it. I guess once a farm girl always a farm girl."

Just then an old pickup appeared from around the bend, coming from the direction of the Big Chumash, and rattled to a stop in front of Mac's tavern. Mac glanced at his watch as he watched two men dressed in camouflage fatigues and fishing vests climb down from the truck and head inside.

"Looks like the noon rush has arrived," he said dryly as he started for the door. As he walked, he turned back, waving the others to follow. "I just took some ribs off the grill. Anyone interested in lunch?"

Jake looked at Kristin, then at Carolyn. "Ladies? What do you think? Ribs all around?"

"Well, I don't know about everyone else," Kristin said, "but I'm starving."

"Normally I'm not much into lunch," Carolyn confessed. "But I've been smelling those ribs smoking on the barbecue all morning. I'm thinking I'm ready to eat about half a cow."

"Well, dibs on the other half," Jake said, extending an arm to each of them. "Shall we?"

Dibs on the other half. Kristin made a face and slid down farther in the truck's seat. Oh brother!

She folded her arms across her chest and stared out the window. She let him think she was resting, but the truth was she was just happy not to have to talk.

You should come up for a tour sometime. She squeezed

her eyes closed tightly, seeing his face as he stood there right in front of her and flirted with Carolyn. Was that his pick-up line—like, come up and see my etchings?

Hitting a pothole, the truck jerked wildly, causing her head to bang against the side of the window.

"Ouch!" She sat up, rubbing her forehead.

"Sorry, you okay?"

"Sure you don't want to go back and try that again. I think there might be one or two potholes you missed."

He laughed, and she let him think she was joking. Little did he know.

The drive back up the mountain wasn't nearly as exciting as the drive down this morning, but then her disposition may have had something to do with it. She was cranky and irritable and...

No! She refused to go any farther with that thought. She had hoped the outing to Vega Flats would give her some perspective, put her back on track as far as seeing things the way they really were. But what a bust it had been.

You could keep your eyes closed the whole way. She turned and looked at him as he watched the road. Whoever had called jealousy a monster must have known what they were talking about. Somehow, someway, it had broken loose inside of her and was running amok.

She couldn't explain it. Something had happened to her when she'd watched him talking to Carolyn. Something totally out of left field. It wasn't that he had been friendly to Carolyn that bothered her. It was the way he *hadn't* been to her that had made her furious.

Her hands balled into fists. Jealous girlfriend—they were two words that had no business being used in relationship to her. She was hardly his girlfriend and she had absolutely no business feeling jealous. It was ridiculous.

Her reaction was completely inappropriate. She was acting as if she'd caught him being unfaithful or something.

"It shouldn't be much longer now," he said, carefully steering around another pothole. "You'll have plenty of time to rest up before we need to get ready for the broadcast."

"Good," she mumbled, turning and looking out the window again.

"Ribs not settling good?"

"No, I feel fine," she lied.

Actually, there wasn't anything "fine" in the way she felt. The lunch had been delicious and there had been every reason in the world that she should have enjoyed herself. Carolyn's Aunt Ruby had ended up joining them and the conversation had been friendly and light. But she had sat there feeling miserable.

She felt awkward and stupid. If she hadn't been there, he probably would have invited Carolyn to go back to the tower with him. He could have given her a "tour," offered her one of his spaghetti dinners, and who knows where things would have gone from there?

Another bump sent her jostling in her seat again, but she didn't care any longer. What a fool she was, making believe he had an interest in her. It just wasn't true, and if she had needed a reminder, she'd gotten a good one this afternoon. Jake Hayes wasn't interested in her, he was stuck with her. Enough said!

Chapter 9

"That's wonderful news." Kristin bobbed around the room, searching for the spot where the reception to her cell phone was the best. She'd come to have mixed feelings about Nancy's phone calls in the three weeks she'd been at Eagle's Eye. While she was anxious for Nancy's updates, she also found them frustrating. She missed her clients, missed taking care of them and wanted to be there in case they needed her. "I can't tell you how relieved I am."

"I thought you'd be pleased," Nancy said. "For a while there, I didn't think she would trust me enough, but I have to say, I think we've had a real breakthrough."

"I've been thinking about Patty so much," Kristin admitted, picturing her young client in her mind. "I had really felt we might be close before I left, which was why I was so worried about going. I was afraid it would have just played into all her abandonment issues."

"I think it did for the first couple of weeks but after

that, she was very angry with you—and me, too, for that matter—but we're working through it,'' Nancy assured her. ''There's once thing I wanted to mention. The service sent me one of your calls yesterday. Do you remember Marie Anders?''

Kristin moved quickly around the table, chasing the cell signal. ''Marie Anders, yes, of course. I worked with her last year. She stopped coming to therapy just when I thought we were making some headway. Has something happened to her?''

''She made a halfhearted suicide attempt the other night,'' Nancy said after a moment. ''She was at the county hospital and called looking for you.''

Kristin felt a wave of nausea wash over her, picturing the curly-haired teen in her mind. She had been referred to Kristin from a teen suicide hot line she had called for help. The troubled young woman had been raised in an abusive home, only to become involved in an equally abusive relationship with a man she had met on the Internet. ''Is she all right?''

''Like I said, it was a halfhearted attempt—a few pills and she threw them right up. She wanted to see you. I explained you weren't available.''

''Damn,'' Kristin groaned, sighing heavily. ''How'd she take it? Is she okay?''

''I think she's fine,'' Nancy assured her. ''She's signed herself into the counseling center for a few days and they're watching her. She's fine for now. I can go by and see her if you want me to.''

''Oh Nancy, would you? I'd feel much better if you would,'' Kristin said, feeling frustration like a tight band around her chest. ''God, this is driving me crazy. I have to get back to work. I'm going crazy cooped up in this place knowing I should be down there. I should be helping her.''

"I know, but hopefully it won't be for much longer. It's only been a couple weeks. Have you heard anything about the investigation?''

"Three,'' she corrected. "It's been three weeks! And no, I haven't heard much of anything. Frankly I'm not sure the police are any closer to catching this guy than they were when I left.''

"What are they telling you?''

"Oh, Ted keeps saying they're following leads, but I'm beginning to think he's just telling me that to shut me up. I have to say, I'm tempted to just pack up my things and head down this mountain by myself.''

"Mountain?''

It was only then Kristin realized what she had said and sighed heavily. "I suppose I shouldn't have said that.''

"No, probably not.''

Kristin snorted inelegantly. "Although, I think even if I did tell you, I doubt if you could find it—I doubt if *anyone* could find it. I've been on top of this mountain for almost a month and you could count on one hand the number of people I've seen.''

"Sounds pretty remote.''

"Remote doesn't begin to describe it.''

Almost on cue, a blast of static all but drowned out her voice.

"Nancy? You still there?''

"I'm here, but I can barely hear you.''

Kristin's mind raced. "I hate this, having to worry about whether I can get a signal or not. What if something happens to Marie? I want you to be able to get in touch with me right away.''

"I could always call your sister…she knows where you are, doesn't she?"

"I'm not sure she knows exactly where this place is. Ted does, but he's not very easy to get in touch with most of the time." She thought for a moment. "I really don't want to put you in any sort of danger, but I have an idea. If there really is an emergency and you couldn't reach me by phone, call the Forest Service. Tell them I'm at Eagle's Eye."

"Eagle's Eye? That's the name of the mountain?"

"I don't think I should say any more."

"Eagle's Eye," Nancy repeated. "And that will mean something to the Forest Service, right?"

"It should."

"Okay, but I don't want you to worry. Like I said, we've got Marie on a watch and I'm hopeful we'll get her through this."

"I hope you're right."

"I've been listening to the show—sounds great."

"Thank goodness for that," Kristin sighed. "I swear, it's the only thing that makes this whole thing bearable."

There was another loud crackle. "Kristin? Can you hear me?"

"I'm still here," Kristin shouted into the phone. "Nancy? Nancy?"

But the signal was gone. Kristin stared down at the phone in her hand, feeling frustrated and overwhelmed. She wasn't sure how much more she could take. She was beginning to feel her life would never be her own again and she would be alone on this mountain for the rest of her life.

She tossed the cell phone down on the bed and walked to the window, gazing outside. The afternoon sky had grown dark. Clouds had been gathering ominously in the distance since dawn and the winds had steadily increased throughout the morning. They blew through the pines now, making the trees sway and whistle.

Despite her mood, she couldn't resist a thrill of excitement as she watched the storm build. There was something so unique and elemental about Eagle's Eye, like nothing she'd ever experienced before. Everything was different—the air, the sky, the weather. Even a rainstorm had a drama all its own. She wanted to go home, she wanted to get on with her life. But it wasn't the rugged landscape she objected to, or the remoteness of the location or the unique nature of life on top of the mountain. If the circumstances were any different, she would probably have found herself enjoying the experience if she just didn't feel so...alone.

It had been almost two weeks since the trip to Vega Flats and if not for the radio broadcast, she didn't think she would see Jake at all. He went about his routine and she went about hers. He was as helpful as ever during the broadcasts, even going so far as to engage her in a little conversation afterward, but it was obvious that his interest in her only reached as far as that. Once the program was over, once he'd "talked" with Jane, he retreated to his world and she to hers. And that silly notion she had that he might have some sort of interest in her seemed like a joke now. He barely looked at her anymore.

She closed her eyes, remembering those piercing brown eyes—and the way she felt when he looked at her. She hadn't realized she would miss them so much....

She opened her eyes and gave her head a shake. She couldn't allow herself to think that way. It was stupid and only made her feel worse. She was convinced he was angry and frustrated—probably as angry and frustrated as she was—just for different reasons. She suspected he wasn't very happy that he couldn't pursue his interest in Carolyn as long as she was around, even though she'd done her best to stay out of his way. Kristin wouldn't have minded exploring the area a little, hike a few of the trails that surrounded them. It would have helped pass the time and the exercise would have done wonders for her. And yet she had resisted the temptation in an effort not to make any trouble for him, not make him feel he had to watch out for her or keep tabs on where she was. She'd allowed herself to become a virtual prisoner in her room during the day, coming out only when necessary, trying everything short of telling him he was free to do whatever he wanted and not have to worry about her "interrupting" anything.

She turned and walked back to the bed to pick up her cell phone. Looking around, she spotted the charger, connected it to the phone and plugged it into the wall socket. Of course, a fully charged battery meant little when there was a weak signal to be had, but she figured it paid to be prepared. Besides, even though reception was iffy, it was still her only link to the outside world and she felt better just knowing it was there.

The knock on the door startled her, but she had no time to react. The door was open and Jake was inside before she had a chance to think.

"I need your help."

"Of...of course," she stammered, her mind reeling. "What's happened? What can I do?"

"I just got a call from Claybe down in Cedar Canyon. They've got a missing mountain biker. He was reportedly headed up this way. They're sending out a crew up the mountain to look for him. I'm going to drive down a ways, see if I can spot him before the storm hits. Do you think I could I get you to monitor the radio in the tower?"

"Yes, of course."

"I'll take one of the handheld radios so you and I can communicate—I thought you could relay any messages from Claybe."

"Absolutely," she said, looking around the room. "Let me just find my shoes."

"And you might want to grab a jacket," he suggested as he headed out the door.

"A jacket, yes," she mumbled absently, trying to figure out how her shoes could utterly disappear in such a small space. She knelt down, pushing up the bedspread and running a hand beneath the bed. Nothing.

She scrambled to her feet and had just decided to forgo the shoes, when she spotted them, neatly waiting for her by the door where she had left them.

"If they'd had teeth, they would have bitten me," she muttered as she dashed across the room and slipped them on.

Jake was already halfway across the driveway by the time she stepped outside. She ran after him, the wind catching her hair and causing it to dance wildly around her head. Inside the tower, she climbed the spiral stairs to the lookout.

"I've got these both on channel five," he said, handing her one of the small radios. "Just push the button when you want to talk, release to listen." He walked over to the large ham radio. "You can reach Cedar Canyon on this. It's all set. If Claybe calls, you just push this button and talk into the microphone." He turned to her then and she almost thought she saw his features soften just a little. "Just like Dear Jane."

"Got it," she said with a stiff nod.

He snatched up the other walkie-talkie and headed for the stairs. "I really appreciate this."

"Not a problem. I'm happy to help."

At the top of the steps, he hesitated for a moment, stopping just long enough to give her a quick look. "Thanks."

She opened her mouth to say something to him, but before she could even formulate anything in her brain, he was gone.

"Be careful," she whispered into the silence.

Jake grabbed the end of his sleeve and wiped it across the inside of the windshield. The fan was on high and the defroster was working at full capacity, but it wasn't enough to keep the windows from fogging up.

The rain was coming down in sheets now and the poor visibility had brought him to a crawl. He'd been making his way down the road for over an hour now but had seen no sign of anyone, and with the storm really winding up now, he doubted he would. If the lost biker had made it this far up the mountain, Jake would practically be on top of the poor guy before he even saw him.

"Kristin, do you read me?"

There was a momentary pause before he got a response. "I read you, Jake. I'm here."

There was something about hearing her voice that had his heart quickening in his chest. "It's getting pretty bad out here, I'm thinking of heading back in." He waited for a response, the moments stretching out endlessly. "Kristin? Do you copy that?" He waited a few moments longer, panic just tickling the outside edges of his consciousness. "Kristin? Can you hear me?"

"I'm here, Jake, hold on. I've got Cedar Canyon on the other radio."

He brought the truck to a stop, sitting back in the seat and waiting as he watched the windshield wipers sweep back and forth across the glass.

"Jake?"

He jumped, catching up the walkie-talkie and pushing the button. "I'm here."

"That was Claybe…they've got him, Jake. Did you get that? They've got him."

"Copy that," he said, breathing a sigh of relief. "I'm heading home."

Home. He wasn't sure he'd ever referred to Eagle's Eye as his home before. Frankly, he wasn't sure he'd even *thought* of it as home before. It had been more like his refuge, his retreat, his place away from the mess his life had become in L.A. Of course, that had been before Kristin.

He edged the truck back and forth across the narrow road, inching it around to head back up the mountain. It was strange how much he felt Kristin's presence, especially considering how little he saw her, how brief their interactions were. After the trip to Vega Flats, he'd gotten the message loud and clear. She appreciated the place to stay and the protection Eagle's Eye afforded her, but beyond that, there was nothing else she wanted from him.

So why wasn't that enough for him? Why wasn't he satisfied that he'd been given the opportunity to meet Jane Streeter, had been able to watch her work, to actually assist her with the broadcast? She'd even gone so far as to sit with him after the show and chat with him about the callers and the topics they'd discussed. How much more did he want from her?

Only, he knew what he wanted. He wanted Kristin. He wanted to know about her, wanted to know how she could be so open and happy one moment, then somber and completely closed off the next. Jane Streeter was the part of her personality that was outgoing and extroverted, but Kristin was more reluctant to open that door. What had happened that made her keep such a tight hold on her emotions? It wasn't something that came naturally to her, because there were those times when she would forget, when she would lower her guard and lose control. But then she would catch herself and everything would change.

He turned the wheel sharply, inching the truck forward just enough to clear an embankment and get himself pointed in the right direction. Stopping just long enough to give the windshield another swipe with his sleeve, he slowly started back up the mountain.

Maybe he really had lived alone too long, maybe the isolation of Eagle's Eye had finally gotten to him, or maybe he just didn't have anything else to concentrate on. He couldn't seem to put things into perspective any longer. He had barely seen Kristin in the last two weeks and she had made it almost painfully obvious she was perfectly content to do without his company. And yet he couldn't seem to get the woman out of his mind.

It made no sense. He'd never been one to let his imagination get the best of him or let himself go off the deep end when it came to a woman—not even for his ex-wife, Valerie. Women had always held a place in his life, but at his time and at his choosing. Yet, there was something about Kristin that seemed to break the mold. Thoughts of her had a way of creeping into his head and into his consciousness and he seemed helpless to stop them.

The rain striking the windshield sounded like bullets and the wind came in powerful, sweeping blasts that rocked the entire truck. As anxious as he was to get back to the dry warmth of the tower, he kept his pace slow and steady. The road was muddy and slippery now and one wrong move could land him in serious trouble.

It was probably because he was concentrating so hard

on the road that he didn't see the large boulder tumbling down the embankment until it was practically on top of him. Hitting the gas, he jerked the wheel sharply but it wasn't quite enough. The boulder clipped the back bumper of the pickup, spinning it and sending it sliding across the road sideways.

Jake struggled with the wheel, fighting for control, but the truck had picked up momentum from the boulder and careened toward the edge of the cliff. The world slowed to a series of moments, one stretching out after the other with a clarity and a cognizance that was surreal and dreamlike. He watched the ledge coming closer and closer. In his mind he could see himself plunging over the side, free-falling down to the canyon floor. He saw himself dying, but strangely it wasn't what bothered him. What worried him was Kristin. What would she do when he didn't come back? She would be all alone on that mountain. There would be no one to watch over her, no one to protect her.

Then suddenly the truck came to a stop. For a moment he could do nothing but sit there staring out the window, hearing the sound of the wind and the rain raging outside. In his mind he was still hurtling toward the bottom of the canyon, falling away from the road, from the mountain, from Kristin.

It took him a moment to realize he wasn't moving, that something had halted the fatal path he'd been on and he wasn't lying in a heap at the bottom of the canyon. He watched the windshield wipers sweeping back and forth across the glass, and realized he was going to live.

Turning his head, he peered out the passenger window. Through the streaks of water, he could see only dark, murky storm clouds as they moved down the mountain.

He was going to live, but he was perched precariously on the edge of the road.

He carefully reached for the gearshift, only then becoming aware of the death grip he had on the steering wheel. He had to consciously peel his fingers free, one at a time, each joint protesting the move.

Shifting the truck into low gear, he eased his foot from the brake and onto the accelerator. He could hear the huge tires spinning, but the truck didn't move. In fact, he felt the rear of the pickup sink down a few inches. He gave it another try, but the action only made the back end sink farther.

He set the brake and turned off the engine. Putting up the hood of his down jacket, he looked at the deluge outside. He wished now he had brought the slicker that hung beside the back door—he was going to get drenched. But it was unavoidable.

He reached for the handle and pushed open the door. Stepping out of the truck, his boots sunk down into the soft mud. He made his way around the truck. It was another boulder along the other side of the road that had stopped his slide, leaving a considerable dent in the truck. But it wasn't the damage that prevented the truck from moving. It was the soft mud. The rear tire was buried nearly halfway in it.

"Damn," he muttered, the wind picking up the curse and sending it out across the canyon.

He made his way back to the cab, his soaked jacket leaving a puddle on the seat. Reaching for the walkie-talkie, he switched it on.

"Kristin, are you there?"

Chances were she wasn't. There would have been no reason for her to stick around the tower if she thought he was on his way back. Still, he felt compelled to try.

"Kristin? Come in. Do you copy?"

While he waited to see if she would answer, he reached behind the seat, searching for the small, collapsible shovel he kept back there. He had just grabbed it, when the walkie-talkie crackled to life.

"Jake? Did you call me?"

"Kristin! Yes! I've got a little problem here."

"Jake? Are you all right? What's happened?"

He told himself the alarm he heard in her voice was simply the concern she would show anyone. "I got a tire buried in mud." With his free hand, he pulled the shovel out of its canvas carrier and started to unfold it. "I'm going to have to dig it out and it's liable to take me a while. I just wanted to let you know. Didn't want you to—" He stopped. It seemed a little presumptuous to think that she would be worried about him. "I just wanted to let you know."

"Is there anything I can do? Can I help?"

"You could give AAA a call for a tow, but I don't think it would help," he joked.

"Want me to call Claybe?"

"No. I'll be fine. Just wet and dirty."

"I'll wait to hear from you. Keep me posted?"

It was stupid, but he liked the idea of checking in with her. "Will do."

The picture of Kristin in the tower was an image that stayed with him during the course of the next grueling two hours. He dug what felt like a mountain of mud from the tire and packed dozens of rocks around it in an effort to give it enough traction to climb out of the hole. But in the end, it was a hopeless battle. The more he dug, the softer the earth became; the more area he cleared, the more mud filled the cavity.

He was becoming exhausted. His shoulders ached and

his fingers had long since lost feeling from the frigid rain. But he labored on, aware that the sky was growing darker and the storm grew worse. Only, he knew he was in trouble when he brought the shovel down hard and a sudden, sharp vibration shook through his entire body.

The edge of the shovel had struck a rock buried in the mud, snapping it into two pieces and bending the handle.

He stared down at the broken shovel for a moment. He was angry—furious actually. After all that work, after all the rain and the mud and the stress on his body—but he was too tired to curse, too tired to do anything but head back for the cab and crawl inside.

Water pooled everywhere. He struggled out of his jacket, tossing it onto the floor, and started up the truck, letting it idle until the engine warmed up. He'd been working so hard his body heat had kept him warm, but now that he had stopped, the cold was beginning to seep in and he started to shiver.

Once the engine had warmed, he flipped the switch, turning the heat on full blast. At first, the air shooting from the vents felt only a little better than the arctic wind outside, but gradually it heated and he began to warm up.

When he was warm enough to stop shivering, he picked up his coat and squeezed as much water out of it as he could, letting it puddle on the floorboard opposite him. The inside was still relatively dry and if he could get some of the moisture from the outside, it would help. He spread the jacket across the dash, allowing the heater vents to blast against the soggy fabric.

"Kristin?" he said, picking up the walkie-talkie. "You still there?"

There was a momentary pause, then her voice sounded through the speaker. "I'm here, Jake. Are you okay? Where are you?"

"I'm still stuck," he said, slipping his free hand under his coat and letting the heat from the vent warm it. "I'm going to have to just sit out the storm and hike back up to the station once it's over."

"But, Jake, I've been listening to the weather reports coming over the radio. This isn't expected to lift until sometime tomorrow. You can't stay out there."

"I'll be all right. I'm inside the truck." He switched the walkie-talkie to the other hand and warmed the cold one. "Do you think you can handle the broadcast on your own tonight?"

"I'm not worried about that," she insisted. "I'm worried about you being out there all night. You'll freeze."

I'm worried about you. Under normal circumstances he probably wouldn't have even thought about those words too much, but sitting there alone in the rain and the mud, they sounded warm and familiar and caring.

"I can start up the truck if it gets cold," he said, reminding himself to keep his imagination in check.

"But you're going to be stuck out there all night. You don't have anything to eat."

Jake didn't relish the thought of spending the night out here either. It promised to be cold, wet and thoroughly miserable. But at the moment, it couldn't be helped. There was gas in the truck, and eventually his coat would dry, so things really could have been a lot worse given the circumstances.

"I won't starve," he assured her. "And I'll start back just as soon as there is a break in the weather."

"Maybe I should call Claybe."

"No, no, I'll be okay—honestly. Just keep the radio with you and say hi once in a while."

"I will."

He had thought she'd clicked off, so when he heard her voice again, he was surprised.

"Jake?"

"Yes?" There was such a long pause, he thought for a moment she wasn't going to answer.

"You're not hurt, are you?"

"I'm muddy—other than that, I'm fine."

"Okay. Talk to you later?"

"I'll be here."

He reached down and turned off the truck engine, not because he was warm but because he had to be careful. It wasn't even three in the afternoon and it was going to get a lot colder and a lot more uncomfortable before the day was through. He would need to conserve what resources he could.

Settling back against the seat, he grabbed his jacket and pulled the dry side over the top of him. Staring out the window, he watched the rain as it splattered against the windshield. The storm was a bad one but he'd been through bad ones before. There would be the usual washout slides, and once he got the truck out of this ditch, he would need to go and check on any danger spots.

It hadn't taken long for the warmth generated by the heater to disappear completely. The interior of the cab became an ice cube—cold and wet. But the hours of digging had exhausted him and the cold didn't seem to bother him as much. He folded his arms across his chest and closed his eyes.

He must have drifted off to sleep, even though he had no memory of having become drowsy, because when he opened his eyes again the sky had grown darker and more menacing. He also realized he was shivering again.

He sat up with the intention of starting the engine and turning on the heat again, but as he started to reach for the key, something caught his attention, something that had him stopping abruptly.

The rain on the windshield made the image blurry and distorted, but he could still recognize the sight in front of him—he just couldn't believe it. There, coming down the road toward him, were two headlights.

Chapter 10

"No," he said, bolting upright. "It can't be."

But it was. As the lights drew closer, he recognized them as those of his SUV—and Kristin was behind the wheel.

He was stunned—so stunned, in fact, he couldn't move for a moment. His mind simply refused to compute what his eyes were seeing. Surely he was hallucinating or dreaming or *something*. It was simply impossible that she was there. He had resigned himself to a long and unpleasant night alone in the truck, but this...this didn't make sense.

He fumbled into his jacket and reached for the door handle. Within moments of stepping out of the truck, he was drenched. The rain beat against his face, making it difficult to see and making the whole scene before him even more surreal.

He stalked through the mud to the driver's side of the

Jeep, yanking the door open. The closer he got, the more real everything felt and the more furious he became.

Somewhere in his brain it registered that she'd been smiling when he yanked open the door, but he'd been too infuriated to consciously notice.

"Move over," he ordered her, shouting above the howl of the wind and rain.

"But I can dr—"

"I said move over!" he shouted again, cutting her off. She seemed to hesitate for a moment, then unbuckled the seatbelt and climbed over the console into the passenger seat.

He stepped up into the driver's seat and slammed the door shut. "What the hell are you doing here?"

"You were stuck. You needed help."

"I was fine," he insisted, shoving the gearshift into the reverse position.

"I thought I could help," she shouted back, her chest rising and falling with angry breaths.

"You thought? You *thought?*" He shook his head. "No, you didn't *think* at all."

"Jake—"

"You could have killed yourself," he pointed out, cutting her off again. "How much help would you have been to me then?"

She stared at him, the fury in her eyes cutting through him like a hot knife through butter. He thought for a moment she was going to scream or hit him. But then suddenly she stopped and he watched as the anger and emotion disappeared from her expression. Folding her arms across her chest, she sat back against the seat.

"Fine," she said in a cool voice. "My mistake. I'm sorry."

He shivered, but it had nothing to do with the wind and

rain. He was furious with her, but there was something about watching that curtain drop down over her emotions that made him want to smash something. How could she do that? How could she just turn her emotions on and off like that? Did nothing matter to her? Were feelings just something she talked about on her radio show?

"You could have gotten hurt or—"

"No, you're right," she said, stopping him with a raised hand. "I shouldn't have come. It won't happen again."

He stared at her for a moment, trying to figure out a way to let go of his anger, a way to vent his fury that didn't involve putting his fist through the windshield. Or kissing her senseless. Finally, he settled for brutalizing the steering wheel, grabbing it with a stranglehold while he edged the SUV around and headed back up the mountain.

He looked at her, but she wouldn't look at him, and he felt the rage in him smolder and burn. One way or another he was going to have it out with her, but this wasn't the time or the place. Somehow, someway, he had to find a way to concentrate on the road ahead and not on the woman beside him. But he wasn't going to let this go. He wasn't going to take the cold shoulder this time. It wasn't over—not by a long shot.

Kristin saw the lights of Eagle's Eye just ahead and breathed a silent sigh of relief. It had taken well over an hour to make the trip back to the station and it was rapidly growing dark. Only, it hadn't been the storm or the harrowing mountain road that had made her anxious for the trek to end. She didn't want to spend another minute in the cab with Jake. The silence between them had gone far beyond awkward, beyond the outside edges of uncomfortable, and had reached the realm of painful.

Maybe striking out on her own had been a stupid thing to do. Maybe it had been foolish and dangerous—but her intentions had been good. Couldn't he have at least acknowledged that? She had only been thinking of him, only trying to help him out of what she had thought was an unacceptable situation. She wouldn't have done it if she hadn't cared.

But he hadn't wanted her caring, he hadn't wanted anything from her, and he'd made that very clear in the most embarrassing and humiliating way that he could. All she wanted right now was to get back to Eagle's Eye, back to her room and away from him as fast as she could.

Her mind was made up. Once the weather cleared, she was calling Ted and telling him to come get her. It didn't matter if the stalker was on the loose or not—she wasn't going to stay where she wasn't wanted any longer.

It was her own fault. She should have seen this coming a mile off and yet she'd ignored all the warning signs. Once again she'd shown someone she cared, only to regret it later. When was she going to learn?

As Jake brought the Jeep into the driveway and to a stop, Kristin reached up and unsnapped her seat belt. All she wanted was to get out of the truck and into her room without having to talk to him or even look at him again.

"Kristin—"

But she opened the door and stepped out into the rain before he could go any further. She wasn't in the mood to listen, wasn't in the mood to do anything but get away from him.

She was across the driveway and almost to the steps before he caught up to her.

"We have to talk," he said, catching her by the arm and spinning her around until she faced him.

"We have nothing to talk about," she insisted, trying without success to break free of his hold.

"You're wrong," he maintained, his hold on her arm remaining firm. "One way or another we're going to talk. We can go inside where it's dry or we'll do it right here. Your choice."

She was ready to put up an argument, ready to stubbornly refuse to let him order her around, but there was something in his expression, something she'd never seen before that told her he would brook no resistance. She stood for a moment longer. The rain was drenching them both, but it gave her a sense of satisfaction watching it pour down on him. Then she turned and stalked across the driveway toward the tower. If he insisted on talking, they'd talk, but they'd do it in the tower. That way she could turn around and leave when she wanted. He could rant and rave all he wanted, it didn't matter any longer. She was in control now and wasn't about to allow him to get to her again.

He refused to let go of her arm, so she rushed across the driveway with it hanging stiffly at her side. He followed her across the soggy gravel and up the stone steps. When he reached for the door, his hold loosened enough for her to pull free. But stepping onto the porch, he reached for her again, catching hold and spinning her to him.

"Do you have any idea how stupid that was?"

"That's your opinion, not mine," she pointed out coolly, pushing her wet hair back from her face.

"It's not just my opinion," he shouted, taking a step closer. "It's a fact. Anything could have happened out there."

"Something did happen," she said. Her heart pounded furiously in her chest but she struggled to keep tight control on her every reaction. "You turned into a jerk." She pulled out of his hold and turned around. "Or maybe you were always a jerk and just couldn't hide it any longer." She turned back around to face him. "I haven't decided which."

"Kristin, my God, do you have any idea how dangerous your driving out there was?" he asked, taking a step forward. His saturated jacket was making a pool at his feet.

"I have an idea," she told him in a deliberate voice. "I was out there, remember?"

The drops of water that clung to the tips of his hair flew in all directions with every move he made. "I realize you thought you were helping."

Her gaze narrowed. "I seem to recall you saying something about me not being capable of thinking."

"I didn't say that."

"No? That's what I heard."

"Well, you heard wrong. I was merely pointing out that if you had thought this out, you would have realized just how foolish it was."

"So now I'm a fool." She could feel her heart beating faster and folded her arms across her chest in an effort to maintain control. "This just keeps getting better and better, doesn't it?"

His hands balled into fists. "Stop putting words in my mouth."

She arched an eyebrow, giving him a deliberate look. "Someone has to. You apparently don't listen to what you're saying."

His fists squeezed tight and his lips narrowed to a tiny sliver. "How do you do that?"

"Do what?" she demanded, her breath coming in short gasps. "What am I doing?"

He tore off his jacket and dropped it to the floor. "Just stand there. Is there nothing inside you, lady?" He reached out and grabbed her by the wrist. "Is that blood in there, or ice water?"

"What are you talking about?" She snatched her arm away and took a step back.

He swiped a hand through his wet hair and gave his head a shake. "Forget it, just…forget it. I don't understand what you thought you would accomplish taking that kind of chance with your safety."

"Gosh, Jake, I don't know," she said, her voice heavy with sarcasm. She could feel the hold on her anger slipping, but at the moment she didn't care. "I guess I was thinking about how much fun it would be to just hop into the old SUV and go. I've got to tell you, I couldn't wait to get out there in the middle of this rainstorm from hell so that you could insult me. I mean, what about that don't you get?"

"I didn't insult you," he insisted, taking a step closer.

"Oh no?" She could hear her voice getting louder, but it was like a dam breaking. The flow had begun and she was helpless to stop it. "You called me stupid. I'm sorry, did I misunderstand? Was I supposed to interpret that as a compliment?"

"I didn't call you stupid."

"Yes, you did."

"I said it was a stupid thing to do."

"Well, my goodness, Jake, I'm sorry. I mean, please, let me apologize for doing such a stupid thing."

"You don't know how to drive those roads, don't know how to handle a vehicle in those kinds of conditions."

There was something in his eyes, something in his manner or attitude she found arrogant and condescending. She wasn't a child, for heaven's sake. It wasn't as though she hadn't weighed the consequences.

"What the hell are you talking about?" She should have stopped right there and walked out. Only, something had snapped, something deep in her belly, and she suddenly felt free and empowered and wonderful. He looked so ridiculous standing there like a drowned rat and she was so angry she didn't have time to think about controls and precautions. "What would you know about what I can and cannot do? For your information, I am a very good driver and I handled that Jeep just fine."

"You were lucky," he roared, glaring down at her.

"I was capable!" she shouted back, hands on her hips. "And if that threatens that overinflated male ego of yours I suggest you get over it."

"Overinflated ego, what are you talking—"

"But you know what, Jake," she continued, ignoring the interruption. "You are right about one thing. It was a stupid thing to do—I can see that now. I mean, here I was sitting in this warm, dry tower, worrying about you spending the night out there in the rain, thinking that maybe you were cold and uncomfortable, that maybe you were hungry or hurt." She laughed, but there was nothing resembling humor in the sound. "You are absolutely right, that really was stupid. What was I thinking?" She stalked toward him. "And you know what else? I never should have done it. I should have left you out there to freeze, you big dumb *idiot.*"

She had been so full of emotion, so intent on getting out all the pent-up anger, she hadn't really been thinking about what kind of reaction to expect from him, and for a moment he didn't do anything. He just stood there, staring down at her. He had been furious with her and she'd been able to see it in his dark eyes and the rigid set of his forehead and jaw. But now his entire expression had changed and she had no idea what he was feeling. She wasn't sure if she should stay and stand her ground, or maybe start heading for the door.

But then the most amazing thing happened. Suddenly he was coming toward her, reaching for her, pulling her close. She probably would have struggled if she'd thought to, but there was something in the way he was looking at her, something that had everything within her coming alive and making it difficult to think at all.

"I could have lost you," he growled, pulling her into him. "I could have lost you."

His words made their way into her heart and burst through her system like fireworks on the Fourth of July. She forgot about being angry, forgot about being careful and staying in control. She'd been careful for too long. Her world was tilting, spinning, moving faster than the speed of light, out of control. Suddenly she understood there were some things worth suffering for—and in that moment she knew Jake Hayes was one of them.

Jake had been angry when he'd spotted her behind the wheel of his SUV but that was nothing compared to the rage he'd felt when she so coolly and so completely dismissed his anger. And the fact that she wouldn't talk to him had only fueled his rage. It was a good thing she had agreed to come into the tower to talk with him, because he'd been prepared to drag her in if she hadn't. He had followed her inside, prepared to keep her there until they'd gotten a few things straight. One way or another she was going to answer him, he was not going to let her dismiss him again.

Only, once they'd gotten inside, everything seemed to change. She had started out with that shield around her—

that damn frosty, detached shield that seemed impenetrable. But then, amazingly, the more she talked, the more emotional she became and the more emotional she became, the angrier she got.

He could hardly believe what he was seeing. Something had finally broken through the layers of indifference, had pierced the shield she hid behind and found the heart of the woman underneath—and it was incredible.

For a moment all he could do was stand there and stare. He didn't care what she was saying, didn't care if she was angry at him or even if she hated him. It was enough that she felt something for him—anything!

He didn't remember actually reaching out to her, didn't remember consciously pulling her into his arms. It was enough that she was there, that he could touch her and feel her and know she was safe.

"I could have lost you out there," he murmured again, only this time against her lips. "I could have lost you."

"Jake—"

But whatever else she had meant to say was lost with the onslaught of his mouth on hers.

It was as if suddenly he'd been transported out into the elements again with the wind roaring in his ears and the fury surrounding him. Her body was soft against his, and despite the cold, dank climate and the sodden clothing, it seared into his like a hot iron, branding him for life. She tasted sweeter than the rain, sweeter than anything he'd ever known and he couldn't seem to get enough.

"I can't lose you," he growled against her mouth. "I can't."

But he gave her no time to answer, no time to respond. He couldn't. This woman who had started out in his life as a voice on the radio had suddenly become his whole world. She had cracked open the door to his soul and he wanted nothing more than to kick it down completely. He'd been existing in a world where the ground rules had been dictated by the sins of the past, by mistake and regret and remorse. But in her arms there was no sin. This was a whole new world—a brave new world with only one purpose, one intent, one woman.

Kristin.

His hands moved over her, finding the zipper to her jacket and yanking it free. Nothing was going to keep him from her—not convention, not the elements and certainly not modesty. He pulled the jacket from her, tossing it to a heap on the floor beside them.

Her neck was warm and felt like velvet against his lips. He could hear the sounds of her breath catching in her throat, tasted the wind and the rain on her skin. It was all he could do to keep himself from tearing at the buttons on her blouse. He had a sense of her pulling at his shirt, but he couldn't concentrate on anything other than the taste and the feel and the sound of her. Only when his skin finally came into contact with hers did things come into focus again.

Kristin felt the fabric falling from her body, felt the rush of cool air on her bare skin, but she was far from cold. Jake's hands left a trail of fire everywhere they touched, burning into her veins, into her blood and turning it into a flame. Desire became a firestorm, something she'd never known and yet instinctively recognized. She wanted him—all of him. It was as if she needed him to breathe. There would be no ghosts from the past holding her back, no protection, no obstacles of any kind. Fate had stepped in and taken control and she was unwilling and unable to do anything but accept whatever it held in store for her.

Jake breathed in the scent of her, reveled in the feel of

her and felt desire coil tight in his belly. Clarity came in a burst of insight. He felt new to the world, like a babe reaching out for the very first time. His hands were wild and restless, wanting to touch and possess every part of her. He caressed the round curves of her hips before moving up to her waist, which was narrow and small. When he touched her breasts, his life changed forever. His existence was no longer dependent on simple oxygen in order to survive. What he needed was her—the feel, the touch and the taste of her. Her breasts were full, firm and softer than anything he could imagine and his fingers stroked and caressed until they were both trembling.

The need in him was almost blinding. It was as if he'd been wanting her all of his life, before he'd known her name, before he'd even known she existed. He had found what he'd been searching for, what he'd meant to have, and like a man teetering on the brink of glory, he trembled with the knowledge of what lay ahead.

She pressed her body into his. He was hard with need and that realization moved like molten lava through her veins. He wanted her—not because of who she was or what she did but because he was a man and she was a woman and destiny had set them on a collision course that nothing could stop.

Gathering her up into his arms, he carried her through the kitchen and down the hall. He couldn't seem to move fast enough, couldn't seem to touch or feel enough of her. He wanted her in his bedroom, in his bed. She was in his head, in his blood, moving through his system like a drug and he couldn't seem to get enough. This was beyond wanting, beyond needing. The fire coursing through his veins bordered on obsession. This was beyond a dream come true, outside the realm of possibility and far and away more than he'd ever hoped for. She had become so much more than a voice, so much more than a personality. Her lips, her neck, her breasts had become his world.

"Jake," she whispered as he lowered her onto the bed. "Maybe we shouldn't—"

"Shouldn't what?" he interrupted, pulling her jeans off her. "Shouldn't be happy? Shouldn't take a chance?" He pulled off the last of his clothes and stood beside the bed looking down at her. "Shouldn't do what I've been wanting to since the moment I saw you?"

"Oh, Jake," she sighed, reaching up and pulling him to her.

His body sank into her in one long, smooth, continuous motion. Kristin didn't turn away, didn't pretend a shyness she didn't feel. She, too, had wanted and if she'd been honest with herself, she would have seen it long before now.

"Jake," she groaned.

She felt his name escape her lips, recognized the sound of her own voice, but it wasn't because she had been calling out to him. It had been a declaration, an affirmation, a proclamation. Jake. He had become the beginning and the end of her journey, had been her motive and her objective. People had come in and out of her life, she had known joy and sadness, peace and chaos, but she'd experienced nothing like him. He had walked into her life and captured the middle and both ends of her consciousness and no one had ever done that—not even a stalker hell-bent on terrorizing her. She had thought she had known what she wanted but now all she wanted was him.

"Jake," she groaned again, pressing her lips against his.

Propelling herself forward, she effectively reversed their positions on the bed. Her body caressed the length of his, arms and legs entwined. Her lips seized his, hungry and brash. She had never felt so bold, so focused, so sure of what she wanted. She had spent the last eight-and-a-half months being hunted by a madman but now she was the hunter, now she was the one in pursuit.

She straightened up, her legs straddling his lean form in an intimate embrace, and gazed down at him. Desire stamped his features as he looked up at her and she felt the need in her intensify and grow desperate. She felt strong and empowered—invincible.

"So beautiful," he murmured, his hands sliding up her body. "So beautiful."

And she felt beautiful. Her body moved along his with a poise and assurance she had never known. With each stroke she blazoned a path, with each caress she broke new ground. She was a woman on a mission who knew exactly where she was going and what she had to do to get there. It didn't matter what dangers lay ahead. A fearless explorer, she was a woman pleasing her man and pleasing herself.

He watched the woman above him. She looked like a goddess rising from the elements—ethereal and elemental and far too beautiful to be real. His hands moved up and over her body—her stomach, her hips, her breasts. They did more than touch and caress, they worshiped. To him she was perfect, idyllic, like the heroine from an ancient myth, from an ancient time. She was Helen of Troy, Aphrodite, Cleopatra—a woman a man would fight to protect and lay down his life to possess.

Only, with every motion of her body, every stroke of man to woman, Kristin to Jake, it was he who had become the possessed. She owned him completely—heart and mind, body and soul. He was on fire and the inferno raging in his belly was like a volcano coming to life. His world was spinning out of control. He held sanity by a thread and that thread was dangerously close to snapping.

Pulling her to him, he spun them around, pushing her beneath him. He had moved beyond reason, beyond intellect, and become a primal being again. He could hear her soft groans in his ears, tasted the hunger on her lips and felt her body grow frantic with need. Like a match to a fuse, it ignited the powder keg building within him. His world had narrowed to this woman, his life to this moment.

Kristin couldn't breathe, she couldn't think, but it seemed she no longer needed either in order to survive. He had become her breath, her heart and the only sustenance she required. She had forgotten all about precautions and protection. She had forgotten Dear Jane and the terror of a stalker. There was nothing else for her but the moment and the man. The coil of desire had grown tight in her belly. Everywhere he touched, every move he made propelled her closer and more precariously to the edge.

And then suddenly she was there. In a vortex of light and sound she was hurled into that glorious chasm, caught up in a storm of hurricane strength and catapulted into the dominion of the gods. She had never known such feelings were possible, that desire could be so sharp and rapture such sweet torture.

Jake heard her cry out, felt her body explode beneath him, and it was the end of him. The thread had snapped and with it his tenuous hold on sanity. His body surged into hers and he followed her over the edge as they descended into the sweet agony of madness.

It was a long time before either of them moved—minutes, hours, days—it was impossible to tell. They no longer existed in the world of time and reality. They rested on a higher plain, a loftier kingdom where mundane things such as time and space were of no consequence.

Kristin felt his breath on her neck, felt the pounding of his heart against her, and a peacefulness settled around her like a cloud. This was what it was like—to cherish another, and to be falling in love. She had tried to deny it, had tried to ignore it and pretend it wasn't there, but it hadn't worked. How foolish she had been to think she could remain immune to such things, that she wasn't susceptible. Her heart felt what her heart felt and she was helpless to do anything but acknowledge and accept. There would be time later to think about reasons and ramifications. For the moment it was enough to lie in his arms and feel love.

Jake drifted down slowly, inch by inch, but awareness was slow in coming. He could almost believe their bodies had fused into one—heart, lungs, arms, legs. But even as reality divided them into two separate beings again, she had become a part of him. He had experienced nothing like this before, had never lost himself so completely, so willingly. He felt weak and exhausted, almost unable to move and yet the feel of her, the sound and the scent of her sent a surge of adrenaline coursing through him.

He hadn't consciously started kissing her, hadn't consciously begun touching and caressing, but it had already become as natural to him as breathing. The slow, easy kisses, the brushes of skin to skin, had his body coming to life.

Feeling him grow hard against her, she opened her eyes. "Jake."

"More," he murmured, against her lips. "I want more."

Chapter 11

Kristin rolled over, forcing her eyelids open a crack and peering through thick lashes. She had no idea how long she'd been asleep. She just knew she felt warm and rested and wonderful.

She turned around and snuggled into the warmth of Jake's arms. Sometime during the long hours they lay together, they had managed to crawl under the covers and drift off to sleep. Outside, the wind howled and she could hear the sound of tree limbs scratching against the bedroom window. The storm had hit in full force and raged furiously outside, a stark contrast to the peaceful serenity she felt in Jake's arms.

She thought of the fury of their lovemaking and felt heat fill her cheeks. She had no idea what had taken possession of her. In her whole life she had never behaved that way before—so bold and so wanton—and had never felt so frantic. What had come over her? What had happened to make everything change? How could they have been standing there screaming at each other one minute and grabbing for each other the next? How had she gone from being so angry to being so desperate?

She closed her eyes, then immediately popped them open again. She didn't want to fall asleep, didn't want to risk the chance of waking up to find this had all just been a dream—a warm, wonderful dream full of life and color. She was in no hurry to return to that cold, barren life she existed in, that life where fear forced her to reach out and hold the world at arm's length.

She turned and looked at Jake as he slept beside her and felt a shiver of excitement. This was no dream, no fantasy she had concocted in her head. This was real—*he* was real and she was exactly where she wanted to be. She could touch him, hear him breathe, feel the pounding of his heart in unison with her own.

Comforted, she closed her eyes and snuggled close again. There would be time later to think about exactly what had happened, to ponder the whys and wherefores, the regrets and repercussions. For now, it was enough just to lie with him—in his arms and in his bed—and savor the moment. She wanted to memorize everything, every touch, every taste, every texture, and imprint it all on her soul so she could bring them out again and again and remember for the rest of her life.

"What time is it?"

She jumped at the sound of his voice and looked up at him. "I thought you were asleep."

He gathered her close, pressing a kiss to her cheek. "I was." His lips moved over her jaw and down the slender line of her neck. "But I'm wide awake now."

She felt him against her, hard and ready, and felt her breath catch in her throat. She would have thought she was devoid of energy, that it would have been impossible to summon even a fragment of reaction, but she'd been wrong. Desire started in an ember but burst to full flame within a moment and she found herself surrendering. It seemed she couldn't get enough of him, nor he of her, and it wasn't long before they were both breathless and desperate with need.

It was a long time before either of them moved after that. They remained in a tangled embrace, arms and legs entwined, the fury of passion having ebbed—for the moment. They were both content just to lie there and listen while the storm raged outside.

"Did we ever figure out what time it was?" he asked after a moment. "It feels late."

"I remember you asked," Kristin pointed out dryly. "But I seem to have gotten distracted before I had a chance to answer."

He turned to her, leering playfully. "I like you when you're distracted, but then…" He pecked her nose with a kiss as he raised up on one elbow. "I just like you." But when he peered over her shoulder to the clock on the nightstand, his entire body reacted. "Oh jeez, no, that can't be right."

"What?" The alarm in his voice, coupled with his violent reaction had broken the playful spell and frightened her. "What is it?"

"Look, the clock, it says ten-thirty," he said, sitting up and reaching for his boxers. "That's got to be wrong."

She turned to the clock beside the bed, its bright red numbers glowing in the darkness. "Ten-thirty? Isn't that right?"

He leaped out of bed, stepping into his shorts. "No, no, no. That can't be right. Maybe the generator isn't working right." He flipped on the lamp beside the clock, squinting against the light to read the time on his wristwatch. "Damn!" he muttered. "Ten-thirty. I can't believe it."

"What's the matter?" she demanded, feeling confused and a little flustered. Only a moment ago he was holding her, peaceful and content, and now he was running around like a madman. "Do you have to go somewhere? What happens at ten-thirty?"

He stopped as he reached for his jeans and turned to her. "It's not what happens *at* ten-thirty," he said in a deliberate voice. "It's what happens thirty minutes after that."

She gave him a puzzled look and gave her head a small shake. As far as she was concerned, he was acting like a crazy man. She wasn't sure what she'd expected from him after…well, after what had just happened between them, but watching him leap around and obsess about the time wasn't it.

"Eleven o'clock?" He paused for a moment, letting it sink in. "You have a radio program to do?"

It hit her like a ton of bricks then. "Lost Loves!" The show was due to go live on the air at eleven and it usually took them the better part of an hour to test and get set up to go live. How could she have forgotten?

"Oh my God," she gasped, tossing the blankets aside and jumping out of bed. "We must have slept for hours. Dale has probably been trying to radio us for the past half hour. He must think something's happened."

There was no time for modesty as they both ran back and forth, picking up articles of clothing and handing the appropriate ones to each other.

"Something did happen," Jake reminded her, catching her by the arm and pulling her close for a quick kiss.

Kristin felt herself growing warm all over and blushing. "Do you?"

He crinkled his forehead and gave her a curious look. "Do I what?"

"Like me?"

There was nothing confused or playful in his expression when he pulled her close again and his kiss was long and fraught with emotion. "What do you think?"

It had probably been foolish to look for something more, to seek some sort of assurance or understanding from him. After all, she had gone into this thing with her eyes open and didn't expect any promises or commitments. She understood the dangers of overanalyzing and examining things too closely. She had advised her callers countless times to live in the moment and not look too far down the road when it came to relationships, and she was determined to take her own advice. Still, the words had been out before she could stop them and she couldn't deny a certain pleasure with his response.

She looked up at him, her brain feeling swimmy from the effects of his kiss. "I think we'd better get this radio show out of the way so we can get back to bed."

He laughed, purposefully setting her away from him and pointing her to the door. "I also like the way you think."

She was still asleep, her breathing slow and steady, and Jake savored the quiet moment. During the night the storm had managed to wear itself out and daylight was slowly beginning to brighten the sky.

He gathered her close, settling back against the pillows, and stared up at the rustic beamed ceiling. Twenty-four hours ago he had lain in the very same spot and gazed up at the same rough, uneven timber rafters, but they had looked entirely different to him then. Actually, the whole world appeared different to him this morning. Kristin Carey was in his life and that had changed how he viewed everything.

An old song played in his head—"What a Difference a Day Makes." He didn't know who the singer was or who had written the lyrics but it wasn't the first time he realized just how true the words could be. One day really could make a difference. He knew all too well how the course of a life could turn on a dime, how something could happen and change everything. The first time it had happened to him, Ricky ended up dead, and that had changed forever the way he felt about his life, his wife and his work as a cop.

And now it had happened again. Kristin stirred in her sleep beside him. Yesterday he thought she was a cold, unfeeling woman with ice water running through her veins. Now he knew better. There was nothing cold in the way she kissed him, nothing unfeeling in the way her body reacted to his. She had looked at him, touched him, and his whole life had changed. Being with her had been like coming home after an epic journey, like finding a warm hearth after wandering alone in a blizzard. She had become warmth and comfort and light to him. She had reached into his cold, emotionless soul and breathed new life into it. He had been living in a void, a place where there was no sun and no moon, no light or sound. He lived on the top of a mountain surrounded by beauty and nature, but his life had been gray and vacant. She had brought him color and warmth and he knew he would never be the same again.

He caught sight of his boxers and her bra dangling from the bedpost and couldn't help smiling at their mad dash last night to get dressed and up the tower to prepare for the broadcast. Going from the soothing comfort of each other's arms to total chaos had been a shock to the system.

But the good news was that they'd managed to scramble both clothing and equipment together in time for the show to go on. The bad news was…well, actually, there had been no bad news. Despite the frenzied start, the show had gone off without a hitch. Once it had ended, they had rushed back downstairs, gotten out of their clothes almost as frantically as they'd gotten into them, fallen back into bed and been there ever since.

He knew he was headed for trouble, knew he was treading on dangerous ground, but for some reason, he couldn't summon the strength to be concerned. She'd asked him if he'd meant it when he'd said he liked her—if she only knew! Somewhere during the course of the last twenty-four hours he had come to the realization that he not only liked her, he was falling in love with her.

The impossible had happened—he was falling in love. He wasn't sure how or when, and if he had been asked yesterday if he was even capable of those emotions, he would have been adamant that he was not—and yet it was true. There had been no clapping of thunder, no parting of the seas. The awareness had come to him clearly, precisely and with very little fanfare. Of course, he could make an *attempt* to convince himself it was just a case of physical attraction, that what had happened between them was merely a combination, the right time, the right place, but he would only be fooling himself. Besides, it wouldn't change anything anyway. It was useless to try to fight it, to kick and scream and attempt to explain it away by calling it something other than what it really was. The simple truth was he was so close to loving this woman and he knew with the same assurance that he knew the sun would rise in the east and set in the west that he would love her for the rest of his life.

He was lucky. She needed him now, needed his comfort, his protection, but that wasn't always going to be the case. Sooner or later Ted was going to find the creep who had been stalking her and give her the green light to return to L.A. and her life. She would leave Eagle's Eye then, leave him—it was inevitable. Which was exactly why he was going to make the most of the time he did have with her.

He glanced down at her, his shoulder pillowing her head, and brushed her hair back from her face. He didn't want to think about her leaving, about what his life would be like without her. Despite its remote location, he had never felt lonely or isolated at the tower. Eagle's Eye represented more than a job to him; it was his home. He loved the solitude and the raw wilderness that surrounded it, but all that had changed the moment she arrived.

Even before he touched her, before he'd kissed her and explored every inch of her beautiful body, he had felt her presence everywhere. Days had gone by when he'd barely seen her, and if it hadn't been for the few short hours they were together during the "Lost Loves" broadcasts, he wouldn't have seen her at all. But that hadn't stopped her from leaving her mark on the place, her mark on him. She wasn't even gone yet, but just the thought made him feel empty and alone.

"Which is why you're not going to think about it," he whispered aloud in the quiet room.

"Think about what?" she mumbled sleepily.

"Go back to sleep," he suggested, surprised to find her awake.

She raised her head up, pushing her hair out of her eyes. "You're up."

"No, I'm not," he deadpanned. "This is a dream."

She smiled sleepily, reaching up and running a hand along his cheek. "You're right about that."

He turned to his side, slipping an arm around her waist and pulling her to him. "Go back to sleep."

She turned toward the window, listening. "It's stopped raining. We should get up and go get the truck."

She was right, of course. He didn't want to leave the truck blocking the road for too long, but he couldn't bring himself to even think about getting up yet. The night had been almost too perfect and waking up with her in his arms had been like waking to a dream. The truck wasn't going anywhere, but he didn't know how many mornings he would have like this. He would indulge himself while he could.

"We can do that later," he said, pressing a kiss against her lips. "Go back to sleep."

She nodded, her eyelids heavy. "You too?"

"Don't worry about me," he insisted, cradling her in his arms.

She had started to drift off. He felt her body relax and her breathing become deep and rhythmic. But then she suddenly roused herself, lifting her head off his shoulder and looking up at him.

"You won't leave, will you?"

He reached up and gently pushed her head back down to his chest. "I'm not going anywhere."

"Good," she muttered against him, stifling a yawn. "I want you with me."

Her words alone were enough for his body to react. If she only knew…if she only knew.

"Cindy's here and wants to talk to you. Hold on, okay?"

"Okay," Kristin said, taking a few steps closer to the kitchen window in an effort to improve the reception on her cell phone. The news from Ted had been good. New leads had led them to a suspect and he was hoping an arrest could be made soon. Of course, this should have sent her jumping up and down with joy, but instead she felt a little as though the bottom had dropped out of her world.

"I'm so excited," Cindy said, her voice sounding faint and far away. "Just think, this whole thing could be over soon. You could be coming home."

"I know," she said, doing her best to sound upbeat and excited. "It's really wonderful, isn't it?"

"Honest to God, I can hardly believe it. I miss you so much, I can't wait until you're home and—" Cindy stopped then and Kristin could hear Ted's voice in the background saying something to her. "All right, all right," Cindy said impatiently as she returned to the line. "Ted says we're not to get our hopes up too high, nothing's certain yet, but I can't help it. It feels like you've been gone forever. You must be going crazy up there."

"It's not so bad," Kristin mumbled awkwardly. She wasn't accustomed to lying to her sister, but she wasn't ready to tell her everything yet either. Of course, if this news had come to her ten days ago, she could have said in all honesty that she had been going crazy, but one stormy night had changed all that.

It had been ten days since the storm, ten days since she'd ventured down that slippery mountain road and rescued Jake from a cold night in the rain, and those ten days had been the happiest of her life. God knows she wanted the stalker apprehended, wanted him behind bars and held accountable for that awful attack against Tori. It was just that now, that came with such a high price. With the stalker gone and the danger over, she would be free to leave Eagle's Eye, free to return to her old life again. Only…she wasn't ready for that yet. She didn't want to

think about going home to an empty apartment every
night, about working weekends and keeping the world at
arm's length. She didn't want to think about leaving Jake.

"Not so bad?" Cindy gasped. "Come on, this is me.
You don't have to be a trooper for me."

"Me? A trooper?" Kristin joked, hoping the humor
would steer Cindy's attention away from guessing the
truth. "When have you ever known me to be a trooper
about anything? I pretty much tell it like it is, you know
that. I even make a living at it!"

Cindy laughed. "Well, I suppose you're right. How's
Jake doing? You never mention him."

"Oh, he's…" Perfect? Fantastic? The most wonderful
man she'd ever met in her life? "Fine."

"You two getting along pretty well?"

"Oh yeah, no problem." Kristin ignored the pang of
guilt. Getting along couldn't even begin to describe their
days—and nights—together.

"I know you two didn't exactly hit it off, but he really
is a great guy. And honestly, I was sort of hoping with
the two of you alone up there, you might—"

Kristin felt something very close to panic and purposely
stepped to the other side of the room in order to make the
cell phone reception dip. "Oh gosh, Cin, I'm losing you.
Can you hear me?"

"Kristin? So much static. I can barely hear you."

"Cin? You there? I'm losing you."

Kristin's thumb slid over the Off button on her cell
phone but she hesitated before depressing it to disconnect.
It was a terrible thing to do, but if she thought she could
have pulled if off, if she could have kept up a pretense
with Cindy, she wouldn't even have considered such a
cowardly way of avoiding the truth. But the fact was, her
sister knew her too well. If she started talking about Jake,

Cindy would have picked up on something immediately and she wasn't ready to talk about it yet. What had happened between Jake and her was too new, too special to discuss with anyone—even Cindy.

Steeling herself, Kristin pushed the button and ended the call. She stood, staring down at the blank cell phone screen, almost afraid to move. She felt awful. How could she do such a terrible thing to poor Cindy?

"You get cut off?"

She looked up as Jake walked into the kitchen. "Yeah, but we were just about finished."

"Cell service is never very good up here," he said, strolling across the room and slipping an arm around her waist. "You're lucky to get a weak signal if you get one at all." He reached up, brushing the back of his hand along her cheek. "It's good news, about the stalker, isn't it? You must be pleased."

The crush of emotion that suddenly seized her heart was unexpected and it was all she could do to keep it under wraps. "Y-yes, it's great. It's almost unbelievable," she sighed. It wasn't a lie, but she felt as though it was. "But when you talked to Ted, did he seem a little vague to you—about the details? I mean, he wouldn't tell me anything about who they're suspicious of or how they found him."

He shrugged one shoulder. "I don't know. You get close on a case you've been working a while, you don't like to tip your hand too soon. Too many things could go wrong."

"You never talk much about when you were a cop. Didn't you like it?"

Something shifted in his expression, something very slight and very subtle, but she felt it just the same.

"No, I liked it fine. I just don't know that I was very good at it, that's all."

She frowned. "That's not what Ted says."

"Ted's my friend," he said in a soft voice, reaching down and giving her nose a peck. "He's got to say that."

"I know something happened, something you don't like to talk about."

"Did Ted tell you that too?"

She shook her head. "He didn't have to."

He shrugged casually, but she felt the tension in his body. "You're right, something did happen, but it was a long time ago."

"Could you tell me about it?"

"I don't talk about it." He bent down and brushed a kiss along her cheek. "With anyone."

His words stung. She didn't like being shut out, didn't like the fact that there were areas of his life that were off limits to her. But she wasn't going to push. It was obvious he wasn't comfortable discussing the subject, and as a counselor, she'd learned you couldn't make anyone talk about what they didn't want to. When he was ready, he would tell her and she would be ready to listen.

"Okay, I get it," she said in a light voice. "The mysterious type, huh?"

"Yeah, that's me, mysterious!" he joked, but she could hear the relief in his voice. Grabbing her hand, he headed for the door. "Come on, I'm taking you on a hike."

"You okay?" He reached down and offered her a hand.

"F-fine," she puffed, grabbing his hand and letting him help her up and over a large rock.

"It's going to be worth it," he assured her. "I promise."

"Oh, I believe you," she said, her chest rising and

falling with each labored breath. "I just can't guarantee I'll be conscious enough to enjoy the view."

"Don't worry. I'm prepared to give mouth-to-mouth if you faint."

She looked up and smiled. "If you must. Just don't expect me to enjoy it."

He laughed. He had made this hike many times and he had to admit this last leg was a struggle. But she had done remarkably well—much better than he'd expected. But then, he was beginning to think there wasn't anything she couldn't do once she set her mind to it. If he'd learned one thing in the last ten days, it was that Kristin Carey was one remarkable woman.

He had always known that given enough time Ted would eventually zero in on the creep who had been terrorizing her. When Ted was on a case, he was like a dog with a bone—tenacious, stubborn and too good a cop to let it go. Yet, when Ted told him they were closing in on a suspect, it had felt as if he'd taken a shot in the chest. All the oxygen had seeped from his lungs and he thought for a moment he would be the one in need of resuscitation.

"Careful along here," he warned, pointing to a dense thicket of bushes beside the trail. "Not too close."

"You mean here?" she asked, reaching a hand out. "It's so pretty, a colorful—"

"I wouldn't do that if I were you," he suggested as he reached for her hand and steered her away from danger. "I don't think it would agree with you."

She straightened up, her eyes growing round. "It wouldn't?"

"Not unless you love to scratch." She looked up at him, confused. "It's poison oak," he said, pulling her carefully past the greenery. "And it can be nasty."

She made a face and moved to the far side of the trail. "I'm not crazy about scratching."

As the trail grew steeper, he heard her struggling behind him. "We're almost there," he said, glancing back. "Just a little farther."

She looked skeptical. "That's what you said about a mile ago."

He winked and reached down, pulling her up onto a large boulder. "I know. But I mean it this time."

She stopped, breathless, and bent over to rest her palms on her knees. "I'd laugh, but I'm too pooped."

"I think this will make you feel better."

He stepped to one side and watched her as her expression changed from exhausted to exhilarated. The rock outcropping jutted from the cliff, hovering over the canyon as though it were suspended in midair. With the air clear and the sky blue, the Sierra Madre stretched as far as the eye could see.

"I thought the view from the tower was the most beautiful thing I'd ever seen," she said, breathless with awe rather than from the climb. "But this..." She gave her head a shake. "Thank you."

"You're thanking me? What for?"

"For giving me this," she said, spreading her arms. "Such wonderful gifts."

Emotion felt thick in his throat and he turned away before he did something foolish like grab her and confess his undying love. He looked out across the magnificent landscape but it wasn't the breathtaking view he was seeing. He was thinking about Kristin and how he found her more amazing every day. He had never felt like talking about the past before, about Ricky and the force and what it had meant leaving all that behind—not even to the department psychiatrist they had made him go see. He'd never seen any sense it dredging it all up again. No one would ever understand how he felt—at least that's what he'd always believed until...

He turned back and watched her as she stood gazing out across the canyon. Why did he feel so comfortable with her? Why did he feel that if there was one person on this earth who would understand, it would be her? Was it merely her training as a therapist, or because he'd listened to Dear Jane for so long on the radio? She certainly hadn't pressed him in any way to open up to her. When she'd asked, he'd said no and she'd backed right off. Did that mean she wasn't interested? Was he being presumptuous to think she'd even want to know that much about him? If she knew the truth, would it change the way she felt?

"You're staring at me."

It took a moment for her words to register. "Am I?"

"Yes." She turned and looked at him.

"You're right," he admitted, tossing his hands up. "In fact, I find I have a hard time keeping my eyes off you."

He hoped he'd sounded playful, hoped to lighten his own mood, but she was having none of it.

"As flattering as I find that," she said, taking several steps toward him, "I think there's something more to it."

He told himself he shouldn't be surprised. He'd only met the woman barely over a month ago and yet already she knew him better than Valerie had after three years of marriage.

He hadn't fully realized what a burden the past had been until that moment, now that he had an almost irresistible urge to liberate himself of it. Suddenly he wanted nothing between them—no questions, no ghosts, no secrets. She had come to know him pretty darned well in the past month, but he'd come to know her too. It wouldn't matter what he said, how many secrets he shared with her. Nothing was going to change what they'd shared.

"There was a man," he started, kneeling down and picking up a few small stones from the top of the rock and tossing them over the edge. "He trusted me to keep him safe and I let him down." And with that, the entire story came spilling out as though he'd held it inside for far too long.

Chapter 12

Kristin poked her nose out from under the quilt and immediately felt the icy bite of the morning air. It didn't seem to matter in this rugged part of the world that Easter was just around the corner and spring had sprung. It was just after six, and far too early to get up, but she'd had all the sleep she needed. In fact, she was wide awake. But she was content just to lie there, snuggled close in Jake's arms, and just think about all the amazing things that had happened.

She wasn't sure who had felt better yesterday—Jake for having finally released everything he'd been carrying around for the last three years, or her for knowing he trusted her enough to tell her all about it. As a therapist, she understood just how much Jake had needed to free himself of all those demons he'd kept bottled up inside. But her reaction had been strictly as a woman. Instinct had her wanting to reach out, had her wanting to comfort and protect.

It was clear from the story Jake told that circumstances completely out of his control had contributed to the death of the witness he'd been assigned to protect, and yet his sense of duty had him bearing all the responsibility. But no one would ever be able to convince him of the truth. In time he would come to that conclusion on his own— at least enough to forgive himself, but he wasn't there yet.

It took a few moments for her brain to compute when she heard the first few notes of the *William Tell Overture* sing out, breaking the silence of the morning—but only a few. Cell phone!

She resisted the urge to leap out of bed. While the chiming overture hadn't fazed Jake, she was afraid her moving would. But she had to answer. A call at this hour had to be serious. As carefully as she could, she slid out of the warm bed and raced across the cold wooden floor. Grabbing the phone from the bureau, she flipped it open.

"Hello?" she said in a low voice.

"Good, you're there," Nancy said in a no-nonsense tone.

"What is it? What's happened?"

"It's my mother, she's taken a turn for the worse."

"I…I didn't know she was ill." Kristin couldn't remember Nancy having mentioned her family. She only knew she'd grown up somewhere outside Boston.

"It's been going on for a while now. I'm at LAX, my flight is boarding in a few minutes."

"Nancy, I'm so sorry." It was bitter cold and Kristin felt herself start to shiver.

"I wanted to let you know I've turned over your files to Tony Ramsey from the clinic. I told him you'd give him a call this morning. I didn't want to say anything about…what's that place again? Eagle something?"

"Eagle's Eye."

"Right. Anyway, I told him you'd give him a call later this morning, get him up to speed."

"Yes." Kristin reached for Jake's shirt and slipped it over her naked shoulders. "Yes, of course. But, Nancy, are you okay?"

"I will be," she said. "Don't worry about me."

"Well, if there's anything— Hello? Nancy?" It was too late, the line had gone dead. But when she looked down at her cell phone, she frowned. "That's funny," she mumbled, staring at the power bars on her phone.

"What is?"

She looked up to find Jake peeking at her from over the top of the quilt. "I'm sorry, I was hoping I wouldn't wake you."

"Everything all right?"

"Yeah, I just lost a call."

"Important?"

Kristin glanced down at the phone again and shivered. "I'm not sure. It was Nancy, she's had to leave town and wanted me to know she was turning over my clients to another colleague."

He pulled back the quilt. "It's freezing, come back to bed."

She nodded, replacing the phone on the bureau and walking back across the room. "It's so strange though."

"That she called?"

Kristin felt a pang of guilt as she freed the shirt from her shoulders and slid back under the quilt. He was aware she talked to Cindy on a regular basis but didn't know she had remained in contact with Nancy—no one did.

"Hmm, you feel wonderful," she said, slipping in close.

"You feel like an ice cube," he joked with a shiver, wrapping his arms around her. "So, is everything okay?"

"Yeah, I guess, but it's kind of odd. I was saying some
thing to her and she just hung up."

"Like I said, cell reception is a little sketchy out here.
You probably just lost the signal."

"That's what I thought at first too." The warmth was
seeping into her skin and heating her blood. "But when
I looked at the phone just now, it was still showing a fairly
strong signal." She turned and looked at him. "I think
maybe Nancy hung up on me."

"Maybe she thought you were finished."

"Maybe," she acknowledged, warming her arms and
her hands along the length of his chest.

"So, been getting many calls, have you? Those boyfriends of yours missing you while you're away?"

"Aren't you funny," she said dryly, making a face.

"Funny hell," he snorted, pulling her to him. "I'm
jealous!"

Nothing would have pleased her more than to think she
could make him jealous, but she knew he was joking. He
was concerned for a very different reason.

"Well, calm down, tough guy," she joked, giving him
a reassuring pat on the chest. "But yes, I confess, Nancy
and I have been talking pretty regularly."

"I thought I heard you say something about Eagle's
Eye?"

She'd been caught red-handed and there was no use
denying it. "*And* I told her where I was," she confessed.
But when he started to say something, she lifted a hand
to stop him. "I know, I know. I promised not to tell anyone, but there was a potential crisis with one of my clients.
I wanted her to know how to get a hold of me if something happened."

"If something happened, all she would have to do is
call Ted."

"I know, but that could take time. You know how hard it is to get a hold of him. Nancy was telling me about this client, warning me that she might be in trouble, and at that moment, I felt—" She stopped and shrugged a shoulder. "I don't know, I guess I felt guilty, you know, for not being there myself to help her through it."

His face softened, but his gaze remained stern. "Divulging your whereabouts wasn't the wisest thing to do. It could put both you and Nancy in danger."

She thought of her telephone conversation yesterday with Ted and felt a knot in her stomach. "Well, that doesn't seem like it's going to be an issue for much longer and Nancy's on her way out of town now anyway. I really don't think it's a problem."

He didn't look convinced. "The point is, you shouldn't be taking chances with your safety—not when it can be avoided."

The concern she saw in his face squeezed at her heart. She didn't doubt he cared about what happened to her, and after the talk they'd had yesterday, she understood why. She understood keeping her safe represented a lot to him, that it stood for more than just a favor to an old friend. It meant shattering old doubts and proving something to that fear he'd held inside for far too long.

It would be so easy to misinterpret his concern, to make it into something more than it was, especially at times like this, when he looked at her with so much emotion showing in his eyes, so much affection on his face.

"Don't be mad at me," she said after a moment, struggling with the knot of emotion in her throat. His point was a valid one, even though she believed the risk had been minimal, but she wasn't in the mood to debate the issue. "It's just Nancy. She's not going to tell anyone."

"Well, okay, but promise me you won't tell anyone else?"

"I promise."

He slid down, bringing them face-to-face on the pillow, and gathered her close. "So, are there any more phone calls I need to know about?"

She smiled. "Not a one."

"And I don't have to worry about some jealous boy-friend finding his way up here trying to beat down my door?"

"Well," she snorted inelegantly. "I can't guarantee that. You know how jealous boyfriends can be."

His gaze narrowed. "I'm not sure. Maybe you would like to tell me?"

Things were just too easy with him, she decided as she gave him a playfully wicked smile. How comfortably they could slip between emotions—serious to superficial, tense to teasing. It was how it should be, how she'd always dreamed it would be with the right person at the right time. Only…her time was just about up.

"Oh, stubborn, possessive," she said, brushing a kiss along his lips. "Pigheaded." She slid her tongue along his bottom lip, feeling him grow hard against her. "Un-reasonable and very, very frustrated."

"Interesting," he murmured, shifting his weight and slipping her beneath him. "Sounds like me."

His mouth sank onto hers and within moments they were both breathless with need. Kristin felt herself soar-ing, transported up and away from a world filled with uncertainty and doubt to a place where there was only touch and taste and the man she knew now that she loved.

The real world had only just begun to take shape again, when they heard a thunderous commotion outside.

"Jake?" Kristin cried out, the serene aftermath shattered. A million things shot through her mind. Had the stalker gotten to Nancy, had he come to Eagle's Eye? "What was that? What's happened?"

"Oh, no," Jake groaned, placing a comforting hand on her shoulder. "It sounds like the shed." He slowly rose up. "I don't remember locking it and I will bet the raccoons have gotten inside. It's happened before." He turned and reached for a pair of jeans, carelessly tossed over the back of a chair. "You stay here and keep warm. I'll go check it out and be right back, okay?"

Kristin nodded, but could feel the wild pounding of her heart throughout her entire body. It surprised her just how frightened she'd felt, to discover how jumpy she still was. She'd felt so safe, so secure since she'd been at Eagle's Eye, she almost forgot what it was like to be afraid.

"Be right back," Jake said, pushing into his boots as he hopped toward the door. "Keep my side warm for me?" he asked, turning back and blowing her a kiss.

But he was gone before she could answer. Kristin waited a moment, feeling her heart slowly return to its normal rhythm, then threw the quilt aside and got up. She had all but moved into Jake's room in the last few weeks, but that didn't make finding her clothes any easier, and by the time she had pulled on her jeans and slipped a sweatshirt over her head, she was shivering again and her bare feet felt like ice. Not able to find a pair of her own socks, she grabbed a pair of Jake's from his drawer and pulled them on. Of course, being sizes too big, they made her running shoes feel tight, but that didn't bother her a bit. Her toes might be a little pinched, but they were also deliciously warm.

Heading down the hall and through the kitchen, she pushed open the door and walked outside. But on the steps, she skittered to an abrupt halt.

"Oh my gosh!" she gasped. "They did all this?"

Jake was standing in the middle of the compound holding a shovel and surrounded by what looked like the contents of their recycling bins, compost pile and trash cans.

"Go back inside," he advised, scooping up a shovel of trash and depositing it in a wheelbarrow. "It's cold and this is going to take me a little while."

"But I can help," she insisted. He was right about the cold though. It bit at her cheeks and showed her breath with each word. But she was undeterred and headed down the steps, reaching for a rake resting against the railing.

"No, no," he said, dropping the shovel and starting toward her. "You need to go back inside."

"I want to help."

"That's very sweet," he said gently. "But what would really help would be for you to go back inside."

"I'm not that delicate. I can pick up after a few raccoons."

"That's just it, my lovely woman," he said with a smile. "This wasn't done by raccoons."

"It wasn't?"

"No." With a hand on either shoulder, he slowly began backing her toward the steps. "So why don't you run up there and close the door and let me take care of this."

"But if it wasn't raccoons," she asked, stopping at the steps and refusing to be pushed any farther, "then who did this?"

"Uh, she did," Jake said deliberately, turning and pointing toward the garage.

When it came to size, the black bear quietly watching from the boulder just beyond the compound was probably not that impressive, but to Kristin's startled eye, it looked like a grizzly.

"Ja—"

But Jake's hand gently covered her mouth, effectively cutting her off. "Shh. No sense getting our friend all excited now."

"B-but it's a...a *bear*."

He laughed. "You're right about that and I suspect she has a couple of cubs close by too, so it would probably be better if we don't get too excited and get her thinking we're a threat to them or anything." He spoke in a calm monotone, as though he were discussing the weather or some equally benign topic, as he backed her up the steps. "So you get back inside while I clean up this mess."

"You can't stay out here, you'll get hurt," she insisted. "The gun, we need the gun from the truck. Maybe I should—"

"No, no," he said with a quiet laugh. "There's no need for a gun. This mama bear is used to me and knows I'm no threat to her or her babies." He walked her up the steps and opened the door. "But the two of us together, she may not be so sure of, so you just wait inside and I'll be in as soon as I'm finished."

"But I worry about you."

He bent down and gave her a quick kiss. "I appreciate that." He stopped and kissed her again, longer this time. "Go inside."

She nodded. "Promise you'll be careful?"

"Oh, if you insist," he joked. "But only if you promise to do something for me."

She reached up and brushed a hand along his cheek. "Anything."

He brushed his lips against hers. "Keep my side of the bed warm."

"Looking for bears?"

Jake smiled and put down the binoculars. After the ini-

tial excitement earlier, the rest of the morning had turned
into a quiet one. He and Kristin had shared a leisurely,
albeit late, breakfast and then gone their separate ways.
She had flipped on her computer to prepare for the radio
broadcast tonight and he had headed up to the tower.

"Why? You packing heat this time?"

She made a face. "Very amusing, Mr. Hayes. Can I
help it if I want to protect you?"

"But I'm supposed to be protecting the wildlife." He
reached for her hand, pulling her onto his lap. "You
know, you need a license to hunt bear in these parts." He
nuzzled her neck, breathing in the clean, heady scent of
her. "You wouldn't want me to have to cite you for not
having the proper documentation, now, would you?"

"Cite yourself. This is all your fault, you know that,
don't you?"

"Excuse me? My fault? How do you figure?"

"Don't you think you could have warned me there
were wild animals around here?"

"I did," he insisted with a laugh. He enjoyed their easy
camaraderie, enjoyed ribbing her without having to worry
she would take something he said the wrong way. He'd
never experienced that with a woman before—and certainly not with his ex-wife. Valerie had been so sensitive,
had always misinterpreted everything he said. He'd forever been hurting her feelings, which might be why he
eventually avoided saying anything to her at all. But not
Kristin—she not only could handle the kidding, she could
give as good as she got. "I distinctly remember saying
something to you about critters when you first arrived. I
warned you to keep your door shut."

"Critters," she clarified. "You said there were critters
around here. Squirrels, raccoons, skunks—*those* are critters. You never mentioned anything about bears."

He leaned her back dramatically and gave her a firm kiss on the mouth. "I stand corrected—critters are squirrels, raccoons and...what was that third one?"

"Skunks," she said, pushing herself up. She stood and grabbed the binoculars, aiming them at the compound below. "And I have to run across to my room. Do you think the coast is clear now?"

He stood up, stretching his arms out and yawning. The afternoon sun had begun to send shadows streaking across the driveway. "I think it's safe to assume mama and her babies are long gone by now." He moved behind her, sliding his arms around her waist. "Probably holed up in some cave somewhere, all cozy and full after feasting on our garbage this morning." He planted a kiss along her neck. "Want me to go with you?"

"No," she said, lowering the binoculars. "I'll try and brave it." She raised the glasses to her eyes again. "So what have you been looking at up here all afternoon?"

"I thought I caught a flash of something down in the canyon there," he said, pointing west toward the road. "Probably just someone on a dirt bike or something." He gestured to the sky. "But see those clouds over there? They could be setting up for a beautiful sunset."

She followed with the binoculars. "And I'll bet it would probably go very nicely with a little wine, some cheese." She shifted her gaze just enough to peek up at him. "Interested?"

He pulled her close and brushed a kiss against her ear. "Oh, yeah."

She started to laugh, but something in the glass caught her eye. "Hey, I think I saw something too. Over there?" Lowering the binoculars, she stepped aside and handed them to him. "What is that?"

He raised the binoculars, his jaw tightening. "Smoke."

"What?" Her eyes grew wide.

He lowered the glass. "Looks more like a campfire maybe."

"Someone's camping down there?"

"No one should be," he pointed out. He reached for a set of handheld two-way radios, switching both of them on.

"What are you going to do?"

"I'll just run down there and check it out." He headed for the spiral stairs. "Want to do me a favor?"

"Sure, anything."

He turned and handed her one of the radios. "Think you'd mind sticking around the tower and monitoring this in case I need to have you call down to Claybe in Cedar Canyon on the ham?"

"Of course I wouldn't mind," she said, looking at the little radio in her hand.

"I'm guessing from where that smoke is, I may have to hike a bit off the road." He held out the radio. "Remember how these work? Push this button to talk. Think you can handle it?"

"Push to talk, I remember," she said with a nod, following as he turned for the stairs again. "Be careful?"

At the top step he stopped and turned back to her. "You always going to worry about me?"

"This is the wilderness," she said, gesturing to the view outside. "There's a lot to worry about around here."

"Squirrels, raccoons..."

"Skunks," she quickly added.

"Skunks," he acknowledged. "And bears."

She grabbed the front of his shirt, pulling him to her. "Especially bears. Take care of yourself?"

Emotion threatened to close off his throat. He wanted to tell her how much she meant to him, how much he cared, but he wasn't sure he would have been able to get the words out even if there had been time to say them.

"Always," he managed to say in a tight voice. Turning, he headed down the stairs.

"Hurry back," she called after him. "We've got a date with a sunset."

Kristin carefully tweaked the focus of the lenses, bringing the lush green brush to flawless clarity. She could see the small thread of smoke wind its way up through the pines to form a faint gray cloud above the treeline. To her untrained eye, the smoke trail hadn't seemed to have grown any denser in the fifteen minutes since Jake had left. In fact, she would have sworn it was fading—at least she hoped it was. Seeing the smoke among all the green really showed her just how vulnerable this rugged world was to fire.

She moved the lenses down, hoping to find the road and catch a glimpse of Jake as he worked his way toward the source of the smoke, but it was useless.

"Be careful, my love," she murmured to herself, lowering the binoculars.

Her love. Jake was her love—he was her heart, her soul and the only man she knew she would ever love. She hadn't allowed herself to think about that too much in the last couple of weeks, preferring to concentrate her scope of reference on a day-by-day basis. But living one day at a time had been a fantasy. Her reality was knowing that Jake Hayes would be the love of her life—the one and only. When he was with her, it was too hard for her to remain in control. But in the quiet of the empty tower, she could admit the truth, and the cold hard truth was it wouldn't matter if he lived in Eagle's Eye and she in Los Angeles, or—as painful as the thought was—if year after

lonely year passed and she never had the joy of seeing
him again—nothing was going to change. She would love
him always, and not even the prospect of a lifetime of
hurt and loneliness would change a thing.

The irony wasn't lost on her. The last eight months had
been the worst in her life, and yet it was the terror of a
faceless, nameless stranger who had set her on this course
that brought her to Jake. She wanted nothing more than
to forget the nightmare, to put all the nights of terror, all
the suspicion, all the fear behind her and move on with
her life. Except, going on meant doing so without Jake.

"Why me?" she mumbled in a flash of self-pity. Walking to the slider, she slid it open and stepped out onto the
deck.

Why couldn't things just have been easy? Why couldn't
they have met in the conventional way—on a bus or at
the grocery store where they could have taken things slow
and gotten to know one another in their everyday lives?
Why did it have to happen when her life was in turmoil
and Jake was recovering from the turbulence of his past?
She'd read enough case studies to know that during times
of great emotional upheaval, it wasn't unusual for people—strangers usually—to turn to one another in an attempt to satisfy a very basic human need. That's what had
happened with her and Jake. They had been strangers,
thrown together by circumstances out of their control. It
was only natural they would reach out to one another.
They were two consenting adults, what harm would it do?

A gust of wind traveled up the stone tower, sending a
shiver through her body. The harm was the price she
would have to pay, the toll it would take on her heart.
She had fallen in love. That wasn't supposed to have happened. Maybe she was too much of a realist, but it seemed
futile to try to hold on to hope, to try to turn whatever

was between them into more than it was. She knew the statistics all too well, knew relationships that began in the midst of such life-altering encounters were usually disastrous. So in that respect, maybe she should count herself lucky it would all be coming to an end very soon. At least this way, she could walk away with a lovely memory.

But standing there, staring out at the breathtaking beauty of Eagle's Eye, she felt anything but lucky. Jake had never specifically told her he wasn't interested in a long-term relationship, he didn't have to. The solitary and isolated lifestyle the man chose to live had conveyed all she needed to know.

A sudden glimpse of movement below had her gaze traveling toward the compound. Leaning forward, she squinted, carefully surveying the bushes and rock outcroppings.

"Mama bear, is that you again?"

Jake may have been convinced their morning visitors were long gone, but it was going to take a little more time for her not to feel jumpy and imagine a grizzly lurking around every corner. The last thing she wanted was another close encounter. She watched and waited for a moment, listening carefully, but the only sound she heard was the whistle of the wind as it swept up the canyon.

She turned and headed back inside, but the tower felt cold and lonely. She had never felt alone, even though it was just the two of them here, but now with Jake gone, the quiet and the solitude made her feel restless and slightly frightened.

The smoke trail was almost impossible to see now and she breathed a sigh of relief. Like the wilderness that was vulnerable to the ravages of fire, she was exposed now too. She'd never considered the life of a forest ranger to be a particularly dangerous one, certainly not compared to that of a cop. But she knew better now. She knew about mudslides and slippery mountain roads, about rowdy campers and illegal hunters, about bears and forest fires and all the hundreds of other things that came up each and every day in this unforgiving region of the world.

She picked up the binoculars and was just about to look through them again, when she heard the footsteps climbing the stairs.

"I can't believe it," she said, her breath catching in her lungs. "You're back so soon—"

Only, when she turned, it wasn't Jake's image she saw appear at the top of the stairs and it took a moment for her mind to compute.

Chapter 13

Jake kicked at the ash with the toe of his boot, stirring up a small cloud and causing it to engulf the black leather with a dusting of white. This was definitely the spot. The circle of blackened dirt and ash stretched better than three feet across. Something had definitely burned here—and not long ago either. Embers glowed red along the bottom of the indentation his foot had made, gleaming brightly with the influx of oxygen, only to quickly fade and go cold.

Kneeling at the rim of the circle, he studied the ashes carefully, searching for anything that might give him a clue as to what might have happened. The small clearing was well off the beaten track, located more than a hundred yards from the road and nowhere near any established trails or hunting areas, which pretty much eliminated any notion he might have had about a campfire. Besides, what- ever it was that had burned here wasn't meant to be a bonfire or a campsite. This fire had gone up fast and hadn't lasted long.

Wind rustled through the trees, catching hold of the ashes and sending them flying. Something flickered in the breeze, something in the ash that was small and light and partially buried among the soot. Reaching down, Jake carefully plucked it up from the powdery ash. It looked like paper, charred and blackened on the ends, but he could see some kind of printing on it.

Catching a glimpse of movement again, he glanced up. The wind had shifted, sending another flurry of ashes swirling into the air and revealing dozens more pieces of paper.

Jake gathered up several more, spreading them out in his palm and examined them closely. The printing on the paper was sporadic and difficult to make out.

"Lose? Lost?" he guessed, trying to fit two of the pieces together like a puzzle. "Lost and…" He took several steps back, catching a stream of sunlight through the trees and shifting the bits of paper around again. "Oh my gosh," he murmured when the random words suddenly made sense. "The *Los Angeles Times.*"

His hand closed around the pieces and he shoved them into this pocket and looked around the clearing again. The hairs at the back of his neck prickled in a way they hadn't since he left the force. Someone had gone to a lot of trouble to hike way up here to burn their *L.A. Times.* And as far as he could tell, they hadn't left behind so much as a match or a footprint, a tire tread, a horse hoof—nothing.

Granted, he had seen a lot of unusual things since he'd been at Eagle's Eye, things that didn't always make a lot of sense—hikers who had tried to create their own trails, rock climbers who had attempted midnight climbs, hunters who liked taking potshots at other hunters. But this was something new.

Looking around the clearing, he shook his head. If someone had been intent on starting a forest fire, they'd botched it pretty badly. In the first place, they hadn't picked a very good spot for it. Given the open space of the clearing, it would take more than some newspapers to ignite the green shrubbery and solid tree trunks. But even if they had been successful in getting the brush to burn, they had to know they'd been in the clear vision of the fire tower. A few runs by a borade bomber would have dropped enough chemical retardant to have prevented the fire from spreading very far.

He knelt down again, sifting through the rest of the ashes, looking for anything else that might help explain what happened, but he could find nothing, which in itself made even less sense. He was hardly an arson investigator, but as far as he could tell, newspapers had been the only thing that had burned. And from the depth of the ash, it would have taken a number of newspapers burning to create a fire circle this size.

"A *lot* of newspaper," he mumbled. "No wood, no charcoal, no kindling, no trash."

Which, of course, only made the whole thing feel all the more bizarre—and it was that, more than anything else, that nagged at him. Maybe it was just the natural suspicions of an ex-cop, but things just didn't add up. He tried to think of a scenario that would make this picture clear, that would help him understand what the person who had done this was thinking. Were they lost? Had this been meant as a signal fire? But if that was the case, where were they now? Why hadn't they stuck around and waited for rescue?

"And these newspapers," he said out loud, rising

slowly to his feet. "Where the hell did all these news-papers come from?"

He suspected the culprit couldn't have been anyone who lived in the area. People who made this wilderness their home learned to live with the constant threat of fire and did all they could to prevent it. He had a hard time believing a local would be so cavalier with their own safety as to burn anything, let alone leave trash in an open area like this.

He stepped back from the circle, retracing his steps in an effort to keep the area as pristine as possible. This wasn't exactly a crime scene, but old habits were hard to break. He walked a wide perimeter, looking for any sign of footprints again, but again could see nothing.

But there was something about the scene that bugged him, something he couldn't quite put his finger on—that is, until he noticed a spot along the edge of ashes, a spot that almost looked as though the dirt might actually have been piled up, creating a small ridge.

"What's this?" he asked the unknown body who had walked the same spot before him. "Did you actually *dig* a pit here, my friend?"

He suddenly realized what it was that bothered him. It was the actual appearance of the burned-out area itself, the unnatural symmetry and bowl-like appearance. It was almost as if someone had taken the time to dig out a shallow pit—but for what reason?

He circled the mound of ashes one more time, then reached for the small, collapsible shovel that was folded in the case attached to his belt. Crime scene or no crime scene, the most important thing was to eliminate the risk of fire. Besides, experience told him there was a set of circumstances that would fit this scenario, he just hadn't found them yet. Of course, experience also told him that even knowing how didn't always explain why. And as far as he was concerned, digging a fire ring in the middle of the wilderness to burn a bunch of newspapers wasn't going to make sense under any circumstance.

He turned the ashes under, burying the fire ring completely and tamping out any embers that might have remained. But working only made him all the more uneasy. By the time he had finished and folded the shovel back into its canvas case, he decided it would be wise to report the incident to Claybe just to be on the safe side. They'd been lucky with this one. This fire had virtually gone out by itself, but it just as easily could have turned into a disaster. While it appeared that measures had been taken to ensure this fire wouldn't spread, a loose ember in a dry patch of grass could have ignited the entire forest. They needed to keep their eyes peeled for any suspicious activity. At the very least, this had been an illegal burn and the person responsible needed to be cited; they might even have an arsonist-in-the-making on their hands.

By the time he had reached the truck, he was breathing heavily and his body felt overheated and uncomfortable. Between the digging and the hiking, he'd gotten quite a workout. But he couldn't take time to rest. He felt a sense of urgency now that had nothing to do with reporting a suspicious fire. The shadows were already beginning to grow long and he had a date for a sunset.

He slid behind the wheel, turning the key in the ignition and shifting the truck into gear. It was a new experience for him to have someone waiting, to have a reason to get done with work and look forward to a little free time. He'd been alone for a long time and had become used to the solitude. He'd thought he was too old to change, too set in his ways, but all that was different now. It seemed that everything had changed when Kristin came into his life. He suddenly remembered just how nice it was to have someone to laugh and be silly with, to share sunrises and sunsets, someone who worried and cared about what happened to him.

Reaching for the radio on the seat beside him, he picked it up and depressed the call button. "Anyone ready for a sunset?" He waited a few moments, then tried again. "Fire tower, do you copy? Kristin?"

The tower should have been in range of the radio, but with the twists and turns of the mountain road it wasn't unusual to lose the signal. Continuing up the road, he negotiated a hairpin turn, bringing the tower into view, and tried the radio again.

"Kristin? Honey, answer me."

But she didn't answer and he felt the hairs at the back of this neck prickle again. Of course, she could have just switched off the radio, or maybe she'd left the tower, but that didn't seem like something she would do.

Clipping the radio to the visor of the truck, he inched his foot down a fraction farther on the accelerator and sped up the mountain road as quickly and safely as possible. The sense of concern he felt was new to him, too, and something he'd experienced only once before: When he had seen the headlights of the Jeep coming out of the storm on the slippery mountain road, a chill had gone through him that had turned his soul to ice.

Just then the radio crackled to life as he heard Kristin's voice through the small speaker. Snatching the radio from the visor, he depressed the button to speak.

"Hey, there you are," he said, relief flooding his body like blood in his veins. "I thought you forgot about me."

Except, when he freed the transmit button to receive her response, her words made no sense. It was as if he were listening to a television program, to a conversation that had nothing to do with him.

"Kristin?" he said again into the radio. "Can you hear me? Are you on the cell phone? I don't understand what you're saying."

He listened for a moment longer. He could hear her voice clearly, could hear the words she was saying but they still made no sense. If was almost as if she was talking to someone else....

"Oh, God," he groaned as realization hit him like boulders tumbling down the mountain.

Someone was with her. Suddenly all those random, disjointed pieces of the puzzle began falling into place. The fire had been set to lure him away from the tower, to get him out of the way. It had been no accident, no arsonist attempting to start a forest fire or some nut burning trash in the wilderness. The fire had been a ploy by someone who had wanted to get Kristin alone.

Nancy. Kristin could hardly believe her eyes. A million things went through her mind. Had something happened to one of her clients? Had Ted sent Nancy here to keep her safe, too? Was the stalker after both of them now?

"Disappointed, aren't you?" Nancy said, her voice sounding unnaturally high. She stepped up from the stairs and into the tower. "Thought it was going to be your boyfriend, didn't you?"

"N-Nancy, I can't...I can't believe it. How did you get here? *What* are you doing here?"

"You thought I was your mountain man and you were going to rush right over here and throw yourself into his big strong arms." Nancy threw her head back and laughed, a loud, harsh sound that had nothing to do with humor. "Oh, my, how romantic."

"Nancy—"

"Shut up!" she snapped, taking another step closer. "All you do is talk, Jane Streeter. Now you're going to listen, now it's my turn."

Kristin felt as though the floor beneath her had suddenly tilted. This wasn't right—*Nancy* wasn't right. The fidgety, excitable voice was completely out of character for her, and there was such a wild, almost fanatical look in her eyes.

"Nancy, maybe you'd like to sit down for a little while. You don't look as though you feel very—"

"I said *shut up*," Nancy screamed. She slipped her hand from her pocket, pulling out a large handgun, its long, silver barrel catching a ray of the fading sun and sending it dancing across the floor. "I feel just fine. But I'm afraid Dear Jane is coming down with something, something bad, and may have to miss the broadcast tonight. In fact, I think she's going to be missing a few of them."

A wave of nausea hit Kristin like a tsunami. This couldn't be happening. Her entire world had changed and she didn't know what to believe any longer. The isolation that had once kept her safe now held her prisoner. Someone she thought was familiar was now a stranger. She felt dizzy and unsteady and thought she was going to throw up—and probably would have if she hadn't suddenly spotted the two-way radio on the counter beside her.

Her mind couldn't comprehend everything so she switched to a kind of overdrive mode, operating on instinct and intuition and blocking out the fear. If only she could distract Nancy, just for a moment, just long enough to reach the radio.

"Wh-what are you going to do?" she asked, hoping the question didn't sound as staged to Nancy as it did to her. There wasn't time to think too much about it, wasn't time to calculate the risks and formulate a plan of action. She needed to act now while she still had a chance. Slowly, she lifted the binoculars and rested them on the counter. "What do you mean I'm going to miss the broadcast?."

"Oh, Kristin, please," Nancy said, tossing her head back with a laugh. "I realize you're surprised but surely you can figure that one out."

Kristin moved the moment Nancy laughed, slipping the binoculars onto the counter in front of the radio, blocking Nancy's view.

"Oh, I think I know," she said, slipping her hand over the radio. "I guess I just want to hear you say it."

"What? Is that supposed to make me feel bad?" Nancy asked, glancing down at the gun in her hand.

The instant Nancy's gaze dropped, Kristin's fingers closed around the radio and she slid it off the counter and into the palm of her hand.

"Nancy, I can't believe this," she said in a loud voice, her finger depressing the transmit button down so tightly it threatened to shut off all feeling. She only prayed that Jake was in radio range, that he would hear them before Nancy discovered exactly what she was doing. "Please, *Nancy,* please, won't you put the gun down?"

"Put it down? Why would I want to do that? I finally got your undivided attention." She lifted the gun, making a dramatic play of examining it, turning it in all directions and letting it catch the light. "You know, it's so amazing how people who have no time for you suddenly find all the time in the world when you have one of these things in your hand."

"Nancy, put it down," Kristin said again in as loud a voice as she dared. She had to resist the almost over-

whelming desire to scream for help, knowing it would
only made matters worse—and serve little purpose in this
secluded spot. Nancy was relatively calm at the moment
and it was important that she stay that way. But Kristin
had worked with too many unstable personalities to know
that violence could escalate at the drop of a hat. "Before
someone gets hurt."

"Too late," Nancy laughed. "Someone has already
gotten hurt, have you forgotten about that? I would think
you'd be feeling rather guilty about it now." She took
several steps closer, waving the gun as she spoke. "Since
it was all your fault!"

Kristin felt an icy chill make its way down her spine.
"You hurt Tori, how could you do that?"

An almost undetectable shadow passed across Nancy's
animated expression, so brief she would have missed it
had she not been looking right at her. But it was enough
to give her hope. Somewhere in Nancy's troubled mind,
a fragment of reason must still exist, a sliver of reality
that could still distinguish between right and wrong.

"Tori was unfortunate," Nancy admitted with a dramatic shrug, nothing in her expression now except an unsettling mask that bore little resemblance to the person
Kristin knew. "I admit it. She was in the wrong place at
the wrong time. Which just goes to show you what happens when you trust someone to do something for you.
No matter how much information you give them, no matter how many details you supply, they still screw it up."
She shrugged, then leveled the gun again. "Which just
goes to prove if you want a job done right, you have to
do it yourself."

Kristin's head was spinning and she struggled to maintain control. Reality had become too unreal, too surreal.
Surely she was going to awaken to discover this was all

just a dream—a horrible, awful dream that made no sense at all.

Only, the knot of terror in her stomach was enough to convince her this was no dream. What was happening was all too real, frighteningly real. The deeply disturbed woman looking at her with such hatred in her eyes was not the Nancy Fox she knew, not the colleague and partner she had worked with for years. This woman was a stranger and she was dangerous.

Kristin tried not to think about how vulnerable she was, how isolated and alone, relying instead on her experience and her years of work dealing with a variety of irrational and volatile personalities to guide her. The only way she was going to survive, the only chance she had would be to keep her head and not panic.

She clutched the radio in her hand again. The feeling was gone from her fingers now but she had to keep the transmission open. Jake had to hear her, he just had to and she had to hold on until he did.

"It was you then, Nancy?" she asked in a calm, practiced tone that came from years of experience. "All this time, it was you? The telephone calls, the letters?"

"Oh, I admit, I had help. After all, I could hardly go all over the country myself making telephone calls and mailing letters, could I?" she asked with a shrug. "My little helper is so fond of me, you know. But men, they're such corruptible creatures. We women can talk them into doing anything, can't we?" She arched an eyebrow. "But then, you already know that, don't you? I must say, it didn't take you long to wrap that big, strong brute of a forest ranger around your little finger. The poor man can't seem to keep his hands off you, can he?" Kristin started to open her mouth to speak but Nancy waved her silent. "Oh yes, I've seen the two of you together—those longing looks, the embraces, the kisses. It's enough to make a girl blush.'' She made a gesture, pointing to the expanse of windows. ''Be careful what you do in front of an open window, even if you are in the middle of nowhere. You never know who might be watching.''

The thought that Nancy had been watching them sent another rattling down Kristin's spine. ''I don't understand, Nancy, why? After all these years we've known each other, all the years we've worked together. Why would you do something like this?''

But something had already sparked in her memory, something she had filed away in the back of her brain but now flashed to consciousness again. It had seemed so innocent at the time, so insignificant, but remembering it now shed a completely different light on things.

It had happened after a broadcast one night. Nancy had been a guest on the program, chatting with callers and answering their questions as the Sly Fox. After the show, Dale had complimented her on what a natural she had been at the microphone. Nancy had laughed and jokingly said that if the ''Fox'' was really sly, she'd get rid of Jane and take over the program herself.

''Why?'' Nancy snorted. ''Why do you think? Are you so arrogant that you think I like sitting on the sidelines and watching while everything works out for you, while everyone raves about Dear Jane and I'm just there to take up the slack? I'm tired of being the second-string Kristin, tired of being in your shadow.''

''You're not in my shadow, Nancy, you never have been.''

''No?'' She threw her head back and laughed, another wild, ferocious sound that spoke more of madness than humor. ''Then maybe you should talk to your bosses about that.''

Kristin's hold on the radio tightened. "What? I don't understand."

"Well, let me clarify it for you." She had begun to pace back and forth in front of Kristin, a nervous, jerky step that looked unnatural in its flow. "I'm a natural, they tell me. I do a great job on the air—as the stand-in. Just not good enough to be given my own show." She saw Kristin's eyes widen in surprise. "You're shocked, I suppose, shocked that someone else might be good at what you do, that you might have some competition. Well, you don't have to worry, they didn't want me. They had the real deal, they had Dear Jane, why would they want another talk-show host." She cradled the gun against her chest, stroking the barrel as though it were a living thing. "But I have a feeling they'll be changing their minds very soon."

Kristin felt light-headed and could hardly believe what she was hearing. How had this happened? How could this madness have taken over Nancy and Kristin not have noticed? Had there been signs that she'd simply ignored?

She thought about the cell phone conversations they'd shared, how she'd thought of Nancy as her lifeline to the outside world. They had talked about the progress of her clients, about strategies and treatment options. How could she have had such intense conversations with this woman and not picked up on how deeply disturbed she was?

But she hadn't, she'd had no idea. Up until a short time ago, she had trusted Nancy completely. She'd trusted her to watch over her clients, to watch over her practice, she'd even trusted her enough to tell her about Eagle's Eye.

"Is that what this is all about, Nancy?" she asked after a moment. "The show? About 'Lost Loves'?"

"I suppose you think I should be content to just fill in for you from time to time. But you see, I'm not. I'm going to have it all, Kristin,'' she said, taking several steps toward her. ''And I'm prepared to do whatever it takes to get it.''

''So that's your plan?'' Kristin asked. It took all the control she had to keep the fear from her voice. ''Get rid of me so you can take over with your own radio show?''

''You've always been so good with your analysis, Counselor,'' Nancy pointed out sarcastically. ''And you could have made this all so easy if you'd just cooperated.'' Nancy turned and walked toward the window. The sun was beginning to set and dark shadows had started to fall across the tower. ''Anyone else would have been frightened off long ago. But not you. Oh no, you had to make it hard on everyone, you had to be brave and struggle despite the fear.'' She turned back and looked at Kristin. ''How noble.''

''So you sent someone to hurt me?''

''Like I said, you didn't make it easy. It should have been you that night in the parking garage, not Tori. If anyone is to blame for her getting hurt, it's you.''

''Are you listening to yourself?''

Nancy was visibly surprised by the change in Kristin's tone. ''What? What are you talking about?''

''I'm talking about denial,'' she pointed out. Nancy had not yet noticed the radio in Kristin's hand and the growing darkness gave her hope that maybe she wouldn't. Still, she wasn't sure how much longer she could keep her hold firm. If only Jake would hear, if only he would come back. Nancy was far too smart—and far too dangerous—to keep distracted for much longer. ''Listen to what you're saying. It's your fault—not mine. Nancy, come on. That's classic denial. You can tell the rest of the world anything you want, but let's at least be honest with each other.''

"Honest? You want to be honest," Nancy challenged. "I want you gone."

"Gone? Or dead?"

Nancy glanced down at the gun in her hand and smiled. "I would have been satisfied with gone, but unfortunately you wouldn't cooperate. I guess I'll just have to settle for dead." She glanced back up at Kristin. "How's that for honesty?"

Kristin wouldn't let herself think, wouldn't let herself consider the consequences. She just plunged forward. "I guess that would depend."

"Oh? Depend on what, Kristin? Enlighten me."

"On just how honest you'll allow yourself to be. Whether you have the guts to face the truth." It was a bold move, and a risky one, but instinct told her Nancy wasn't going to be content with just talking for too much longer. The woman hadn't come here looking for passive compliance. She wanted confrontation, wanted to get all the anger and resentment off her chest. Maybe getting her angry, getting her arguing, would help release some of that pressure and buy Kristin a little more time. "And the truth is, you're a bully…"

"What?" Nancy gasped.

"A jealous, mean-spirited bully," Kristin continued without stopping. "And you think you can intimidate and threaten and coerce the world to play by *your* rules. Well, I'm here to tell you, Nancy, that's not the way it is. The world doesn't revolve around you."

For a moment she thought she had gone too far, pushed too hard. Nancy just stood there and stared at her, the barrel of the gun drooping in her hand and pointing downward. The expression on her face was unreadable and Kristin didn't know if she should take that as a good sign or not.

"Clever," Nancy finally said after a long moment. "Turning the tables on the accuser. Very good, but then your clinical technique was always good."

"The truth is, an innocent person suffered and nearly died because you, Nancy—not me. And you can bluster around here and try to make excuses, but you can only fool yourself for so long. You were a good therapist once. You know the problem with denial is that you can only keep it up for so long. Has the truth come back to haunt you yet?"

Nancy did nothing, just stood there staring at her and for a moment Kristin thought she may have gone too far. How could she even think she could predict what the woman would do? Nothing about her resembled the woman Kristin thought she knew.

"Oh, are you finished now?" Nancy asked dryly, suddenly springing to life. But Kristin heard the change in her voice, could see the heightened color in her face. Something in what she had said had struck a chord. "Is this the part where I'm supposed to break down, have an attack of conscience, throw myself at your feet sobbing and ask for your forgiveness?" She tilted her head down, giving Kristin a long look. "It's not going to happen, you know that, right?"

Kristin paused for a moment. A strange, almost eerie calm had settled over her. Nancy was the one holding the gun but it was she who felt fearless.

"What isn't going to happen?" she asked, leveling her gaze with Nancy's. "You breaking down? Or me forgiving you?"

"So strong, so brave," Nancy said with a small laugh. "Right to the end."

As though in slow motion, Kristin watched as Nancy raised the gun. She had played her hand out, had gone as far as she could and had nowhere else to go. With her hand still clutching the radio, her mind scrambled but she could think of nothing else. It was as if she had lost the ability to do anything other than simply stand there and stare. Was this how it was to end, with her standing there just watching while Nancy pulled the trigger?

When she first caught a glimpse of Jake moving up silently behind Nancy, she truly believed she was hallucinating, thinking she had literally willed him to appear. But then clarity hit and adrenaline pumped through her veins like fire through a forest.

Jake grabbed Nancy from behind, startling her and causing the gun to discharge. She struggled violently against his hold, kicking and trying to pull the trigger again.

Kristin didn't think, she just moved. She sprang across the room like a place kicker, her foot swinging up and making contact with the hard steel. The gun shot from Nancy's hold, flying across the tower and landing with a crash against one of the windows. The shattered pane held together for a brief moment, then collapsed into a thousand pieces.

For a moment Kristin just stood there, her mind reeling and trying to make some sense of everything. She turned slowly, watching while Jake clapped handcuffs around Nancy's wrists.

It was over—all of it. There were no more threats, no more danger, no more stalker. She wasn't sure what she was feeling, then realized she was numb and wasn't really capable of feeling anything at all.

But as she glanced up, she caught Jake's gaze and emotions flooded back. With no more danger, there was no longer a reason to stay.

Chapter 14

"*I don't understand, Jane, I would have done anything for her. I loved her. She'd told me she'd never been so happy—not ever in her life. So why did she leave?*"

"*I wish I knew, Cal. Maybe she didn't think it mattered to you—if she stayed or if she left.*"

"*Of course it mattered, she knew how much it mattered.*"

"*Did she? You told her?*"

"*I didn't have to. Women know those things.*"

"*Really, how does that work?*"

"*Well, you know, you're a woman. It's that female intuition thing. Men aren't good with words, they don't know how to talk about feelings.*"

"*And this makes women mind readers?*"

"*No, but they know more about that stuff than men do.*"

"*Oh, Cal, my dear, you really do need some advice. Let's hear from some of you women out there, what do you think? What advice do you have for Cowboy Cal?*"

Give us a call, 1–800–NIGHT TALK. I'm Jane Streeter—
Dear Jane—and you're listening to 'Lost Loves.'"

"Cal, I feel for you," Jake mumbled, reaching for the
bottle of wine. He leaned forward just enough in his chair
to fill his glass to the brim. The sound of Kristin's voice
moved through his bloodstream like a narcotic, potent and
addictive and making him feel more alive than he had in
five long days—five days, eleven hours and—he glanced
down at his watch—thirty-seven minutes, give or take a
few seconds.

This was her first day back on the air since Nancy Fox's
arrest and the first time he'd heard her voice since then.
Closing his eyes, he could picture her in the studio, headset pushed back against her long, golden hair, doodle pad
in front of her on the desk. Only this time she wasn't
broadcasting from a lookout tower in the middle of the
wilderness. She was back in a studio a hundred miles
away and back to a life that was light-years from here.

He opened his eyes and took a drink of wine. He didn't
think he would ever forget the fear and the fury that had
gone through his mind when he'd realized what it was he
was listening to over the handheld radio. It still amazed
him to think she'd had enough wherewithal, given the
circumstances, to even think of the radio, let alone attempt
to broadcast from it, but nothing about the woman surprised him anymore.

He pushed himself up from the chair, slowly rising to
his feet and walking around the deck. The night was
black, with only the light of a million stars illuminating
the sky, and dead quiet. The silence had never bothered
him before—in fact, he'd always found it soothing. But
that had been before Kristin, before she had come to Eagle's Eye and changed his world forever. He found no

comfort in the silence any longer, just isolation and lone-liness.

He walked to the sheet of plywood he'd used to board up the window that had been blown out, remembering how the explosion of Nancy's gun had shattered the si-lence then. It was a wonder he had reached the tower at all, given the speed he had driven up the mountain road, but at the time, spinning off the edge of the mountain had been about the last thing he'd been thinking of. All he'd been thinking about was Kristin alone with that crazy woman. And the look on Kristin's face when she saw him creep into the tower behind Nancy was something he would never forget.

They'd had so little time together after that. Almost within moments of his arrival at the tower, the sky had opened up with light and sound as the Fire and Rescue helicopter arrived with Ted and a swarm of FBI agents and crime scene specialists. Between their investigation and their questioning of Nancy, they were able to piece together a picture.

It had been the arrest and subsequent confession of Ted's suspect, a salesman who traveled the country selling advertising for the radio network that broadcast 'Lost Loves' who had implicated Nancy and alerted Ted she was at Eagle's Eye. Nancy had easily manipulated the man into doing her bidding. While he was the one who had made the phone calls and attacked Tori, it had been Nancy behind all of it. Angry when she could find no interest for a Sly Fox talk show she'd been pitching, she'd set out to get Kristin and 'Lost Loves' off the air, any way she could.

Kristin had been so strong, holding herself together through it all. Yet all he'd wanted to do was pull her into his arms and comfort her, to assure her everything was going to be okay, to assure himself she *was* safe. But it was as though everything conspired to keep them apart. Between the FBI agents, the questions and the crime scene, they'd had no time to be together, then, suddenly, it was time to leave.

Ted had expected Kristin would want to ride with him down the mountain in the helicopter. Of course, he had no way of knowing how difficult this was going to be, that they had become...*involved.* He'd thought he'd been doing her a favor, thinking she was anxious to get home after so many weeks away. But the thought of standing there and watching her just disappear into the night sky had been too much. Besides, he had to complete the assignment he'd been charged with and deliver her back to her life safe and sound.

He'd managed to make some excuse to Ted, saying something about Kristin being uncomfortable riding in a helicopter with Nancy, and gratefully Ted hadn't pushed. But their long drive down the mountain hadn't been an easy one. Neither of them had felt like talking and he'd been hoping every mile of the way she would change her mind and tell him to turn the truck around and take her back with him. Only...she never did, so despite the many miles and late hour, it seemed they arrived at her house all too soon.

Jake walked back across the deck and picked up his wineglass, draining it in one gulp. He could still see her, standing on the small front porch. It was so uncomfortable, they were so awkward with one another, it was almost embarrassing. Of course, they had smiled and laughed and promised to keep in touch, but this was the end and they both knew it. He'd given her every opportunity to stay, but she'd made her choice and he couldn't blame her for that. It was just that standing there alone in the darkness with her, it was all he could do to stop himself from pulling her into his arms and begging her to change her mind.

When she'd reached up and given him a kiss on the cheek, he'd nearly lost it, and where he'd found the strength to lean down and kiss her, he'd never know.

He sank onto the chair again, his head resting against the back. He could still taste the salt from that one lone tear that had fallen from her lash and down her cheek. He had thought leaving her that night had been the hardest thing he'd ever done—at least he had until the next night. It had been more difficult, as had each subsequent night. Living without her was hard and it just wasn't getting any better.

"We're back and we've got Becky on the line. Becky, what do you think? What advice do you have for a sad cowboy whose lady has left?"

"I think he should wake up and smell the coffee. Female intuition? Give me a break. If he wanted the woman to stay, he should have just asked her."

"Short and to the point, thanks, Becky. Let's hear what Kathy from Kentucky has to say—Kathy, you're on the air, what have you got to say to Cal?"

"Well, you can just tell Cal I don't buy all that about men not being able to talk about their feelings. My husband has been using that excuse for years. I say if you love the woman, tell her."

"Okay, thanks, that's two for talking Cal. What do you have to say about that?"

"I—I don't know what to say."

"Well, Cal, tell me something, will you?"

"Sure."

"You said you loved this woman, did you mean that?"

"With all my heart."

"*Then don't you think you should tell her?*"

"I told you, she knows, she—"

"*No, Cal, she doesn't. Oh, she may think you do, may hope you do, but she doesn't know it and she won't until you tell her. Let me ask you something else, cowboy. You said you would do anything for the woman. Why won't you do this? Don't you think she has a right to know? Don't you think you should tell her how you feel?*"

"I...I suppose. But, Jane, is love enough?"

"Yeah Jane," Jake murmured, rubbing a tired hand across his eyes. "Is love enough for you?"

"*I happen to think it is, but I guess you'll never know unless you try, will you?*"

Jake opened his eyes and sat up.

"*Think about it. Happiness could be just a phone call away. Don't you think it's worth the risk? What about my fellow travelers out there on the rocky road to love, what do you think? This is 'Lost Loves' and I'm your host, Jane Streeter. Let me hear from you. 1–800–NIGHT TALK.*"

He suddenly felt as though he'd taken a punch to the stomach—dizzy, unsteady and unable to breathe.

"The tear," he mumbled aloud, his wineglass slipping from his hand and landing in pieces on the deck. But he wasn't thinking about the broken glass. His mind was reeling. Scattered, fragmented pieces were suddenly falling into place, making sense out of chaos, reason out of rhyme.

Why hadn't he seen it before? Why had he overlooked something that was so obvious? He knew better than anyone what a tight hold Kristin kept on her emotions, how adept she'd become at hiding her feelings behind a facade of indifference. Except that night on her porch, that night he had delivered her home and walked away. Something had penetrated that iron hold of hers, something had broken through the facade.

"That tear," he murmured again.

That one lone tear; she hadn't been able to stop it. It would have taken some pretty powerful emotions to have caused it to slip by that iron hold of hers.

But were they powerful enough? He was in love with her. Was it possible she had feelings for him? Could it be that she had fallen in love too?

Suddenly everything seemed so clear. He'd wanted her to stay, but just like the guy on the radio, he hadn't asked her to, either. He'd assumed she would have stayed if she'd wanted, just as he'd assumed she knew how he felt. He'd never thought about asking her to stay because he'd assumed his love hadn't been enough to offer. Now he was wondering if he'd assumed too much.

He bolted inside, reaching for the ham-radio mike. "Cedar Canyon, this is Eagle's Eye, anyone awake down there?"

"Just call me a night owl."

"Claybe! Thank God." Jake ran a shaky hand through his shaggy hair. "Buddy, I need a favor."

Kristin adjusted her headset and waited for Dale's cue. The show was nearly over and yet she felt as though she could go on all night. Not because she wasn't exhausted but more because she didn't relish the thought of going home to an empty house again. She wondered if it was always going to be this way, wondered if she was always going to miss him.

She was still reeling about Nancy and only beginning to realize just how truly disturbed the woman was. It was clear Nancy's problems had begun long before Kristin and the stalking. Deep-seated issues going back to her childhood were at the core of it, unresolved issues that had been left to fester and grow dangerous. In her troubled mind, Nancy had fixated on Kristin, wanting to take over Kristin's life in an effort to escape her own. But Kristin consoled herself with the fact that Nancy was where she could get help now. Tori was on the road to recovery and life could get back to normal again—or something close to it.

Only, Kristin was no longer sure she knew what normal was. She was back in her home, back with her sister, her friends, her practice, her job—and yet her life felt anything but normal. Was it normal to cry yourself to sleep every night? Was it normal for your heart to ache when the sun rose and to break when it set? Was it normal to miss someone so much you thought nothing was ever going to feel normal again?

"Back in three seconds," Dale's voice prompted through the earpiece.

She nodded. *"And we're back, and we've almost made it through another long, lonely night, my friends. We've got one last caller on the line with a sad story to tell. It's—"* The words scrolling across her prompt screen had her heart lurching in her chest and her brain skittering to a stop. She looked up and turned to Dale in the control booth. He merely glanced back and calmly pointed to the On Air sign glaring in large red letters. *"Uh…oh, it's Mountain Man. So…talk to me, Mountain Man, you have a story to tell?"*

"A sad one, I'm afraid, and I need your advice, Jane."

The voice in her headset sent Kristin's world tilting sharply and the air in her lungs escaping in one harsh gasp. *"M-my advice?"*

"You see, Jane, there's this woman. We met in a very turbulent time in her life and things happened pretty

quickly between us. But then circumstances changed and she had to leave. Like Cowboy Cal earlier, I would have liked for her to have stayed, but we live in two different worlds. Her life is somewhere else—her family, her career.''

"You…wanted her to stay?" Kristin's heart hammered in her chest. *"Why?"*

"Jane, I'm in love with her."

"You never told her."

"I know. Is it too late?"

Tears began to burn her eyes. Could this really be happening? Could dreams really come true? *"I don't think it's ever too late for love."*

"But is it enough, Jane? Her job, my job and all the miles in between, how do we work that out?"

"Oh, Mountain Man," Kristin's voice cracked and her hands trembled. *"Don't you know? Love will find a way."*

Catching sight of movement beside her, she turned quickly. Jake stood in the door of the broadcast booth, his cell phone to his ear.

"I love you," he whispered.

"Oh, Jake, I love you too," she sobbed, yanking off her headset and rushing into his arms.

She never heard the static through the speakers when her headset hit the mike, never heard Dale's voice over the airway closing out the program. All she knew was Jake was there, holding her, and she felt right for the first time in five long days.

"Are you sure?" he growled, holding her so tightly she could barely breathe. "Because when I get you back on the mountain, I'm not letting you go again—not without me."

"I'm sure," she cried, tasting her own tears on his lips. "Yes, yes, I'm sure."

Everything happened in a blur after that. There were tears and laughter and gasps and sighs and then that very long drive. But then, at last, there was the mountain, the tower and the bed.

"I was afraid," he said, pulling her close as they watched the sun start to peek over the top of the mountain. They had begun making love from the moment they'd reached Eagle's Eye and greeted the dawn spent and exhausted.

"Afraid." Kristin pulled back just far enough to look up at him. "You? The man who shares his front yard with bears and any number of other wild beasts, what could you possibly have been afraid of?"

He glanced down at her. She was joking, he knew, but how could he make her understand? She had done so much for him, had done what all the department shrinks and three years alone on the mountain hadn't been able to. She'd helped him get rid of all the demons, all the ghosts from the past once and for all. There were things he would always feel badly about, like Ricky and his failure with Valerie. But Kristin had helped him realize that life didn't come with any guarantees. It was trial and error for everyone and basically we were all just feeling our way along. What defined a man wasn't his successes or failures, it was his ability to persevere, to pick up the pieces and go on and give it the best that he could. And for the first time in his life, he was ready to do that.

"The thought that I was wrong, that maybe you really didn't care after all. That maybe I'd be standing there in that broadcast booth only to have you send me home alone."

"And yet you came anyway."

"I did. I had to." He smiled and pulled her close again.

"Because the thought of living without you terrified me even more."

Kristin's heart swelled in her chest, and she almost thought it would burst. "Even more than bears?"

He laughed, bending down and giving her a kiss. "Hey, you can always shoot a bear."

"As long as you have a license," she pointed out.

"That's true. Unfortunately, there's nothing on the books about open season on dangerous females." He slipped her beneath him. "So I guess I'll just have to improvise. There's another kind of license that just might work."

"Oh really." She smiled when she felt him grow hard against her. "What did you have in mind, Mountain Man?"

"I'm thinking a marriage license just might take care of the problem. What do you think?" he murmured, sliding into her in one, smooth stroke. "Marry me? Love me forever?"

Kristin felt her breath growing short as the real world began to slip away. Jane Streeter knew all about heartbreaks and heartaches, but Kristin had some advice for her. In the end, love really was all that mattered. It made the future bright and the past irrelevant and wiped the slate clean. The road to happiness was a rocky one, but despite the obstacles, love could always find a way.

"Forever," she whispered.

* * * * *

eHARLEQUIN.com

For **FREE online reading,** visit
www.eHarlequin.com now and enjoy:

<u>Online Reads</u>
Read **Daily** and **Weekly** chapters from
our Internet-exclusive stories by your
favorite authors.

<u>Red-Hot Reads</u>
Turn up the heat with one of our more
sensual online stories!

<u>Interactive Novels</u>
Cast your vote to help decide how these
stories unfold...then stay tuned!

<u>Quick Reads</u>
For shorter romantic reads, try our
collection of Poems, Toasts, & More!

<u>Online Read Library</u>
Miss one of our online reads?
Come here to catch up!

<u>Reading Groups</u>
Discuss, share and rave with other
community members!

For great reading online,
visit www.eHarlequin.com today!

✂ **Your opinion is important to us!** Please take a few moments to share your thoughts with us about your experiences with Harlequin and Silhouette books. Your comments will be very useful in ensuring that we deliver books you love to read. *Please take a few minutes to complete the questionnaire, then send it to us at the address below.*

> Send your completed questionnaires to:
> **Harlequin/Silhouette Reader Survey, P.O. Box 9046, Buffalo, NY 14269-9046**

1. As you may know, there are many different lines under the Harlequin and Silhouette brands. Each of the lines is listed below. Please check the box that most represents your reading habit for each line.

Line	Currently read this line	Do not read this line	Not sure if I read this line
Harlequin American Romance	❏	❏	❏
Harlequin Duets	❏	❏	❏
Harlequin Romance	❏	❏	❏
Harlequin Historicals	❏	❏	❏
Harlequin Superromance	❏	❏	❏
Harlequin Intrigue	❏	❏	❏
Harlequin Presents	❏	❏	❏
Harlequin Temptation	❏	❏	❏
Harlequin Blaze	❏	❏	❏
Silhouette Special Edition	❏	❏	❏
Silhouette Romance	❏	❏	❏
Silhouette Intimate Moments	❏	❏	❏
Silhouette Desire	❏	❏	❏

2. Which of the following best describes why you bought *this book?* One answer only, please.

the picture on the cover	❏	the title	❏
the author	❏	the line is one I read often	❏
part of a miniseries	❏	saw an ad in another book	❏
saw an ad in a magazine/newsletter	❏	a friend told me about it	❏
I borrowed/was given this book	❏	other: _____	❏

3. Where did you buy *this book?* One answer only, please.

at Barnes & Noble	❏	at a grocery store	❏
at Waldenbooks	❏	at a drugstore	❏
at Borders	❏	on eHarlequin.com Web site	❏
at another bookstore	❏	from another Web site	❏
at Wal-Mart	❏	Harlequin/Silhouette Reader	❏
at Target	❏	Service/through the mail	
at Kmart	❏	used books from anywhere	❏
at another department store or mass merchandiser	❏	I borrowed/was given this book	❏

4. On average, how many Harlequin and Silhouette books do you buy at one time?

I buy _____ books at one time ❏

I rarely buy a book ❏

MRQ403SIM-1A

5. How many times per month do you shop for any *Harlequin and/or Silhouette* books?
   One answer only, please.

1 or more times a week	❏	a few times per year	❏
1 to 3 times per month	❏	less often than once a year	❏
1 to 2 times every 3 months	❏	never	❏

6. When you think of your ideal heroine, which *one* statement describes her the best?
   One answer only, please.

She's a woman who is strong-willed	❏	She's a desirable woman	❏
She's a woman who is needed by others	❏	She's a powerful woman	❏
She's a woman who is taken care of	❏	She's a passionate woman	❏
She's an adventurous woman	❏	She's a sensitive woman	❏

7. The following statements describe types or genres of books that you may be
   interested in reading. Pick *up to 2 types* of books that you are most interested in.

I like to read about truly romantic relationships	❏
I like to read stories that are sexy romances	❏
I like to read romantic comedies	❏
I like to read a romantic mystery/suspense	❏
I like to read about romantic adventures	❏
I like to read romance stories that involve family	❏
I like to read about a romance in times or places that I have never seen	❏
Other: _____	❏

*The following questions help us to group your answers with those readers who are
similar to you. Your answers will remain confidential.*

8. Please record your year of birth below.

   19 _____

9. What is your marital status?

   single ❏   married ❏   common-law ❏   widowed ❏
   divorced/separated ❏

10. Do you have children 18 years of age or younger currently living at home?

    yes ❏   no ❏

11. Which of the following best describes your employment status?

    employed full-time or part-time ❏   homemaker ❏   student ❏
    retired ❏   unemployed ❏

12. Do you have access to the Internet from either home or work?

    yes ❏   no ❏

13. Have you ever visited eHarlequin.com?
    yes ❏   no ❏

14. What state do you live in?

    _____

15. Are you a member of Harlequin/Silhouette Reader Service?

    yes ❏   Account # _____   no ❏   MRQ403SIM-1B

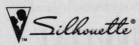

COMING NEXT MONTH

SIMCNM0903

INTIMATE MOMENTS